The
OUTSIDE
of a
Horse

The
OUTSIDE
of a
Horse

a novel

by
Ginny Rorby

Dial Books for Young Readers
an imprint of Penguin Group (USA) Inc.

DIAL BOOKS FOR YOUNG READERS
A division of Penguin Young Readers Group
Published by The Penguin Group
Penguin Group (USA) Inc., 375 Hudson Street, New York, NY 10014, U.S.A.
Penguin Group (Canada), 90 Eglinton Avenue East, Suite 700, Toronto, Ontario,
Canada M4P 2Y3 (a division of Pearson Penguin Canada Inc.)
Penguin Books Ltd, 80 Strand, London WC2R 0RL, England
Penguin Ireland, 25 St. Stephen's Green, Dublin 2, Ireland
(a division of Penguin Books Ltd)
Penguin Group (Australia), 250 Camberwell Road, Camberwell,
Victoria 3124, Australia (a division of Pearson Australia Group Pty Ltd)
Penguin Books India Pvt Ltd, 11 Community Centre, Panchsheel Park,
New Delhi - 110 017, India
Penguin Group (NZ), 67 Apollo Drive, Rosedale, North Shore 0632,
New Zealand (a division of Pearson New Zealand Ltd)
Penguin Books (South Africa) (Pty) Ltd, 24 Sturdee Avenue, Rosebank,
Johannesburg 2196, South Africa
Penguin Books Ltd, Registered Offices: 80 Strand, London WC2R 0RL, England

Book design by Jasmin Rubero
Text set in Adobe Caslon
Printed in the U.S.A.

2 4 6 8 10 9 7 5 3

Rorby, Ginny.
The outside of a horse : a novel / by Ginny Rorby.
p.   cm.
Summary: When her father returns from the Iraq War as an amputee
with posttraumatic stress disorder, Hannah escapes by volunteering
to work with rescued horses, never thinking that the abused horses could also
help her father recover.
ISBN 978-0-8037-3478-4 (hardcover)
[1. Horses—Fiction. 2. Horsemanship—Therapeutic use—Fiction.
3. Amputees—Fiction. 4. People with disabilities—Fiction.
5. Emotional problems—Fiction.] I. Title.

PZ7.R69Ou 2010
[Fic]—dc22

2009025101

Dedicated to my father,

Noel Rorby,

and all he might have been

There's nothing so good for the inside of a man
as the outside of a horse.

OLD ENGLISH PROVERB

1

SATURDAY, FEBRUARY 11, 2006

Hannah, I need you, please," Sondra calls again, this time from the top of the stairs.

I pin myself to the wall in the kitchen and hold my breath.

My baby brother starts to wail.

"Blast it," she says. I hear the floorboards creak as she goes back down the hall to the nursery.

I tiptoe to the kitchen door that leads to the garage, open it carefully so the hinges don't squeak, and slip out. If I tell Sondra I'm going to see the horses again, she'll come up with a day's worth of things for me to do. She doesn't care that it's Saturday. When Dad gets home, she'll have to quit trying to make me her slave.

I close the kitchen door silently, get my bike, and push it through the trees in our yard rather than ride it down the driveway where she might see me leaving.

It's warm for February, so I know the horses will be out of their stalls and in the paddocks. There's an old, sway-backed white one I call Silver 'cause he looks old enough to have been the Lone Ranger's. He raises his head when my bike brakes squeal. The big brown one that looks like a racehorse, the black one with a white stripe on his hip, and the one with a white face all look up for a moment, then go back to eating the green winter grass.

I don't have anything for them today. In the fall I brought apples off our trees and bowled them into the pad-docks, but this time of year it's carrots, and then only the few I can steal without Sondra noticing how many have disappeared. Every once in a while she asks where all the carrots have gone, and I tell her I ate them. She pretends to believe me and says she's only asking because she's worried the whites of my eyes will turn orange. I promise to cut back—like I'm addicted or something. We've been doing this little dance—pretending to get along—since Daddy got sent to Iraq.

I didn't even know there were horses this close to our house until after my mom died and I had to start taking the bus to school. But it wasn't until Daddy left that I started coming here. He and I love everything about horses, espe-cially racehorses, so I watch them for both of us. It makes me feel like he's not so far away.

When my mother was dying of cancer, Dad and I used

to sit in her hospital room on either side of the bed, each holding one of her hands while she slept. It was one of those times when he first told me about running away from home to become a cowboy in Nevada.

"It was the best summer of my life, Hannah." He looked past me and out the window, his eyes soft and wistful. "We rounded up whole herds of wild mustangs."

"What would you do with them?"

"Most were sold." His sad eyes drifted to my mother's sleeping face. "Do you remember when we're riding the waves coming in from fishing, the wind in our faces, blowing your momma's hair? Those horses were that beautiful." He sighed, then smiled. "The roundup boss let me break a few of the young ones, and at night I slept on the ground— spread my dusty bedroll near the campfire, used my saddle for a pillow, and slept near our horses."

"I'd like to camp like that someday."

"Someday we will."

"How come you came back?" I asked him.

"Breaking wild horses is pretty dangerous work. I got bitten and kicked, once so hard it broke three ribs, and . . ." He pushed his hair aside so I could see the scar on his forehead. "This is where one reared up and nearly killed me. An inch or two closer to my temple and I'd have been toast. After a summer of that kind of work I decided fishing with my father wasn't all that bad."

There's a thick patch of blackberries between the road and the paddock fences, so I've never been nearer the horses than this bike path. Even if there were no blackberry vines, I think his stories have kept me from wanting to get any closer.

From down the road, I hear the roar of a souped-up car engine—high school boys, no doubt, racing up Sequoia Street. Before they come into sight, I feel the boom of their radio in my chest. I don't know why I want to hide from them, but there's no place to go anyway. When they're next to me, they blast the horn and one of them pounds the side of the car door with his fist and shouts, "Hey, baby. Let *me* be your horsey."

"Giddyup," another whoops. They all laugh and blow the horn again.

I suddenly feel like crying. All the horses whinny and run in a panic toward the far fence. The big brown one throws up his hind legs, like he's trying to kick the noise away. The two mangy dogs that live under the old run-down trailer across the road start barking at me too. I turn my bike for home.

My life sucks in so many ways right now. My mother died five years ago, my dad's been in Iraq for over a year, Madison, my best and only friend, moved to Oregon, and I'm stuck with my stepmother. I guess she's not as bad as

I sometimes make out, and I do have a new baby brother who looks exactly like Daddy did when he was about the same age. Sondra bought a frame that holds both their pictures and put it on the mantel above the woodstove. Side by side, they look like the same baby, except the picture of Daddy has faded.

My name is Hannah Gale. "Gale, as in a strong wind," my dad likes to say instead of spelling it for people. He's a fisherman. To him a gale means wild and dangerous seas, but to me it is a wind as strong as a racehorse pounding around a track, blowing by every other horse that ever lived.

Momma died in October of 2000. For a year or so afterward, Dad and I made a go of it on our own. We shared the cooking and cleaning, and when the salmon season opened, I took care of myself. I thought we were doing pretty good, until he met Sondra at the Knights of Columbus Crab Feed and married her a month before my tenth birthday.

We live in Fort Bragg, on the north coast of California, so there wasn't much opportunity for Dad to be a cowboy. Work here is timber or fishing, and not enough of either one anymore. My grandfather was a salmon fisherman all his life. Dad decided to carry on with the family business. He and my grandfather were building Dad a boat, but my grandfather died before they ever put it in the water. I was born four months later and Daddy named his salmon troller the *Hannah Gale* after me.

That May, when I was three months old—a month younger than Jeffy is now—Sea Hero won the Kentucky Derby. Dad told me he thought it was his father smiling down on him. He and Mom, who were high school sweethearts, had married, had a baby—me—and a boat of his own, then a horse named Sea Hero won the Derby. Dad said it was the best year he could remember since Nevada.

The first time Dad called from Iraq, I told him about the horses at the stable and how maybe when he gets back from the war I'd take a few riding lessons; then we could go on a camping trip and sleep under the stars.

"It's a promise, Hannah Banana," he said. "I haven't been on a horse in twenty years; maybe I'll take a lesson with you."

2

WEDNESDAY, FEBRUARY 22

Today is my thirteenth birthday. When the phone rings, my heart leaps. I don't know how, but I know it's Daddy. He's only allowed to use his cell phone when he's inside the wire—not out on a mission—and the last time he called was just before Thanksgiving. Since then, every time the phone rings or a strange car pulls into our driveway, I think it may be news of him and my heart nearly stops. But not today. Today it's him. I know it.

"Hello."

"How's my girl?" Daddy says. He sounds strange.

"I'm great now. Where have you been? We've been worried."

"It's a long story."

"Are you okay?"

"Pretty much."

There isn't the usual long delay our voices take to reach

7

each other when he calls from Iraq. He sounds like he could be next door.

"Where are you?"

"I'm in D.C."

"Washington, D. C.?"

"None other."

"What are you doing there? Are you coming home?" I can see my reflection in the kitchen window; I'm smiling.

"Soon, sweetie. Pretty soon."

I'm thrilled, thinking he's saved this news just for today.

"This is the best birthday present ever."

There's a pause before he says, "I'm sorry, Hannah Banana, I forgot it was your birthday."

"Oh." He's never forgotten my birthday. "It doesn't matter. You're coming home. That's all that counts."

"It will be a couple of months . . ."

Just then Sondra comes in with a load of groceries.

"It's Daddy . . ."

"Oh my God." She dumps the grocery bags on the table, spilling cans and oranges. She runs her fingers through her hair as if he can see her, grabs the phone, then hugs me excitedly. "The baby's in the car," she whispers to me. "Get him, please, and the rest of the groceries." She shoos me toward the door. "Jeff." Her voice cracks with emotion. "Oh Jeff, sweetheart. I've been so scared."

When I come in with Jeffy, Sondra's sitting with her back to me. The phone is in its base. "Did you hang up? I didn't get to tell him good-bye."

She doesn't say anything, but I see her shoulders shaking.

"What's the matter?" I put Jeffy's car seat on the table.

She turns; her cheeks are wet.

"He's been wounded. He was calling from Walter Reed."

"The hospital?" My stomach flip-flops. "Where was he wounded?"

"His leg." She chews a cuticle.

"How bad?"

Sondra doesn't say anything for a minute, then kind of shakes her head.

"If it was really bad, I'd have known."

She takes a napkin from the holder and dabs her eyes. "How would you have known?"

"I just would. Somehow." She forgets that Dad and I are related by blood and all we've been through together.

Sondra keeps watching me, so I open the fridge, not looking for anything in particular, but since she's sitting right here staring at me, I take a carrot just to keep up the charade. When I turn around holding it like a candle, Jeffy is smiling and kicking his legs. I reach to poke his belly with it, but the expression on Sondra's face stops me. She's staring at his fat little legs.

"Can you watch the baby?" she croaks.

Before I can answer, she jumps up and runs from the kitchen. The back of her chair hits the dishwasher, then crashes to the floor, scaring Jeffy, who starts to scream.

3

SUNDAY, MARCH 5

A couple weeks after Daddy's call from Walter Reed, I come in from visiting the horses to find Sondra paying bills at the kitchen table.

She heaves a sigh. "I wish you were old enough to get a job this summer," she says. "Money is going to be tight for a while."

"How old do I have to be?"

"I don't know. Sixteen, probably." She smiles. "If you'll lie, I'll swear to it." She's trying to kid, but I know she means it. She's a bank teller and we're pretty much living off her paycheck. Even if Dad gets disability until he can go back to fishing, it's going to be rough.

I'm tall for my age. Five seven. I wanted to be a jockey when I was little, but I passed that mark on the kitchen door frame over a year ago. With a little makeup, I can pass for sixteen, maybe older.

I'm sure Sondra pictures me working at McDonald's or bagging groceries at Harvest Market, but the minute she mentions me getting a job, I know exactly where I want to work: Redwood Springs Stables.

In spite of knowing every winner of the Kentucky Derby from Secretariat in 1973 to Giacomo, who won last year, I've never actually touched a horse. But after Sondra put the idea in my head to get a job, there's no place else I want to work.

We live on the western end of Sequoia Street on the north side of the road. After school, I have to ride the bus all the way up Simpson, right past my house, and out Mitchell Creek, then back again because the school bus won't pick up or let us off where we have to cross our busy road. The ride home—twice past the stables—is my favorite part of the day.

The tops of the stall doors are always open and the horses sometimes look out as we pass. If the weather is nice, they are in the paddocks wearing loose blankets and eating the grass, which is green from the winter rains. In summer it turns golden and the horses wear mesh masks over their eyes to keep the flies from bothering them. Each horse has its own fenced rectangular patch of grass and clover, though I think they like each other's company, because I see them standing side by side all the time as if they're gossiping over the fence. It makes me miss my friend Madison more than I already do.

I ride on one side of the bus going up Sequoia and move to the other side coming home. Another girl, who always sits near the front, does the same thing. I think her name is Lacy. She's in my math class at school but is always with a bunch of friends, so we've never talked.

The week after the conversation with Sondra about getting a job, I decide it's time to do more than just watch the horses. I get up early, put on jeans, one of Dad's plaid flannel shirts and the cowboy boots he sent me when he was in basic training. I hear Sondra in her room goo-gooing Jeffy as I creep downstairs. I steal a few carrots, get on my bike, and head up Sequoia to the stables.

I've been there dozens of times in the last year, but I've always stayed on the bike path behind the blackberries. Today I stop at the top of the driveway by the row of mailboxes to gather my nerve. Those two mangy-looking dogs jump up from where they are lying in the shade of a junked car. They're usually tied up, but today they run toward me barking. The one that looks like some kind of pit bull mix comes across the road, growling at me with the hair on his thick neck sticking straight up.

"Beat it," I say, trying not to show any fear.

The car that's coming barely slows down. It honks at the dog, whose rear end is in the traffic lane. "You're gonna get your dog killed, cowgirl." It's one of those boys who yelled at me before.

The car distracts the dog and I coast down the driveway.

The same white truck that's always there is parked near where they pile the horse manure, but I don't see anyone around. The horses look up for a moment, see it's me, and go back to grazing. Silver comes over and I toss him a chunk of carrot.

"I'm here to ask for a job. What do you think of my chances?"

He blinks and chews the carrot. Nothing I can interpret as support. I push my bike a little farther down the driveway, then lean it against the fence and keep walking. Silver follows me.

If I'm going to ask for a job, I'd better get brave and at least try to touch a horse. I step up on the bottom board of the fence and hook my elbows over the top railing. Even as old and swaybacked as he is, Silver still looks huge as he walks toward me. My heart sounds like the clop of hooves beating in my ears, but when I raise my hand to touch his nose, he steps back and stands just beyond my fingertips.

"Horses are prey animals, not predators," a woman's voice says. "That one hates men and is a little spooky around women he doesn't know." She's carrying a pitchfork full of hay toward an open stall. "Try keeping your hand where he can see it. It's hard for them to see between their eyes, and they can't see at all behind their ears, or the backs of their necks."

"Thank you," I say to her, then to Silver, "Sorry," I whisper. "I didn't know you might be afraid of me too."

Silver puts his head over the fence about four feet away from where I'm standing. I get down and walk over to him, put my hand out, palm flat, so he can smell it. When he doesn't move, I bring it up. His nose feels warm and moist against my skin, but when his tail suddenly switches, I jerk my hand away. I glance toward the woman, but she's gone into the stall with the hay. I imagine "rejected: scared of horses" written in big red letters across my job application.

She comes out and smiles. She's a little taller than me, thin and pretty with short blond hair. "His name is Jack, but I call him Ole Blue Eyes."

Jack. Not Silver. "He sure has blue eyes all right."

"I was thinking of a certain singer." She looks at me. "You're too young."

"Too young for what?" Does she know why I'm here?

"To know who Frank Sinatra was. His nickname was Ole Blue Eyes. Ask your mother about him. Or maybe your grandmother."

"I will," I say.

"What can I do you for?"

"Are you the owner?"

"No, I'm the manager."

"I live down the road a mile or so and I love horses . . ." I take a breath and feel my good-luck necklace move against

15

my skin. It's a flat piece of cobalt blue glass wrapped in gold wire. Momma and I found it at Glass Beach. I curl my fingers around it. "I'd like to work here."

Her eyebrows pull down in a V. "We don't really hire help. We just board the horses and every owner takes care of his or her own."

"I'd do anything and you wouldn't have to actually pay me."

"Not much of a job then, is it?"

I look at my feet. "I guess not."

She walks away.

Blew that.

I start back toward my bike and have a foot on the pedal when she comes back with another pitchfork full of hay. "Ever been around a horse before today?"

Could I count standing at the fence and staring at them? "No," I say. "It's just my dad was a cowboy once and he's been in Iraq and I want to surprise . . ."

She stops at the stall door and turns. Her lips are compressed. Maybe she's one of those "Women in Black" people who stand outside Town Hall on Friday evenings to promote peace. I start to tell her that he was in the National Guard and didn't want to go.

"How long's he been gone?"

"Fourteen months. But he's coming home . . ." I duck

my head and stare hard at the dusty toes of my cowboy boots.

Her eyes soften before she turns and goes into the stall. "How old are you?" she calls to me.

I hesitate. "Fifteen?"

She comes out and closes the bottom half of the door. "This is Super Dee's stall." She points to the tall brown horse in the paddock next to Jack's. He's been standing at the gate watching her put hay in his stall. "He's a grandson of Seattle Slew. Seattle Slew won—"

My eyes widen. "*The* Seattle Slew?"

"Yep." She walks over and rubs Super Dee's forehead. "Such a good boy," she says, her lips against his nose. "How do you know about Seattle Slew?"

"I know all the Kentucky Derby, Preakness, and Belmont winners. He was the 1978 winner of the Triple Crown. My dad was born in 1973, the year Secretariat won, and I was born in 1993, the year Sea Hero won the Kentucky Derby."

"Well, now I am impressed."

I lower my head. Did she catch my lie?

"You're tall for thirteen, but about right for fifteen."

"I'm sorry. I didn't think you'd hire a thirteen-year-old."

"I wouldn't, or even a fifteen-year-old, but I could use a volunteer muck-raker."

"I'm your girl," I say. *Muck-raker?* "What is that?"

"Cleaning the horse manure out of the stalls and the runs."

I laugh. "Wait 'til I tell my dad."

"Will he mind?"

"Oh no, ma'am. He's gonna say I was born to start right there. He calls me the family optimist."

My new boss looks at me like she doesn't see the connection.

"My stepmother is a worrier and a pessimist. Dad told me the difference between her and me was if there was a stall full of horse manure, she'd see the manure and I would be digging through looking for the pony."

She laughs. "I guarantee you *will* find ponies." She takes her glove off and puts out her hand. "My name is Dillon."

"Hannah Gale."

"Well, Hannah Gale, why don't you report for 'work'"— she makes quote marks with her fingers—"tomorrow, and when you do, lose the cowboy boots. Don't want to muck up those fine-looking things."

4

SUNDAY, MARCH 12

The morning after Dillon says I can come help out at the stables, I wake early and am too excited to go back to sleep.

Sondra's in the kitchen pumping breast milk to fill Jeffy's bottles for the sitter. "Where are you going? You look like you should be wearing a straw hat and picking your teeth."

I have on an old pair of jeans, a ratty T-shirt, and Dad's plaid work shirt. "I got a job."

She smiles like I'm joking.

"I did. At the stables up the road."

She looks kind of impressed but says, "I don't know, Hannah. That could be dangerous."

"I'm just cleaning stalls when the horses are in their paddocks."

"What's a paddock?"

Sondra's not into horseracing like Dad and me. "It's a small fenced field where the horses can run around and eat grass."

"You're not in there with them, are you?"

"No. Of course not."

Her nose wrinkles. "Would you really rather clean up horse poop than work someplace nice?"

"What, like McDonald's?"

"Not necessarily, maybe at one of the nurseries. You could water plants and weed."

Her thinking of a nursery surprises me. That would have been my second choice, if I'd thought about it. "That'd be okay, but I already got hired by the stables."

"How much are they paying you?"

She's boiling bottles on the stove. I turn off the burner and carry them to the sink so that I don't have to be looking at her when I lie. "A couple bucks an hour, I guess."

"Minimum wage is five fifteen."

"Well, that's it then. She said minimum, but I didn't know how much that was and didn't ask."

"Well, we'll have to see what your dad says."

She's filled three bottles. "He'll think it's great." I open the fridge and put them on the shelf.

"Maybe he will."

"You're not going to ask right away, are you? I want it to be a surprise for when he gets home."

"You promise you're not actually around the horses?"

"I promise."

"Okay. We'll wait."

"Thanks." I give her a quick hug.

At the stables the stall doors are still closed. I don't want Dillon to find me waiting; she might think I'm going to be a pest. I turn around and ride back down the road, then cut into the forest on a horse trail that winds its way down to Digger Creek. I sit on a log and watch the water flow over the rocks. No sun gets through the redwood branches, so after a while I get cold and decide to start back. Someday, when Dad's all healed, and after I learn to ride, I'll bring him this way through the woods and we'll water the horses here in the creek.

Dillon's truck is there when I ride down the driveway the second time, but like yesterday, I don't see her anywhere. She's opened the top half of each stall door and the horses are lined up looking out. I lean my bike against the fence and walk to the first stall on the right and start to read their names, which are on white boards on the bottom half of each door, along with an owner's name and phone number.

The black horse with the white stripe on his hip is Indiana, with quotes around his nickname—"Indy." This is the first time I've been close enough to see that the stripe on his hip is a line of white hair. He's busy licking the door frame and ignores me. Super Dee is next to Indy. He's eating oats but lifts his head to look at me, his nose covered with bits of grain. He's huge and I don't get too close. Next is poor Jack with his scarred face and runny eyes. He lets me touch his cheek. On the other side of Jack is the white-faced horse whose name is Bobby. He sticks his neck out and shows his teeth like he's trying to bite my face. I jump back.

Next to Bobby is a hay shed, then two empty stalls, then a storage shed full of funny-looking pitchforks, and three rows of white bait buckets full of water—ten in all. Bridles, ropes, brooms, and shovels hang from nails in the walls. There's another hay shed, then an enclosed lean-to with a lawn mower and an ancient, rusting tractor parked side by side. Against the outside wall is a line of wheelbarrows, and beyond—far enough away so I can't smell it—is a small mountain of horse manure.

I still don't see Dillon, so I turn to start back the way I came and run right into her.

"Good morning." She's pulling on gloves.

"Am I too early?"

"Not at all." She turns and crooks her finger for me to follow.

There's a big barn to the west of the stalls. Attached

to it is a small kitchen and bathroom. Outside the barn, there's a picnic table and a matching one in the kitchen. A single lightbulb hangs from a cord in the beamed ceiling and the only window is dirty and full of cobwebs. On the outside wall of the barn is a hose and a muddy slab of plywood where, Dillon tells me, the horses stand to get their baths.

She leads me to the kitchen and starts going through the piles of things on the table. "I'm trying to find you some gloves to wear."

"It's okay. I don't need gloves."

"Oh yes you do. Ah, here. These are Meg's, but I doubt she'll mind."

"What do you keep in the barn?"

"Barn? Oh. It's not a barn . . ." She opens the door. "It's an arena. In the winter we play with the horses in here."

She stands aside to let me look in. It's about the size of our gymnasium at school, with a dirt floor. The only light is coming through skylights in the roof. There's a row of white plastic chairs lined up behind some orange traffic cones. To my right is a pile of blankets, which smell of horses. Directly in front of me is a set of three steps and to my left strips of heavy plastic hang from a metal frame. There are four white barrels out in the center, a blue tarp like we use to cover our firewood, a huge blue rubber ball, and a big square of bubble wrap. I want to ask what all these things are for, but I already feel like I'm keeping her from what she was doing.

"I've come by sometimes and seen all the cars and wondered where the horses were. I thought you were riding in the woods."

"We do that too, but it's drier and warmer in here and we can let them run at liberty."

"What does that mean?"

"No halters, reins, or ropes. When you come next Saturday, you can watch."

I follow Dillon to the far end of the stalls, where we each get a wheelbarrow and roll it to the shed.

"This is a muck-rake." She smiles and hands me one of the odd-looking pitchforks. "It's nice to have a helper."

"Thanks for letting me be here."

"One rule: I don't want you in an occupied stall."

"Okay."

"It's every owner's job to muck her horse's stall, but no one's going to complain about a little help. I own Bobby and Indy, so we'll start with them."

"Who owns Jack?"

"Meg. He was her first horse, but he's gotten too old to ride. She also owns Super Dee. She'll be here after a while."

"Is Super Dee still fast?"

"Probably not. Meg never runs him hard. He's got too many aches and pains from his racing days."

There's a box on the side shed that makes a clicking sound every few seconds. Dillon sees me look at it. "Along the top of each run is an electrical wire. It keeps the horses from chewing the wood. It can give you a bit of a jolt if you touch it."

I nod. I don't like electricity, not since I stuck a safety pin in a light socket when I was five and charred the tips of my fingers.

Dillon parks her wheelbarrow outside Indy's stall. He sticks his head out and she kisses his nose, then takes a halter and rope from a peg by the door and puts it over his head. She opens the bottom half of his stall and leads him out and across to a paddock. I love the clompy sound of his hooves crossing the gravel driveway. She opens the gate to the paddock, leads him in, then takes his halter and lead off, brings them back, and hangs them by his door. "We never leave their halters on when they are in their stalls or the paddocks. They could get caught on something."

"Okay." I like that she bothers to tell me this.

I step inside Indy's stall and start raking the poop into a pile.

"Turn it the other way," Dillon says, "and scoop."

"Oh. That is easier."

Dillon goes to Bobby's stall and takes a rope halter off

the nail by his door. He bounces his big head up and down, then shakes it side to side. "Hold still," Dillon snaps. He sticks his neck out and lifts his upper lip like he did to me. She ignores his teeth and puts the halter over his nose and behind his ears, then opens his door and leads him to the nearest post and ties him up. When she starts to brush him, dust and hair rise in a cloud.

I'm in the doorway of Indy's stall with the first wheelbarrow full. Super Dee is taller than Bobby, but Bobby, especially this close up, is massive and he's blocking the walkway in front of the stalls. I either have to duck under his chin or walk around behind him, both of which I'm afraid to do. "Does he bite?"

"No, but he's very oral." Dillon leans her head to the side a little and looks at his rear end. He rotates around to face her just as if she'd asked him to move. I'm thinking that was cool, when she taps his nose and says, "Gimme some tongue."

He lolls his fat yellow and pink tongue out the side of his mouth.

"He'll do anything for a carrot. They're in that cupboard." She points to the big wooden box between the stalls.

I get one from the bag and hold it out to him.

"Break it into chunks and give it to him a piece at a time with your palm flat."

Bobby stretches his neck toward me and flaps his lips,

showing those yellow teeth again. He slobbers on my hand, which I wipe on the front of my shirt.

"Can I take one to Jack?" He's watching me with his sad, bloodshot blue eyes.

"Sure."

I break another carrot into chunks and bring them to Jack. Bobby's head is turned to watch me and when he sees me look at him, he lolls his tongue out again. I laugh, maybe for the first time in a year, and give him the last chunk.

At home that night, I smell like a cowboy, all horses and hay. I hide my shirt so Sondra won't find it and wash it.

5

LAST MAY

Two months after Dad and Sondra got married inside the Point Cabrillo Lighthouse the war started and a year after that Daddy got sent overseas, leaving the two of us here alone.

I like Sondra okay and I didn't actually mind them getting married. She's always been nice to me and she made Daddy happy, but after he left, she tried to mother me, which definitely didn't work. Even Dad told her I was used to taking care of myself. Then she tried being my friend, taking me to lunch and a movie on the weekends. I went twice, but both times we couldn't agree on which movie to see and ended up sitting in different theaters.

The first and only leave Daddy got was Christmas before last. It was a wonderful two weeks but, just before he left to go back, he told us his National Guard unit was being redeployed for another six months. I think Sondra took the news better than I did, but when she found out she was pregnant with Jeffy, she totally changed, got all needy and helpless, crying at the drop of a hat.

I really did feel sorry for her, but my way of dealing with Dad being gone is to go off by myself and think about him. I'm not a good crutch.

The sorriest I ever felt for her was last May. We were both squeezed into the chair in front of the computer waiting for our Skype connection to come up to Dad in Ramadi. Sondra was nearly five months pregnant. At the time, we thought he had only four months to go on his redeployment and that he'd be home for the baby's birth near the end of September. When his face appeared on the monitor, I saw his lips move, then about ten seconds later we heard his voice. "How are my girls?"

"We're good," we said in unison. "How are you?"

"Fine. Fine." He didn't look right into the camera when he answered. "It's about a hundred fifteen degrees here. How is it there?"

"Cool," I said. "Fifty-seven. And it rained last week."

"Still seeing whales?"

Every spring Dad and I took his boat out to watch the gray whales migrate past on their way back to Alaska. We'd see them really close, but I hadn't been out on the ocean since he left. I would have said no anyway so he wouldn't feel like he was missing that too. "I think the migration is over."

"I sure miss you both."

"And we miss you," Sondra said.

"Dad, do you know what yesterday was?"

"Let me guess." He smiled.

I knew he remembered it was the Kentucky Derby.

"I give up," he said, and winked at me.

"You lie."

"Sweetheart, you're being careful, aren't you," Sondra interrupted. "The news from over there is frightening."

"I'm being as careful as I can, baby. Try not to worry.

"So, Hannah Banana, who won?"

"Giacomo. He just came out of the blue."

"What was his time?"

"Two minutes, two and three-quarter seconds."

"Do you remember Sea Hero's time?"

The fact that I was born the year Sea Hero won the Derby makes him Dad's and my favorite racehorse.

"Of course. Two minutes, two and two-fifths."

"If our Sea Hero had been in that race, Giacomo would never have gotten past him."

"The baby's due September twenty-ninth," Sondra said. "You'll make it in time, won't you?"

I saw him look away and that's when I knew they'd extended his tour again.

"Six more months," he said.

"What?" Sondra said.

"It's not up to me, sweetheart. They don't have the troops to replace us."

Tears rolled down Sondra's cheeks. She pushed herself to her feet and went into the bathroom for a Kleenex.

"Daddy, it's okay. Don't worry about us."

He winked at me from all those thousands of miles away. "Did you have a bet on Giacomo?"

"You're funny. I'll bet you he wins the Preakness, okay? Two bucks."

"You're on, but let's make it five. Can you remember the last horse to win the Derby and the Preakness?"

I was trying to think of the answer when Sondra came back poking her stomach out as far as she could so Daddy would notice, which he did.

"I'm sorry I can't be there with you, honey, but Hannah will take good care of you, won't you, baby?"

Sondra put her arm around my shoulders and nodded. "I know she will."

"Sure, Daddy. We'll be fine," I said, though I wanted to cry too. Six more months. Then I remembered the last horse to win both. "It was Smarty Jones in '04," I yelled, but the connection was gone.

Almost two years have passed since Daddy and I sat on the sofa and watched President Bush fly in and land on the aircraft carrier *Lincoln*, then stand with the "Mission

Accomplished" sign behind him and everyone cheering, as if we'd won the war. I believed it. A week or two earlier, we'd watched the Iraqis pull over the statue of Saddam Hussein, then drag it down the street whacking it with their shoes.

"Mark my words," Daddy said. "This war isn't over, it's just beginning."

"It looks over to me," I said. "Wanna bet?"

"I'd be stealing your money."

The day after Bush took a bow in front of that "Mission Accomplished" sign, Funny Cide won the Kentucky Derby. As the news about the war got worse, Daddy started calling that banner "Bush's funny sign."

Dad joined the National Guard after 9-11. He said flying the American flag off your antenna wasn't enough. He wanted to be here to protect me and Sondra and our country. He chose the National Guard because the recruiter told him he would never have to leave home. That man lied to my dad.

I don't know if all fishermen are a little superstitious, but even before the war started, during the 2002 running of the Kentucky Derby, Dad had a premonition about having to go fight. He and I were watching it together and cheering for our favorite, but when War Emblem won, Daddy sat on the sofa staring at the TV, his hands clasped between his knees. "That's not a good omen, Hannah Banana," he'd said over the roar of the crowd at Churchill Downs.

6

SATURDAY, APRIL 22

H annah, are you dressed yet?" Sondra shouts up the
stairs.

Today we're driving down to get Dad at the VA hospital
in Palo Alto, and she's been running around like a lunatic
trying to get herself and Jeffy ready.

"Yes," I yell back, then go to the railing.

"I'm forgetting something." She's standing on the landing looking around at nothing, then up at me. "Just hurry,
okay? We should have left twenty minutes ago."

She so doesn't get it. I don't have to *get* ready; I've *been*
ready. Ever since he left, I've been waiting for Daddy to
come home.

Last week he finally phoned from Walter Reed to say
they were releasing him. Sondra was on the kitchen phone
and I was on the one in Dad's office.

"I'm as healed as I'm ever going to get in this dump," he'd

said. "They're shipping me to the Palo Alto VA, where you can pick up the remains." He laughed, a flat, dull laugh.

"What did he mean, as healed as he's ever going to get?" I'd asked her after we hung up, but she didn't answer. She just sat at the counter with her head bowed. It scared me a little, but then I decided his leg probably still hurts and he's gonna have to use a cane or even crutches for a while.

"Do you have Jeffy's diaper bag?" I say.

"That's it. Where did I leave it?" She pulls on her chin.

She's wearing one of Dad's sweaters draped around her shoulders, but a small wet spot shows on her blouse. "It's in the downstairs bathroom and you're leaking."

She pulls her shirt away from her chest, curses under her breath, then gathers the sides of the sweater together and knots them in her fist.

I don't blame her for being discombobulated. I'm having trouble thinking straight myself. He hasn't been home since Christmas of 2004—a year and four months. I was only eleven then. Well, almost twelve, but still. Since then I've grown five inches and my hair is long; it was short when he left. I worry he won't recognize me.

Sondra snaps Jeffy into his car seat and turns. "Dear God, Hannah, why are you dressed like that? You look like you're going to work at the stables rather than going to see you father for the first time in over a year."

I have on clean jeans and my flannel work shirt so when

I hug Dad, he'll smell the horses. "You don't understand," I say. She's wearing one of her church dresses and enough perfume to choke a horse.

She shakes her head like I'm a complete mystery, and gets behind the wheel.

I roll my window down before I get in, but I still sneeze and wonder if you can get nose cancer from secondhand perfume.

The drive south to Palo Alto takes about five hours, though by the time we get there it feels more like fifty. Sondra doesn't want to talk. When she gets quiet, I know she's letting herself get worked up imagining all kinds of things.

When I'm nervous, I chatter. I start telling her about the time Dad ran away from home to become a cowboy.

"Good Lord, Hannah, please be quiet. And close your window before you give Jeffy a cold."

I read the MapQuest directions, and we find the Foothill Expressway okay but miss the turn to get on Miranda Avenue. By the time we pull up in front of the VA hospital, Dad is waiting near the front doors in a wheelchair. An orderly is standing beside him holding his crutches.

I wave at Dad, wishing I could leap from the car and run to him. He lifts his hand and smiles, but it's an odd kind of smile, like Mom's when I came to the hospital and talked about things I wanted to do when she got better.

The orderly lays the crutches across the arms of the wheelchair and Dad holds them in place as he's pushed toward us. Sondra jams the car straight from drive into park without putting her foot on the brake so that it bucks through reverse. Without turning off the engine, she leaps out. The crutches are in her way, so she goes around to the back of the wheelchair and throws her arms around Daddy's neck. I turn off the engine and jump out the other door. Jeffy starts to cry.

"Oh Jeff. Jeff," Sondra cries against his neck.

Daddy closes his eyes and leans his head back against her cheek.

"Hey there, Hannah Banana. How's my grown-up girl?" he says when he opens his eyes again and sees me.

"I'm fine, Daddy. How are you?"

"I'm good," he says, then reaches up and pats the back of Sondra's head.

I open the rear door to get Jeffy out of his car seat. His little face is wet and red. He holds his arms out to me. It's when I turn with him that I see Daddy's legs. It's windy, and his uniform pants are snapping around his ankles— his ankle. His right leg is there, but the left one is gone. There's just a shoe and an exposed two inches of metal rod. Our eyes meet.

"If I was a horse they'd have shot me," he says.

Pain erupts in my chest as real as if I'd been kicked in the heart. I glance at Sondra, whose face is still buried against Daddy's neck. When I look back at Daddy, he's looking at Jeffy, who's screaming. I want to say something brave, but nothing comes to mind. I close my eyes, hug Jeffy tight, and let him scream for the both of us.

When I open my eyes again, Sondra has straightened, leaving a damp circle of tears on Dad's uniform collar. She comes around the chair and takes the baby from me. "Jeffy—sweetheart—this is your daddy." She holds him out to Dad, but Daddy doesn't raise his arms, and for a second, it occurs to me they might be gone too. They aren't, of course. He just doesn't have the heart to hold his son right now. He closes his eyes and lowers his head.

"He's wet, Sondra. Let me change him first." I take Jeffy and lay him on the backseat.

"It will be all right, sweetheart," Sondra says. "You're home. That's all that matters."

If she just saw his leg, she's awfully calm. I turn to look at her. Dad has his crutches and is trying to stand. Sondra has her arm around his waist and I realize she's known all along that he'd lost his leg. He's my dad. She should have told me when I asked her how bad. Instead she let me believe I'd have known. I hate her.

"Wait, sir," the orderly says.

"I'm done with waiting," Daddy says, but his first try to

get up doesn't work. His jaw tightens with determination like it used to on our boat in high seas.

After I finish changing Jeffy, the orderly touches my shoulder and hands me the crutches. He straddles Daddy's legs and lifts him to his feet. Daddy grimaces as the orderly holds him steady, then takes the crutches back and helps him balance himself. When Dad's standing on his own, the orderly folds the wheelchair and asks me to open the trunk.

Dad keeps his balance with the crutches, but when he tries to move toward the car, he nearly falls. His face scrunches with the pain. The orderly's lips compress as he jumps to help Daddy. He takes a crutch away and wraps Dad's left arm around his neck. Daddy hops to the car, turns, and lets the orderly lower him into the passenger seat.

Sondra runs around to the driver's side as I wait for Dad to catch his breath. He looks at me for a moment. I've seen that look before: the last afternoon I came into Momma's hospital room from school. Daddy was sitting on the far side of her bed, holding her hand, his forehead against their knotted fingers.

"Is she asleep?" I'd whispered.

He looked up and nodded, his eyes red-rimmed and dull-looking. It wasn't until I took her other hand and felt how cold it was that I realized he meant asleep forever. It scares me now to see his face so empty of hope and that sad look again.

Daddy puts his hands under his thigh and lifts his leg into the car. The material of his uniform pants sags against his metal knee cap and the rod they've given him to replace his missing leg. The orderly puts his hand on my shoulder and speaks against my ear. "Be strong for your dad."

7

THE SAME DAY

I sit in the backseat of the Honda with Jeffy, holding his bottle for him, but I can see Sondra's eyes in the rearview mirror. She's glancing at Daddy, then at me, then at Daddy. I can't understand why she didn't tell me he'd lost a leg. I just stare back at her.

"You look good." She smiles at him.

"Feel good. Glad to be home." We were on 101 near the San Francisco airport. "Take the 380," Daddy says.

"Why?"

"The 380 to 280 to Brotherhood Way. We can get on Sunset and miss all the traffic on Nineteenth."

"I got us here, Jeff, I can find my way home."

"I know, sweetheart. It's just all the traffic and noise makes me . . . Never mind, I'm just trying to show you a shortcut to the Golden Gate."

"Guess what," I say. "I got a summer job at the Redwood Springs Stables and I've already started working there on weekends."

He looks at me through the gap between the seats. "That's wonderful, honey." His smile doesn't reach his eyes. "You're being careful, right? If you walk behind a horse it might kick you."

"I'm just cleaning the empty stalls."

"Good."

"Dillon—she's my boss—told me it's safe to cross behind a horse that knows you as long as you walk real close and keep your hand on its butt so it knows you're there."

"Just be careful." He smiles at me, then glances at Jeffy, who's finished his bottle and has fallen asleep. "That boy's a keeper." He's talking to Sondra, trying to be his old cheeky self, but Sondra doesn't get it.

"He's not a fish, Jeff."

"Do you remember how I met this beautiful woman?" He's taken Sondra's right hand and is gazing at her like she's another long-legged relative of Seattle Slew.

"Yeah," I say, and stare out the window. A picture pops into my head of Daddy asleep by a campfire. A single boot stands at the foot of his bedroll, and his saddle lies nearby with the left stirrup cut off. I bite my lip to keep from crying.

By the time we get home I'm so ready to have this ride

over with I want to applaud when we make the turn off Sequoia Street.

Our gravel driveway is long and winds through a small, second-growth stand of Doug firs, so it isn't until we pull up in front that it dawns on me that we live in a two-story house and all the bedrooms are upstairs.

Sondra turns off the engine and stares at the front door. There are three stairs just to get up to our porch. "I guess I thought with the prosthesis you'd be able to walk," she says. "How's this going to work?"

Dad opens his door. "Hand me those crutches, Hannah, will you?"

"Wait, both of you," Sondra says. "Let's get the wheelchair first."

"Where are we going to wheel it?" I ask.

"From here to the front door."

"If we pull into the garage, there are no steps up into the kitchen."

"Good thinking, Hannah," Sondra says. "Go open the doors for me, will you?"

I jump out, run and swing the two garage doors open. The floor of the garage is dirt and it's uneven. I go through and open the door into the kitchen. Dad's workbench takes up three feet of the twelve-foot wide garage, which doesn't leave enough room for his wheelchair to get by when the car's inside. I hold up my hand when Sondra starts the engine and begins to roll forward. "There's not enough room. Let's get him out and in the house first."

Through the windshield, I see Dad put his head back and close his eyes. I'm talking to Sondra about him—in the third person—as if he is no longer able to think or speak for himself. "Don't ya think, Daddy?"

He doesn't answer.

Sondra pulls the trunk release. I open the wheelchair and put the wheel locks on like I used to do for Momma, then I reach to help Dad swing his right leg out. I start to slip my hand under his left thigh and feel the back of my knees tingle. The thought of touching where his leg was cut off makes me queasy. "I'll do it, Hannah." He pats my cheek like he understands. "Put the chair right here beside me."

Daddy lifts his leg up, but not high enough. He bangs the shoe against the door frame. His teeth clench in pain. "I'm okay." He closes his eyes and groans. "It's okay."

I watch him as he slowly swings his left leg out and carefully puts his fake foot on the ground. I suddenly hate all of those men who drummed up this phony war, then sent my father into it. It was supposed to be a one-year tour of duty; now it's a life sentence.

He stands up on his good leg, holds on to the door, turns, and flops into the wheelchair.

Sondra has carried Jeffy into the house and is in the doorway watching us, her face full of pity. I give her a dirty look. I don't want Daddy to see her looking at him like that.

"I think we can set up your office as a bedroom, don't you?" she says.

"That's what I was thinking," Daddy says. "Just move a few things around. That will work until I get used to this thing."

Between the two of us, Sondra and I clear enough out of Dad's office to make room for a rollaway and give him a clear path to the bathroom. We push most of his furniture against the file cabinets that line one wall. The rollaway is a single and the same one we used when Mom came home and was too weak to climb the stairs. We make the bed with the only twin-bed sheets we own—the ones with blue and yellow balloons that I picked out to cheer Mom up. I wonder if Daddy will remember and feel sadder.

The door from the garage into the kitchen must have been wider than the inside doors, because when we're done and invite him in for a look, his wheelchair won't fit through either door—office or bathroom.

"There's a crowbar on the pegboard over my workbench, Hannah. Get it for me, will you?"

"What are you going to do?" Sondra looks worried.

"Take the molding off."

"It will look awful."

"What would you rather I do, sleep sitting up in this thing and pee in a jar?"

"Jeff. Really."

"Sorry. There are some pills in my duffel. Get them for me, will you?"

He is downing a few with water when I come back with the crowbar. He doesn't just push it between the door frame and the interior molding that keeps the door in place, he jams it in as hard as he can. Pieces splinter and fly into the room.

Sondra looks at him. "I'll go fix dinner."

I pick up all the pieces while I tell him about the stables, Dillon, Super Dee, Jack, and the others.

"A grandson of Seattle Slew? Really?"

"Oh yeah, Dad. And he's huge too. Seventeen hands. That's four inches per hand, you know?"

"I remember."

"I'm hoping Dillon will teach me to ride one day . . ." I hesitate. "Then we can go on that camping trip . . ."

"I'm not sure when that's going to happen, Hannah Banana." He glances at me and must see how sorry I am that I brought it up. "Just give me some time, okay?"

"Sure, Dad. When your leg stops hurting."

"We'll have to take it one day . . . one door at a time." He pops off the last of the molding.

The door frame has taken an awful beating, but when he's finished, the chair fits through both doors and Dad wheels himself into his new life.

8

SUNDAY, APRIL 23

It's Sondra who suggests I go to the stables this morning. I'm glad. It's weird here. She and Dad are stiffly polite to each other and she's being really nice to me. Too nice. She asks how I want my eggs cooked. She never does that. She usually slaps a bowl and the cereal box on the counter. I roll my eyes when she calls me sweetie. She saw me, I guess, 'cause that's when she said, "It's a beautiful day, Hannah. You should go visit those horses."

Today is Sunday. The fun days to be at the stables are Saturdays and Sundays, when they play games with the horses. Weekdays, Dillon comes by in the morning, opens the tops of the stall doors, feeds and waters all the horses, and, if the weather is nice, lets them out into the paddocks. In the afternoons, both Meg and Dillon come after work at their day jobs to clean stalls, feed and water. Meg's a nurse at the hospital and Dillon has an online site that sells saddles and other stuff for horses.

The first few Saturdays at the stables, after I helped muck the stalls, I sat on the pile of blankets in the arena and watched them work the horses. Dillon and Meg led Bobby, Indy, and Super Dee into the arena, then closed the tall doors so nothing could scare them. After the first two times there, I learned their routine and now Dillon lets me help. We brush the horses first. When we're done, we take their lead ropes off and the horses follow Dillon and Meg to the center, where, just by pointing the direction they want them to go, the horses begin to trot around the arena. They thunder by my perch on the blankets, manes and tails flying. I close my eyes and listen to them pound down the backside and I begin to tremble when I hear them charging back again. This must be what it feels like to stand at the railing during the Derby.

After the horses have burned off their excess energy, the women play games with them. Without leads or ropes, they ask the horses to do bowties around the barrels, walk sideways perpendicular to the wall, and jump PVC pipes set on blocks. They have them walk across the bubble wrap, which pops and snaps. The horses don't even flinch.

There's a platform about the size of a small trampoline just to the left of where I sit, and all Dillon or Meg have to do is point and Super Dee or Bobby or Indy will step up and stand on it. I haven't seen them use the beach ball or the tarp yet. Dillon says those are for teaching horses that are still using the right side of their brains.

All these horses have been trained by a gentle, natural method, which makes them use the left side of their brains—the thinking side—and helps them overcome their instinct to flee in a panic, which comes from the right side of their brains. The training imitates the games they play with each other and the relationships they had with their mothers. It's called Parelli. The Parellis have a show on TV, but we only have cable, not Dish, so we don't get it. I think maybe the Parelli method is kind of what Robert Redford used in *The Horse Whisperer*—my favorite movie.

When I get to the stables this afternoon, Meg's and Dillon's cars are there, but no one is around. Just Jack—alone in a paddock.

"Where'd they go?" I ask when he comes and hangs his head over the gate. I rub under his forelock, then walk across the driveway to get a couple of carrots from the bag in the cupboard. There's a note thumbtacked to the door of Bobby's stall: *Gone for a trail ride. Figured you'd stay home with your dad, so didn't call. Hope he's well. D.*

Hope he's well? I walk to where Jack waits for me, breaking the carrot into bite-size chunks. I feed them to him one at a time, then lay my arm on the fence railing and put my forehead against it. I breathe deeply and imagine I can still smell my dad in the flannel. "He's not, Jack. He's not well at all." I feel his warm muzzle against the back of my neck and start to cry.

Daddy's shouting wakes us. Sondra and I come out of our rooms at the same time and rush down the stairs. I beat her to the den, where Daddy is on the floor all twisted up in his balloon-print sheets.

"Daddy, wake up," I cry. He's flailing like a fish on a hook, so it's hard to get close enough to touch him. He works his leg out of the twisted sheet and pivots on his left hip, kicking and screaming for us to get away. I'm near his head, but when I reach to touch his shoulder, he tries to bite me. He curses, then shouts for his friend Shorty.

Sondra pulls me away from him. "Jeff! Jeff. Wake up!"

Upstairs, Jeffy starts to scream.

Daddy gets an arm free and drags himself toward the bookcase. "Get those kids away," he yells. He starts tearing books from the bottom shelf of the bookcase—the ones he can reach—and knocks over the dictionary stand. "My leg," he screams. "Oh Christ, my leg. Help me." His hand closes like a vise around my ankle and he drags me down.

"Let go," I cry, and kick his shoulder.

He lets go and grabs his stump. "God help me. My leg."

I crawl into the corner between the office chair and the table that holds the fax machine.

Sondra runs from the room and I think she's gone up to Jeffy, but in a moment she's back. There's a full glass of water in her hand and she throws it in Daddy's face.

His eyes have been open the whole time, but now he sputters and looks at us, confused for a second until he sees what the room looks like. "I'm sorry," he croaks, then clutches his pajama top and starts gasping for air like he is having a heart attack.

I drop to my knees to search for the phone. I find the base, but it's a moment longer before I find the receiver, which had spun across the bathroom floor, hit the tub, and split open. The battery is dangling out. My hands shake as I fit it back in and start to dial 911.

"It's okay, Hannah," Sondra says. "Hang up."

"He's having a heart attack."

"No. It's a panic attack and he's hyperventilating. My dad had these for years after Vietnam.

"Shhhh, Jeff." She sits down beside him and strokes his head. "Jeff, it's okay. You're home." That's all she says, over and over—in the calmest voice.

He keeps gasping for air, but when she cups a hand over his nose and mouth, he grabs her wrist and jerks his head away.

"Get me a Ziploc from the kitchen," she says to me. "Jeff, try to relax."

Daddy claws at the neck of his pajama top, which is

soaked through with sweat. "I can't breathe," he gasps, his eyes wide with fear.

"Go!" she screams at me.

I run to the kitchen.

"Jeff. Listen to me," I hear her say when I come back. "You're hyperventilating. That's all it is."

Sondra grabs the Ziploc, opens it, and holds it over Daddy's nose and mouth. "You have to breathe your own carbon dioxide for a moment or two. Trust me."

Watching her face, Daddy does as she says until his breathing slows. "I'm sorry," he says when she takes the bag away.

Sondra puts her palm against his cheek. "It's okay."

It isn't, of course.

9

MONDAY, APRIL 24

I've never seen my dad have more than a cold beer or two after fishing all day, but the next night he drinks a lot and still wakes us up again shouting. This time Sondra and I come quietly out of our rooms. She takes my hand and pulls me toward the top step, where we sit to listen to him relive the war. After a few minutes, she puts her arm around my shoulders and the side of her head against the side of mine. Tears stream down our faces.

"I'm not sure I can go through what my mother went through," she says.

I look at her. "Your dad got better."

"Eventually."

"Months or years?"

"Years and years."

———

Every morning Sondra has to get Jeffy ready to go to Mrs. Watson's, help Dad dress, and get herself ready to be at the bank by eight, so this morning I volunteer to cook breakfast. While the bacon is frying, I pack up Jeffy's milk bottles and make sure there are plenty of Pampers in his diaper bag.

I feel wrung out after two night of practically no sleep, but Dad, when he wheels in, looks like he's been mugged and left in an alley. I don't know who I feel sorriest for as we eat in silence. I guess it should be Daddy, but Sondra's the one with deep, dark circles under her sad eyes. At least she and I can get away for the day. I can't imagine what Dad must think about, sitting home alone all day, me at school, Sondra at work, Jeffy with the sitter. He tries to act cheerful—thanking me for fixing his eggs the way he likes them and telling Sondra how beautiful she looks—but between his nightmares and the pain in his stump, it's hard to fake, even for as long as it takes us to get ready and leave.

It's seven thirty-three when I hear the school bus go by headed east. I have about nine minutes to finish getting ready when Dad says, "There's a guy coming by this morning who may buy my boat."

I turn from taking bottles of breast milk out of the refrigerator and Sondra turns from the pile of dishes in the sink. "What?" we say in unison, then look at each other.

My first thought is that he has no right to sell a boat named after me. I know we need the money, but if he sells it, Dad will never fish again unless it's working for someone else.

"No," I say. "You can't do that."

"Are you sure?" Sondra says, ignoring me.

"What choice do I have?"

"This is your third day home. It's too soon." I shoot Sondra a butt-out-of-this look, which she also ignores.

"We'd be able to save the dockage fees and maintenance," Sondra says.

"If he sells it, he'll never have another one," I say. "What happens when he wants to start fishing again?"

"We have to be realistic," Daddy says.

"Not after just three days we don't," I say.

"Hannah, it's your father's decision."

I spin on Sondra and yell, "No it isn't. That boat belongs to our family, not to yours."

"Hannah, don't talk to Sondra like that."

"Then tell her to butt out." I hesitate only a moment. "What do you think Mom would say if she knew that you were giving up like this?"

If Dad could have reached me, he might have slapped me, but he couldn't. I run from the kitchen, grab my backpack, and leave.

I don't feel bad about what I said to Sondra. She shouldn't be part of the decision to sell or not sell the *Hannah Gale*. She's only thinking about the money and not about what it would mean to Dad to know he'd never fish again.

Mrs. Watson lives three houses away. To save money, it's my job to pick Jeffy up when I get home from school at three thirty, but I don't want to go home today. As soon as the last bell rings, I go to the office and use their phone to call Mrs. Watson and ask her if she can keep Jeffy until Sondra gets there. She says she can.

There's a school bus stop just past the stables. Lacy, the girl in my math class, turns and actually gets on her knees to watch me walk back toward the stables. I don't think she can hear over the bus engine, but the horses nicker and whinny when they see me coming.

The dogs across the street bark at me but they're tied to one of the concrete blocks a junked car sits on, so I yell at them to shut up. It's a breezy, warm spring day and most of the horses are in their paddocks. Jack comes to the fence and lets me rub his ears.

"I came straight from school, so I don't have anything for you," I tell him, then remember there's an apple in my backpack. I get it and bite off chunks so he won't choke on them, spit them out and feed them to him one at a time.

I start down the driveway and he follows me like we're friends walking side by side.

Muck-raking gives lots of brain space for thinking: Mom and me and Dad on the boat; Mom helping to pull the baited lines and me watching from the wheelhouse, where they made me sit so they didn't have to worry about me falling overboard; Daddy taking me with him when Mom first got sick and I was too young to be home alone.

Dillon's truck comes down the driveway. She waves. "Hey kiddo. You're early."

"Yeah, I didn't feel like going home."

The rake handle is propped against my shoulder as I rewrap a scrunchie around my ponytail.

"How's your dad?"

I shrug. "He's okay."

Dillon doesn't move, and I go back to scooping the poop and putting it in the wheelbarrow. "You ever want to talk or anything . . ."

"Thanks."

"I'll bring you a bag of rice hulls. Keeps the run from getting too muddy."

"Okay."

She goes out but is back again a second later. "Hannah, it's not my business, but a lot of the guys coming back from Iraq have problems adjusting. I know. My dad was in Nam."

"My grandfather was in Vietnam. He got exposed to Agent Orange and died of leukemia a few months before I was born."

She looks at me with the same sadness in her eyes that I see in Sondra's now that Dad is home. "So I mean it— about talking."

I nod. If I open my mouth to say anything, I'll start to cry, and if I do, I won't be able to stop.

"Where were you?" Sondra meets me at the door.

"At the stables."

"Why didn't you tell me you weren't going to pick Jeffy up?"

"Mrs. Watson said *she* could keep him until you got home."

"Yeah, well, you didn't call me, so I didn't know where he was. Don't do that again."

I look at her. "Don't give me orders. You're not my mother." I take the stairs two at a time, slam and lock my bedroom door.

By seven, I'm starving. Dad and Sondra are in the living room with the TV on. *Jeopardy!* has just started. There is no way to get from my room to the kitchen without them seeing me unless I tie my sheets together and drop out the window.

"Hannah," Dad says, when he hears me on the stairs.

"Yeah."

"Come here."

"If you're going to rag on me, forget it. I'm not sorry."

"Just come here."

I walk over and stand with my arms crossed.

"The guy I was talking about this morning came and he did make an offer—a pretty good offer."

"So you called me in here to tell me that nothing I said made any difference?"

"No. I wanted you to know that I didn't accept his offer."

"You didn't?" I let my arms drop to my sides.

"No. I—" He smiles at Sondra, who doesn't smile back. "We decided to hold out as long as we can. You were right. There'll never be another *Hannah Gale*."

I throw my arms around his neck. "Thank you, Daddy. You'll see. You'll fish again. I know it."

Sondra looks at me with no expression at all, then turns to face the TV and closes her eyes.

10

SATURDAY, MAY 6

For the first time since Funny Cide won the Kentucky Derby in 2003, Dad and I will watch it together. Dad's in his wheelchair at the end of our sofa. He looks at me and we smile.

Sondra said horseracing is cruel and she didn't want to watch them whipping the horses to make them go faster.

"They're so pumped on adrenaline, they don't feel a thing," Dad said.

I nodded in agreement but wondered if that was really true. I love horseracing and don't want to think anything bad about it, but if they don't feel it, why do they run faster when they are whipped?

Sondra left and took Jeffy to her mother's house. Her mom, Mrs. Lutz, will babysit while Sondra, who says she needs to get out of here anyway, goes to the movies with her friends from the bank. It will be good for her to get away and like she told me in the kitchen, she doesn't need to stick around when Daddy's got another excuse to get drunk.

What does she expect? His leg hurts and he can't sleep. She says she's worried about all the stuff he's taking: painkillers, something for depression, and something else to help him sleep. All the drugs are prescription. The VA doctors should know better than Sondra and it does seem to help, so I think she should lay off him 'til he gets better.

I'm microwaving popcorn, and run to the kitchen when the bell dings.

"We're supposed to be drinking mint juleps," Dad calls.

"What is a julep, anyway?" I have to yell to be heard over the TV.

"A drink with mint in it."

"I know the mint part." I come back with the bowl of popcorn, and put it on the coffee table. "Why's it called a julep?"

Dad shrugs. "Google it sometime. I don't think they'd go all that well with popcorn anyway." He's drinking Jack Daniel's and tips his glass to me. "Who ya picking?"

"Barbaro. Who are you picking?"

"Brother Derek looks good, but I kind of like Bob and John."

"Is that one horse? Bob and John?"

"Yep. Guess they couldn't decide."

The race is supposed to start at two o'clock our time—five more minutes. Dad's been pacing himself, but he's already pretty toasted.

I heard somewhere that fat soaks up alcohol, so I go to melt some extra butter for the popcorn, when right on time, the paddock judge calls, "Riders up!" I run back to the living room to watch as each horse is led out of his stall and, one at a time, the jockeys, like a row of dominos, get boosted into their saddles, starting with number one and ending with number twenty. Some horses prance and act nervous. Barbaro—number eight—is calm.

The microwave bell dings while thousands of spectators sing the traditional "My Old Kentucky Home." I know the words by heart and sing along as I gallop in to get the butter and more napkins.

I put my five-dollar bill on the table beside Dad's drink. We always bet on the race. We have since I was little. Daddy used to tell me who he thought would win, then that was the horse I'd pick. Of course, now I pick my own horse. Unlike Giacomo, who came from nowhere to win last year, Barbaro, though not the odds on favorite to win, is favored second behind Sweetnorthernsaint. He's five times undefeated going into this race, but the reason I want him to win is his foaling date.

"I don't know about Barbaro," Dad says. "Matz has never

trained a Derby winner, and the best Prado, his jockey, has ever done in the Derby is a third."

"I don't care." I take a big fistful of popcorn, tilt my head back, and trickle the kernels into my mouth.

"And I'm not sure what Matz was thinking laying him off for five weeks. No horse has won after that long without running since Needles, fifty years ago."

"I'm still picking him." I tap my fiver. "Where's your money?"

He leans to one side in his wheelchair and digs into his pocket. He takes out some folded bills held together with his Point Cabrillo Lighthouse money clip. He looks at it for a second and I know he's thinking about Sondra.

Daddy takes a five from his thin pack of bills and puts it next to mine on the coffee table. "They're in the gate. Last chance to change your mind."

"No way. Did you decide?"

The odds have changed and Brother Derek has moved into the number one spot. "I guess I'll have to take Brother Derek, just to make it interesting."

"If he's the favorite, shouldn't you give me better odds?"

"I think it's even enough. Whatcha basing all this confidence on anyway?"

I look at Dad. "Barbaro's foaling date was April twenty-ninth."

His eyes get warm and sad-looking. He nods. April 29 was Momma's birthday. Daddy's read all the stats; he knew that. He'd have chosen Barbaro if I hadn't. He's handing me another chance to win.

I grab my blue glass necklace when the announcer shouts, "They're off."

I think I see Barbaro stumble to his knees right out of the starting gate, but there are so many horses, I'm not sure. I scoot to the edge of the couch trying to pick Barbaro out of the field of twenty horses as they merge into an enormous pack. Dad's leaning into it, as if he's on one of the horses himself.

It's nice to see him almost like his old self—the man who used to sing Willie Nelson's "Mamas Don't Let Your Babies Grow Up to Be Cowboys" while he baited his troll line, except he made it *daughters* and *cowgirls* for me.

For the first half mile, the announcer doesn't even mention Barbaro's name. At least I don't hear him. They pass the opening half mile in forty-six seconds.

". . . a grueling pace set by Keyed Entry," the announcer yells.

Daddy grins. "Has your slab of horsemeat left the gate?"

"Funny. Ha-ha. Just you wait."

Big blobs of dirt fly as they sweep toward the midpoint 5/16 pole. I see him then. Barbaro is fifth, then fourth.

The sound of the hooves is thunderous. The crowd is roaring. The announcer's screaming the horses' names. Sinister Minister is leading; Keyed Entry has slipped out of the running. I see Barbaro on the outside just as the announcer shouts, "And here comes Barbaro."

I'm on my feet. "See. See!" I shout.

Dad is in the moment. He has his hands in front of him like he is holding the reins. His body pulses with the rhythm of hooves hitting the ground. I want him to win.

They are in the back stretch and Barbaro is neck and neck with Sinister Minister. Daddy pounds the armrest with his fists.

"Look at that," he says in an awed whisper as Barbaro pulls away from the others. "Prado never even used his whip."

With a quarter mile left to go, Barbaro has a three-length lead. All the other jockeys are whipping their horses, frantically trying to squeeze out something that's not there to get. Not Prado. Barbaro's heart is running him for the win.

"I'll be a son of a gun," Daddy says.

"It's all Barbaro," the announcer's croaky voice screams as my horse crosses the finish line six or seven lengths ahead of whoever came in second.

Daddy puts his hand up and we high-five. "That there is one heck of a horse. He's got Triple Crown written all over him." He shakes his head, then smiles. "You sure know how to pick 'em."

I sit on the edge of the sofa and hook my arm around his neck. We stay like that for a while listening, with our cheeks together, as they show the finish over and over.

11

SUNDAY, MAY 7

Barbaro's final lap time was the fastest since Secretariat won in 1973, the year my dad was born. At the stables, I ask Dillon what she thought of the race.

"Was it yesterday?" she says.

"You didn't watch the Derby?" I can't believe it.

"Never do. Hate horseracing. Hate rodeos."

I get the broom and start sweeping loose bits of hay and oats out of Bobby's stall. "How come?"

Meg's been mucking Dee's stall and passes with a wheelbarrow full of manure. "They start racing them way too young," she says. "It puts too much stress on their muscles and skeletons. Hundreds are injured every year."

Her eyes are pale blue, just like Jack's. With her soft, light blond curls, she looks more like one of the carpool moms than a woman who'd own a retired racehorse.

"How old should a horse be to race?" I lean the broom against the wall and follow her to where we dump the manure.

"At least four, preferably five."

The Derby is for three-year-olds. "They sure look full grown," I say.

"Well, they're not. Most aren't even three." Meg upends the wheelbarrow, empties it, and we start back. "All race-horses are given a foaling date of January first in the year they're born."

"Barbaro's three." I don't want to think about them being too young. "He was born April 29, 2003."

"How do you know that?" Meg asks. She looks impressed.

"April twenty-ninth is—was my mother's birthday. She died."

"I'm sorry."

"It was five years ago." I shrug, like I'm okay now, but she's never out of my head for long, especially now that Daddy's home. "How old is Dee?"

"Twelve. He was born February 22, 1994."

"You're kidding."

"Why would I kid?"

"I was born on the same day in '93." A chill runs through me as if this is somehow monumental news—an omen or something. I think of Dad and his premonitions about things and wonder what this means for me.

"How long did he race?"

"About seven years, but he never broke his maiden."

"What does that mean?"

"He came in second and third but never first. He probably sold for a half a million as a yearling, earned it all back and then some, but when I got him, his owner owed more in stable fees than he was worth. He was starving and was going to be sent to slaughter if I hadn't taken him. I bought him for his back stable fees."

I stop. "What do you mean sent to slaughter? Like a cow?"

"Exactly." She props the wheelbarrow against the outside wall. "You don't want to know."

"Yes I do." I follow her toward the hay shed.

"In a lot of countries, people eat horses: Japan, France, Belgium, lots of places. We even ate them here during the Second World War, and the ones that are too far gone for human consumption go for pet food."

I believe her, but I don't want to. I look over at Super Dee, grazing near the redwood tree in his paddock, and remember Dad kidding me—calling Barbaro a slab of horsemeat. He must know about this.

———

Dad's first disability check arrives in Monday's mail. I bring it in from the mailbox when I get home from school.

In the week before the Derby, Dad seemed more like himself. Sondra drove him to the VA for a new prosthesis, which he said felt better. His stub is still sore, so he only uses his new leg when he goes to physical therapy, but he did go every morning without Sondra having to nag him. She drops him off on her way to work and he takes Dial-A-Ride home.

I feel sad after he opens the envelope. For one thing, it isn't for the amount he's supposed to get. It's for eight hundred and sixty dollars instead of thirteen hundred.

He waves it at us. "When the government recognizes you're half a man, you can take it to the bank."

"They owe you," Sondra says, and snatches the check out of his hand. "Besides, it's just temporary, 'til you're on your . . ."

Daddy looks at her. "Feet again? I'm not a lizard missing its tail." He wiggles his lopped-off leg. "This will not grow back."

"Don't be such a defeatist. When you adjust to your new leg, you'll be able to do all the things you used to do. Look at the guys who run marathons with no legs."

"That's something to look forward to." Daddy rolls across the kitchen to the refrigerator. Sondra tenses.

"When they show those guys pulling bait-lines full of salmon in twelve-foot seas, I'll send the checks back." He gets a beer.

"What about peg-leg pirates, and Captain Ahab?" I pipe in, then wish I hadn't.

"Like in the movies?" He looks at me.

I shrug.

12

SATURDAY, MAY 13

When I get to "work," there's a short, heavyset older lady with maroon-colored hair in the center of the arena with Indy facing her. Dillon is giving her a Parelli lesson. I slide in and sit on the blankets to watch.

Indy's neck stretches, trying to nibble on the cookie bag attached to the woman's belt. He loves to lick stuff: walls, the barrels, the palms of hands, anything. When he licks her vest, the woman steps back.

"*Don't* let him back you up," Dillon says. She's sitting on one of the white barrels in the center of the arena. "Use the Carrot Stick."

Dillon lent me a booklet about the Parelli method of training horses, so I know what the Carrot Stick is for. All the seven Parelli games are played using it to give directions. I thought it was called a Carrot Stick because it's orange, but it's really because it's a cross between the carrot used to bribe a horse and the stick used to make a horse do what you want it to do. The stick part is four feet long, and attached to one end of it is a five-foot long rope, not as thin as string, but not very thick either. The whole thing looks like a flimsy whip.

Every Saturday I've watched them play these games with their horses, but this is the first time I've seen someone learning how to use them. In the booklet Dillon lent me it says the games are meant to give a horse confidence, build trust, and develop a partnership through communication, all of which make for a safer ride.

With the string end of the stick touching the ground in front of her, the woman moves it with a couple little jerks of her wrist and Indy backs up.

"Now put the string over his back . . ."

Swinging the string is called the Friendly Game and is the first of the seven games. It's supposed to feel like the switching of a mother horse's tail.

"Sophia, this is Hannah," Dillon says. "Sophia's getting a Premarin mare."

"Hello," I say. I've heard of Morgans and Arabians and Pintos, but never Premarins, but rather than show how little I know about horses, I keep quiet.

"I'm lucky to have heard of Dillon," Sophia says, lobbing the string rhythmically over Indy's back. "She's a top trainer and I want the poor thing to have the best chance at a new life."

"Was she mistreated?" I ask.

Indy has drifted toward a barrel and is licking it. "Point the direction you want him to go," Dillon says.

Sophia points, slaps the string into the dirt opposite her extended arm, and Indy takes off trotting, nearly brushing the walls as he goes.

"Yes, Hannah," Sophia says. "She was abused."

"Don't disengage," Dillon says. "When you want him to stop, lean a little and look at his butt."

Sophia waits a moment, then does just that. Indy stops immediately, walks over, and stands facing her. She gives him a cookie and strokes his blaze. "Good boy."

"How did you train him to stop and come to you when you look at his rear end?" I ask Dillon.

"It is one of the end results, if you'll excuse the expression, of the Porcupine Game."

In Porcupine you press the Carrot Stick against the part you want them to move and increase the pressure until they do. I quote the booklet. "Air, hair, skin, muscle, bone." Only having to point is air. Hair is just the lightest touch, skin is a little harder, and so on until they move.

"Very good. Come sit over here." She points me to the other barrel.

I always sit on the sidelines, so it's cool to be invited out to the center of the arena. I hitch myself up on the barrel opposite Dillon.

"Mercy me," Sophia says. "You two look like sisters."

I grin. We do kind of, especially since I cut my hair short.

"Flattery will get you nowhere," Dillon says, and smiles at me. "To answer your question, horses nip each other on the rump when they are playing, so if we want them to come and stand facing us, we start with the sting of the string, like a nip, and soon, just looking at the rear end is all it takes. You're too indecisive," she says to Sophia. "Pointing says go that way, then don't do anything else until you want him to come back."

"What happened to her horse?" I ask Dillon.

"Work both sides of him," Dillon instructs. "He needs to go the opposite direction now."

Sophia nods, points left, and slaps the string on the ground. Indy trots off clockwise this time.

Dillon holds her hand up to stop me from talking. "Good. Now try Sideways."

Sophia gets Indy to put his feet over the PVC pipe, then walk sideways along its length. He does fine until he gets near the barrel at one end, stops, and starts to lick it.

"Get his attention. He's supposed to be looking at you."

Sophia swings the string side to side, hard, so it pops in the dirt, then she crooks her finger at Indy. He walks up and stands still.

"Now get him to hook on to you," Dillon says.

Sophia turns and starts walking. Indy follows for a few yards, then drifts toward Dillon.

"Don't walk in a straight line. Go left, go right, make circles. If you walk straight, he'll get bored and drop off again."

When the games are over, Dillon gets Indy ready to saddle. "I usually give lessons using a western saddle. Which do you prefer?" she asks Sophia.

"English, I think."

"Are you just learning to ride?" I say.

"No, but I haven't ridden since I was a little girl."

"So what happened to your horse?"

Sophia's putting chaps on. The stirrup leathers on English saddles pinch. "Being a Premarin mare is what happened, but you're way too young to know what that is," she says.

"I thought Premarin was a breed, like Arabian."

She and Dillon laugh.

"Premarin is a hormone replacement therapy drug prescribed to postmenopausal women. It's made from the urine of pregnant horses. That's where the name came from—Pregnant Mares' Urine, or PMU for short."

"Women swallow pills made of horse urine?"

"That's not the disgusting part," Sophia says. "It's how the horses are treated. At any one time, forty to fifty thousand mares are on the 'pee lines.'"

A picture of someone following a mare with a bucket pops into my mind. "Do they get urine like they get milk from a cow?"

Sophia leads the saddled Indy over to the wooden steps they use to get on the horses. Indy stands right next to them. Sophia is so short that she hops up, lies across Indy's saddle, then works her right leg over his back and sits up. Dillon helps her fit her feet in the stirrups.

"When they are in their third or fourth month of pregnancy," Sophia says, "the mares are put in stalls that are eight feet long, three and a half feet wide, and five feet high. They are tied so they can't move their heads more than a few inches in any direction, or even turn around, then a urine collection device is inserted. The mares stay like that for the next six to eight months, standing in their own feces."

Sophia puts her hand on Indy's neck, but stares at me with no expression.

"Relax," Dillon says. "This isn't the time to let your anger take over. It makes your whole body rigid, and Indy can sense that."

"I'm sorry," I say. "I shouldn't have asked."

"You didn't know," Dillon says.

Sophia sags a little in the saddle and her eyes soften.

"Just mosey a bit. Relax your hands. Relax your legs. Feel his sway." Dillon is back on her barrel opposite me.

I try to imagine what it feels like to be sitting on Indy as he circles the arena.

"Soften your rib cage," Dillon says. "That's it."

Sophia and Indy come past me and I can hear the creak of the saddle.

"Now push on the sway," Dillon says. "Your legs should be your only means of steering. Look left and your body shifts. That's all he needs. Good. That's it."

Somewhere I heard that watching a ballet or any kind of dancing is like watching poetry in motion. That's what it's like to watch Sophia ride. On the ground, she looks a little like Humpty Dumpty, but on Indy's back she's graceful, confident, and elegant. There's no bit in his mouth, yet he moves forward, backward, and sideways, first one way, then the other, with just the pressure of her legs. I want to be up there and sink into the smell and sound of the saddle. I imagine riding Indy would feel like the motion of being on Daddy's boat and how it rocked when the seas were calm. "Dillon, how much do you charge for a lesson?" I blurt out.

"Forty."

I have about twenty-nine dollars saved. "Oh."

"How long have you been *working* here?"

"Two months."

"Well, when we're done here, let's talk about giving you a raise." She winks at me, kind of like Dad used to do.

A raise? Since I don't get paid anything, I don't know what she means.

"Pick up your sway," Dillon says to Sophia.

"What do you mean—a raise?"

Sophia's rhythm increases and Indy begins to trot.

"Well, more like a trade." She smiles. "Does a lesson for every month you work here sound fair?"

I want to jump off my barrel and hug her, but I don't think Dillon is big into hugging, so I just nod. "Very fair. Thanks."

I sit quietly for a few minutes. If I listen and watch closely to what Dillon tells Sophia to do, maybe when I take my lesson, I'll impress her with how much I already know. I'm grinning like an idiot on the inside, trying to act cool on the outside, when I'm suddenly hit by the words *pregnant mares.* Mares that are pregnant. "What happens to the babies?" I ask Sophia as she rides by me again.

Indy stops as if I was talking to him. "The fillies are sometimes raised to be the new generation of Premarin mares, but most of the colts . . ." Sophia looks over at Dillon, who shrugs.

"She should know, I guess," Dillon says.

"Most of the colts are shipped to Japan," Sophia says. "The tender meat of young horses is prized in Japan."

"They eat baby horses?"

Indy begins to move again.

"Do you know what veal is?" Dillon asks me.

"No."

"It's a milk-fed calf. We eat them. I think it's more humane to kill a foal instantly than it is to raise a calf in a crate for six months, then kill it."

"What do you mean in a crate?"

"A veal calf isn't allowed to move. If it moves around, its muscles develop, which makes the meat tougher. So it is confined in a tiny stall away from its mother and fed milk until it is slaughtered. The meat is super-tender."

"But a baby horse! That's like cooking and eating a kitten." I feel cold and my body trembles.

Dillon looks at me. "Horses can live thirty or more years, Hannah, but most never make it to their fifth birthday, especially racehorses."

My cheeks start to burn. I want to tell her to stop talking now, to stop telling me this stuff.

"In this country alone over thirty thousand racehorses a year are born," Dillon says. "What do you think happens to the ones who don't make it, or are injured, or the ones that do race but, like Dee, are finished by the time they're six or seven? In the racing industry, foals that don't meet some standard or other are killed moments after they're born. If they stand up and begin to nurse, the stud fee has to be paid." Dillon is watching Sophia and Indy. She goes on talking without looking at me. "As many as a hundred thousand horses a year go to slaughter."

I jump off the barrel, cross the arena, and go out through the kitchen. If the sadness here equals the sadness at home, I don't know where to be anymore. My bike is leaning against the picnic table. I glance back. Dillon is standing in the doorway.

"I'm sorry," she says. "I shouldn't have told you that much."

"I wonder if they killed Sea Hero."

"You might be able to find out on the Internet. There are websites that trace what happens to Derby winners."

I put my bike down and walk back. When I'm beside her, she puts her arms around me. I close my eyes for a second and pretend she's my mother.

13

THE SAME DAY

There was something on the news not long ago that showed cattle going to slaughter. They were alive and terrified, but the one the camera focused on had a broken leg and couldn't get up. Over and over she tried, but her legs kept slipping and sliding on the wet, slimy concrete. As she flailed and twisted, a slaughterhouse worker drove into the picture, then pushed and shoved her to her death with his forklift. I can't stop picturing that or them doing the same thing to horses.

When I get home, I switch on the computer, and wait for the squawky dial-up sound to end. My screensaver is a picture of Dad and Mom on the *Hannah Gale*. I took it with my first camera. It's not a very good picture. The boat was rocking, so their faces are blurry. Still, it's my favorite one of them together. Before Daddy left for Iraq, he had it scanned and put it on my computer. I move all the icons as far to the left side of the screen as I can pack them, then I stare at the picture until I begin to feel the boat rocking again and see them topple into each other's arms and laugh.

I type *Wikipedia* into the Yahoo! search engine, then stare at its jigsaw globe for a moment before I get the courage to type in *Sea Hero*. What I already knew about him is there, but I didn't know that he'd been a 13:1 long shot to win the Derby, or that he never had another "major win." He was retired at age four and sold to a stud farm in Turkey.

The first thing I think is he must be dead. I look to see if there is a link with more information. The column on the right has his earnings at $2,929,869. Nearly three million dollars and his owners sold him to some place in Turkey. There's a reference section at the bottom of the page with a link to information about him. I click through and scroll down to *Important Offspring*. In parentheses it says "a work in progress." Does that mean he's still alive and fathering babies, or that the web-person is still gathering information? I look down the list at his offspring and find two that were sired in 2005—in Turkey. Just a year ago. Maybe he is still alive.

I go back and type in *Secretariat*. I'm sure he's dead. He'd be thirty-six, but I want to read about him. The article is long and interesting. For one thing, he still has the combined fastest time, beating all the other Triple Crown winners.

"In the fall of 1989, Secretariat was afflicted with

laminitis, a painful and often incurable hoof condition. He was euthanized on October 4, and buried at his home in Kentucky." The article says that his blood flows through many notable racehorses, including Smarty Jones, and that one of his grandsons was sired by a daughter of Seattle Slew. I try to figure out whether Super Dee could also have Secretariat's blood in his veins, but guess that even if he does, I'm never going to know.

One of the last things the article says is how when the vet autopsied Secretariat, he found the biggest heart he'd ever seen—twenty-one pounds. The average is eight. I'll have to remember to tell Dad that he was born the same year as a racehorse with the biggest heart ever.

The days are getting longer and Sondra's already started hinting I should take over from the babysitter a few times a week once school is out, but I said no way. "I have a job, remember?" Neither she nor Dad knows I'm not getting paid.

If Sondra gets home early enough on the weekdays, by five anyway, there is still time for me to go to the stables for an hour or so and be home long before dark. The minute her car pulls in the driveway, I head up the road to see if anyone is still around who'd like help feeding, carrying water, muck-raking, or grooming. I love brushing the horses.

Sondra hates it when I leave that late.

"Why do you care?"

"Well, for starters, we have to save dinner for you."

Like we enjoy eating together anymore. "If you'd let Dad watch Jeffy until you get home, I could leave earlier and wouldn't get home so late."

"He doesn't know how to care for a baby."

"He took care of me when I was little."

"That was a long time ago and a lot has changed."

I know she's afraid he'll be too drunk in the afternoon to hear Jeffy cry or that he might try to change his diaper and drop him or something. "He's been better lately."

"I said no."

"It's not fair."

"Life's not fair, in case you haven't noticed."

I hate answers like that. There's no comeback.

The thing is, I know she's right. Dad isn't Dad anymore. When I was little, though not as young as Jeffy, Mom used to let him take me fishing. If the seas got rough, or I got tired and cranky, Dad would put me down for my nap in the bait well. I must be the only person alive who finds the smell of fish comforting. Mom never had to worry. Now, even if Sondra said it was okay, I probably wouldn't leave Jeffy with Dad either.

Still, I don't want Dillon to think I'm not dependable, so I told her if I'm not there it's because I have to babysit.

"That's fine, Hannah. It's not like I'm paying you. I just appreciate you helping out."

That was nice of her since I'm not really doing much of anything. She still doesn't want me in a stall with a horse by myself, in case I do something by mistake that frightens him. So the only real work I'm doing is helping to muck-rake, carrying water buckets, sweeping and putting alfalfa, oats, and hay in their stalls when they're empty. I don't care. Being there is the happiest I've been since before Mom died.

The weather is getting warmer and they are starting to use the outside field to play with the horses. A couple of days after I met Sophia, Dillon let me bring Jack down and just hold his lead while he grazed near the edge of the sand pit.

"Why does Jack hate men?"

Dillon's saddling Bobby. "He was broken the old-fashioned way and when he resisted being ridden, his owner hit him in the face with a two-by-four."

I flinch. "How long ago was that?"

"Thirty years. Horses have memories as good as any elephant's." She puts her hand against his cheek and strokes him. "He was so abused when he was young, the damage was almost impossible to fix. He's a sweet horse, but the right side of his brain still dominates."

I touch one of the long, deep scars on his face. If horses remember what they've gone through, I wonder if my dad will ever get over Iraq.

14

SATURDAY, MAY 20

Today is the running of the Preakness, which is the second leg of the Triple Crown. Dad is as sure as I am that Barbaro will win—easy, smeasy. I offer to flip a coin to see who gets to bet on him, but Dad says he was mine in the Derby and that gives me automatic first choice. Some things about Dad haven't changed.

We've talked so much about Barbaro and the Derby, Sondra thinks she missed something. She's planning to run to the store and get home in time to watch it with us.

She's in the shower and I'm in my room on the Internet looking up the stats on the other horses for Dad. When I come down the stairs from printing them out, Dad has Jeffy, who was seven months old last week, and is bouncing him on his right knee. There's a lot of pre-race stuff going on and they are facing the television. Dad has an arm on either side of Jeffy for balance, and his big hands curl over

Jeffy's, holding the phone cord like reins. When Jeffy tips back against Dad's shoulder and laughs, Daddy tilts his head so their cheeks are touching.

Dad never mentions my mother in front of Sondra, but when I hand him the stats and put Jeffy in his playpen, he glances at the stairs, then says, "Can you remember the time your mom made a special cake and decorated it with green trim and brown icing like a mud track? It even had a little white fence."

I actually do remember, though I was only five or six. I nod.

"And the time just before our new carpet went in and all the furniture was stacked in the garage. She brought two bales of hay into the living room for us to sit on while we watched." He smiles to himself.

I don't remember that, but I don't think he's expecting me to answer.

It's still a couple of hours before the race. Jeffy's down for his nap, Sondra's gone to the store, and Dad's in the garage doing something. I decide to find a recipe and fix mint juleps for them. I think they are only a Derby thing, and I probably shouldn't encourage Dad to drink, but I don't care. It's a special occasion.

I peek in once to make sure he's busy and won't wheel in and ruin the surprise. He's pulled up next to his workbench and seems to be sorting his fishing equipment. His back is to me, but I see him take something out of a drawer, hold it in his hand, turn it over, then toss it into the box he's put by his chair. He tosses spools of line, a dive belt, his weights, and a pair of fishing gloves. The shelf used to hit him waist-high, now it is chest-high and he has to raise himself off the seat of the wheelchair with his good leg to reach the stuff hanging on the Peg-Board. He takes his fishing lures off one at a time and pitches them into the box. I close the door silently. It's not lost on me what he's doing. Between the constant pain and his memories, he's giving up on his old life a piece at a time. I shake off the thought that he might be giving up on life itself.

There's a two-step ladder in the gap between the refrigerator and the pantry. I open it and put it in front of the cupboard where Sondra has stored all Mom's cookbooks. The ones she uses are in a row on the countertop.

Momma's *Joy of Cooking* had belonged to her mother. I find the mint julep recipe and am stumped before I start. We have dried mint, but the recipe calls for a sprig of fresh mint per serving. I start to close the book when I see something written faintly in pencil in the margin. *First make syrup*. I touch the words with my finger. It is in Mom's handwriting.

"Dad," I call, as if I don't know where he is.

"In the garage, Hannah."

When I open the door, he's pushed the box entirely under the workbench and is spraying his wheels with WD-40.

"Dad, I'm going to run over to Mrs. Watson's for a second, will you listen for the baby?"

"Sure."

I prop open the door so he can hear if Jeffy cries, then run from the house and get my bike to make the trip faster. She's three houses down, but our lots are five acres each.

"Mrs. Watson," I say when she opens the door. "Do you have any real mint?"

"Sure. It's a garden pest. Have lots of it. How much do you need?"

"Enough to make mint juleps." I grin.

"What's the occasion?"

"Today is the second leg of the Triple Crown."

She laughs. "Well, that certainly clears it up. What's the Triple Crown?"

"Can I explain later? I left Jeffy with Dad."

"Sure, honey. Come on out to the garden."

Back home, I find Dad parked beside Jeffy's playpen. He's propped his chin on a fist and his other hand is splayed across Jeffy's little back. "He hasn't moved a muscle," he whispers when I come up beside him. "Sometimes, Hannah, in my nightmares, I see him like the others, covered in blood."

The memory of the day Daddy lost his leg is always just beneath the surface.

"I'm sorry, Daddy. You should try not to think about it anymore." I put my chin on the top of his head and drape my arms over his shoulders. His hair smells oily. He doesn't bathe as often as he used to. It's so hard for him to get in and out of the shower, where he has to balance himself long enough to sit on the stool that's in there for him.

He nods. "I wish trying not to think about it was all it took."

I don't know what to say to make things better for Daddy. "I'm making a surprise; will you stay in here and out of the kitchen?"

"Sure. Don't blow the joint up."

"Funny."

The recipe for mint juleps is long. I find the powdered sugar and get Dad's bourbon out of the liquor cabinet. The recipe says to use only bonded bourbon, tender, terminal mint leaves for bruising, and very finely crushed or shaved ice.

Geez.

It also says they should be served in silver mugs. I'm lucky to find a couple of tall iced tea glasses. I put them in the freezer to chill, then wash the mint, shake the water off, then dip the sprigs in the powdered sugar. In a mixing bowl I make syrup out of two teaspoons of sugar and two of water, then heat it for twenty seconds in the microwave to make the sugar dissolve faster. It says to bruise six mint leaves with a muddler. I'm standing there trying to decide what a muddler is when Sondra comes in from the garage.

"Don't look." I turn my back and hold my arms out to block her view.

"What are you doing?"

"Nothing. It's a surprise. Go away."

"I have groceries in the car."

"I'll get them. Dad's in with Jeffy." I glance at her over my shoulder.

When she's gone, I start bruising the leaves with a spoon, kind of mashing them, which I consider pretty bruising.

The next ingredient is a dash of bitters. Since I don't know what that is, I figure they won't miss it if I leave it out.

Add one large jigger of bourbon whiskey. I don't know what a jigger is either, but it sounds substantial. I measure a quarter of a cup full and pour it in with the sugar and the bruised mint. The clock says it's two thirty. The race should start in about thirty minutes. I poke my head into the living room. The TV is on to the pre-race stuff about each horse. "I'm almost done. How much longer?"

"The riders are up. I'll call you when they play 'Maryland, My Maryland,'" Dad says.

"Okay."

I take the two serving glasses from the freezer and pack them with crushed ice from the dispenser on our refrigerator door. I'm supposed to strain the mint, bourbon, and sugar mixture into the ice and stir, but we don't have a strainer. Mom used to, but I don't know what happened to it. I decide a coffee filter will work. I fit one over each glass and divide the liquid, filtering out the mint leaves. I mix this with a long iced tea spoon and add more ice. Next it calls for a pony of whiskey. I think a pony of anything is a pretty cool measurement, but I don't know how much a pony is or if whiskey is the same as bourbon. Time's running out. I decide a jigger is probably a quarter cup, a pony should be a half a cup. I pour a half cup into each glass.

"Hannah, come on," Dad yells.

I can't find a serving tray, so I get two nice plates from the cupboard, put a napkin on each and start through the doorway when I remember the sugar-coated mint leaves. I go back, put one in each glass, and run cautiously for the living room.

"Ta-da."

Dad turns in his chair. "Whatcha got there?"

"Mint juleps."

He smiles, then laughs out loud. "Well, I'll be dipped."

Sondra doesn't look quite so pleased.

I put the dishes on the table.

Dad turns up the sound, takes one of the chilled glasses, tips it my way, then takes a sip. "Whoa," he croaks.

"There's a pony of liquor in each," I say.

Sondra has the other glass in her hand. "Do you know how many ounces that is?"

"No. But I figured it was more than a jigger, and a jigger is a quarter of a cup, isn't it?"

Sondra puts the glass down and stares at it like it might blow up. "A jigger is an ounce and half. A pony is an ounce."

"Oh." I look at Dad.

He winks at me. "Sondra used to tend bar, you know. We'll just let the ice melt a little."

"There's the favorite—number six—Barbaro," the announcer says. "We're about to see if this is a super horse or just a very good horse."

All the horses are being led into the starting gate. There are only nine, not twenty like in the Derby. Barbaro is behind gate number six. When they are all in, a silence falls. I suck in my breath and hold it.

"Barbaro broke through the barrier," the announcer shouts.

There's Barbaro, the only horse on the track. Prado, his jockey, reins him in and turns him back toward the gate.

"He's ready to run," Dad says, and grins at me.

"That does not bode well for the favorite here, folks," the announcer says. "That is not a plus."

"Why?" I say.

"Nonsense," Dad says.

"Ninety-five out of a hundred that do that, do not go on to win," another voice says.

The camera shows two men, their arms linked around Barbaro's rear end as they force him back into the gate.

I hold my breath again.

"They're off!" the announcer shouts.

The horses come thundering out of the gates. I scoot forward, trying to see where Barbaro is in the pack. I can't pick him out, but it doesn't matter. He'll catch them in his own good time. I glance at Dad. He reaches and squeezes my shoulder.

Jeffy has been awake for a few minutes, but he suddenly screws up his face and starts to cry.

Sondra gets up.

"Barbaro!" the announcer shouts.

I jump up to see over Sondra's rear end as she reaches into the playpen for Jeffy.

"Barbaro," the announcer cries again. "I believe he's being pulled up by Edgar Prado. He's out of this race."

I look at Dad, then back at the TV.

The camera is on Barbaro, who's trying to run on three

94

legs. The bottom half of his right rear leg flops out at an odd angle. Every time it touches the ground he jerks it up, yet he keeps trying to use it.

I look at Daddy again. He's staring at the screen, his mouth open in disbelief.

"What happened?"

Daddy's face goes red. "Damn them," he shouts, then bashes his armrest with a fist.

Daddy's yelling scares Jeffy, who starts to scream. Sondra lifts him up and runs from the room.

"What happened?" I say again.

Daddy shakes his head, then covers his face with his hands.

The race ends, but there's no cheering, just the stunned faces of people in the crowd and the repeated shots of Barbaro holding his foot high off the ground. Prado has jumped down and is looking at Barbaro's leg. People are running out onto the track. A horse ambulance rolls up.

Earlier, there was a picture of Matz, his trainer, smiling in the stands. Now they show his grief-stricken face for a moment before he turns and pushes his way through the crowd. His wife covers her mouth and tries not to cry with the camera on her.

"Don't kill him," some woman screams from the stands.

"Oh, Daddy. What's wrong with his leg?"

"It's broken," he whispers, then he raises his fist and

slams it down on his lost leg. "They've killed that magnificent horse," he cries, and hits his stump again. "They've killed him."

"Stop," I cry. He's hurting himself without seeming to feel it. I get on my knees on the end of the sofa and try to pin his arms. "Don't, Daddy. Please don't."

He grabs me and hugs me so hard, I can barely breathe. The arm of his wheelchair is jammed against my ribs. "Oh God, Hannah, the pain. You can't imagine the pain." He loosens his hold on me and cries against my shoulder.

He's flashing back to when he lost his leg again, but I know he also means Barbaro.

Sondra comes and stands in the doorway to the kitchen. She is bouncing Jeffy and biting her bottom lip.

Daddy begins to moan from what he's done to his leg. "Get me something for the pain, Hannah. Please." He lets me go.

Sondra turns and goes into the kitchen. When I go in, she has his pain meds out and hands them to me. We just look at each other and say nothing.

By the time I get back to the living room with his meds and a glass of water, he's finished his mint julep and has started on Sondra's. On TV they keep rerunning the shot of Barbaro's leg flaring out grotesquely until I turn off the set.

15

SUNDAY, MAY 21

The Sunday morning copy of the Santa Rosa *Press Democrat* has pictures and a long story about Barbaro. His leg is broken in twenty-plus places, but I don't want to read about the repairs they made. Reading about that will make me imagine all the stuff Dad went through, and I don't want to, so I leave the paper on the coffee table.

I'm in the kitchen when Dad wheels in and starts reading the story to Sondra. She's making French toast.

"'The bones were put in place to fuse the joint by inserting a plate,'" he says, "'and twenty-three screws to repair damage.' It says his chances of survival aren't good. Fifty-fifty at best." He looks at her back. "They should have put him down."

She doesn't turn, so she hasn't seen his sad eyes watching her. I feel like he's reading this to be reassured.

"No they shouldn't," I say. "I'm glad they are trying to save him."

Dad's eyes darken. I'm the one who said what he wants to hear instead of Sondra. "He's worth millions as a stud, that's why they're trying to keep him alive," he says.

It seems since Dad has decided that he can't earn a living fishing and Barbaro can no longer race, they are alike—worthless as human and horse. It makes me mad. "I think it's because they love him."

"Don't be a sap, Hannah. Racing is all about making money."

Suddenly the whole kitchen is full of people feeling sorry for themselves—me included. "I'm not a sap. If they loved him when he could run, they still love him."

"I'm sorry . . ." I hear him call after I slam out of the kitchen.

I ride to the stables wondering if they even know what happened since none of them watch horseracing. Of course they do. It's all over the news.

Dillon says she thinks they should have put him down rather than make him suffer the surgeries and the pain. Meg thinks it's worth trying to save him.

"Hannah, why don't you get Jack out and you can start learning the Parelli games," Dillon says. "He knows them all."

"Really? Can I?" I don't say so to Dillon, but I'm hoping, in time, I will learn enough to do something for horses like Meg has done and Sophia is doing.

"Sure. Meg will be glad to have someone play with him. And he likes you."

The fog is rolling in, seeping through the tops of the redwoods. I get my flannel shirt out of my backpack and put it on over my T-shirt. Jack sees me coming and bobs his head. "Hey, old man."

Jack is wearing his halter, which means Dillon planned this. I get his lead from the peg by the door, snap it on the halter ring, and open his stall.

With lots of slack in the lead, Jack and I walk side by side toward the arena. The fog floats around us like a ghost. *Watch this, Momma,* I think—just in case she's near.

Because of the fog it has turned cold; they've taken the horses to the indoor arena. When Jack and I come through the tall double doors, Meg and Dillon are standing in the center and Super Dee, Indy, and Bobby are running at liberty around the arena. They come thundering toward Jack and me, throwing up clods of dirt. When the women signal, the horses stop, walk over, and stand facing their owners.

Dillon walks over with Bobby following her like a puppy. Indy stops to lick a barrel. "Ready?"

"I think so."

"I have a little story I tell myself to remember the seven

games. A Friendly Porcupine Drives his Yo-Yo around the Circle Sideways and Squeezes into traffic."

I raise my eyebrows.

"Kind of dumb, huh?"

"I guess it's like Kings Play Chess On Fine-Grain Sand."

"What do you use that to remember?"

"Kingdom, Phylum, Class, Family, Order, Genus, Species."

"That's a cut above a porcupine driving a yo-yo." She smiles and hands me a Carrot Stick. "So the first is the Friendly Game. It's the rhythmic swinging of the string and it's meant to show your horse that you can be trusted not to hurt him."

"Super Dee used to freak if anything touched his legs," Meg says. She swings the string so it wraps completely around Dee's front legs. He doesn't move or even lift his head. Head up, I've learned, can be a sign of alarm. Head down is relaxed.

"The key," Dillon says, "is to approach, touching the horse lightly with the string, smile and retreat, over and over, until the horse becomes desensitized. Then you can do it with a blanket, his rain blanket, his fly mask, the ball . . ." She pokes the huge blue beach ball they bounce around the horses and put on their backs. "Before you start, you have to learn how to use the Carrot Stick correctly."

She pats Bobby's neck, gives him an apple-flavored oat cookie from the little bag on her belt, then taps his nose when he tries to help himself to another. "Come stand out here and swing the string slowly."

I do as she says, swinging my arm fully from side to side. The string kind of flops here and there.

"You look like you're swinging a dead snake." She rolls the ball out. "Try to drape it over this without swinging your whole arm, but add a little wrist."

After a few more tries, I lay the string over the ball with a snap.

"Watch your rhythm. It's all one motion."

I try again.

Bobby has moved in right behind me. I feel his breath on my neck. I take a step forward.

"Don't move. The one who moves their feet first loses." She takes my shoulders and turns me around. "Use the stick to back him out of your space, like this." With the string end down, she flicks the Carrot Stick with her wrist and Bobby takes a step or two backward. I do it and he doesn't move. "Do it again and increase your energy. It's about respect."

"Can he smell that I'm afraid?"

"Are you?"

I shrug. "He's big."

"Size isn't everything. I'm alpha mare around here and he knows it. All you have to do is gain his respect by not backing down or letting him inside your bubble." Dillon swings the Carrot Stick so that the string causes a little explosion of sand, then she flicks it insistently until Bobby moves back a couple of yards.

"Let's practice with Bobby first. His hide is tough." She smiles at him and crooks her finger. He comes back, twists his neck, and tries to munch her face. When he's playing, his tongue is always working. "If they're licking, they're thinking," Dillon says. "If they are thinking, they are in the left side of their brains."

She lays the Carrot Stick string across Bobby's back like a feather landing. "You try it."

In my mind, I flick the line across his back with one fluid motion, but my arm stays at my side. "I'm afraid I'll do it too hard and hurt him."

"Ha. You can't hurt him."

I lean back like I'm going to cast a fishing line and swing the stick. The string sails through the air and falls across Bobby's neck. I pull it off like I'm reeling in a fish.

"Close. Lob it on, take it off quickly," Dillon says.

I watch her, then try to copy what she did. Both our strings land on his back. "Perfect." She reaches for a cookie, then laughs. "I was going to give this to you as your reward."

"Have you ever tasted one?"

"I have. They taste like bone-dry apple and oat-flavored sawdust."

With Jack as my new victim, I work on gently laying the string across his back, his neck, and his rump. He stands with his head low, ignoring me. He's not licking or blinking. I'm not even sure he's awake.

Meg and Dillon are going through all the rest of the games with their horses, but I catch Dillon checking out my progress. She gives me a thumbs-up, so I don't tell her that I'm bored with this and so is Jack.

After a few more minutes, she comes over. "Ready for the Porcupine Game?"

"Yes, and poor Jack is too."

When I get home, Dad's so drunk, he can't hold his own head up.

"Where's Sondra?"

He opens his eyes and blinks at me. "Her mother's."

I'm suddenly angry. "You're going to drive her away, you know."

He lifts his head, finds where I'm standing, and wags his finger at me in slow motion. "You're absolutely right, Hannah Banana. You've hit the nail on the head."

"Don't you care?"

"I do indeed. 'Deed I do."

I remember Sondra throwing water in his face when he was hyperventilating. I want to do that to him. I march to the kitchen, fill one of the iced tea glasses with water, and carry it back to the living room. I hold it at my side. All I need to do is lift and pitch it at him. His chin's on his chest again.

On the mantel, Sondra has added another picture of Daddy—the one taken in his full dress uniform with the flag behind him. She put a little circle of Velcro on the frame and attached his Purple Heart to it.

I look down at the glass in my hand, then put it on the coffee table. There are white hairs on my sleeve. They are from hugging Jack.

Daddy looks up, his eyes soft and sad. "Do you feel bad, sweetheart?"

"I do, Daddy. I feel awful."

He holds his arms out. I kneel beside him and put my head on his chest.

"Don't be mad at your ole man." He strokes my hair.

"I'm not, Daddy. I'm not."

16

SATURDAY, MAY 27

Sophia's Premarin mare is coming today. She's supposed to arrive about eleven. I get my chores done—my laundry, my room, and the breakfast dishes—and slip out before Sondra thinks to try to guilt-trip me into babysitting so she can have a day off.

I'm so excited you'd think I was getting a horse of my own. I come whizzing down the driveway a little before eleven; the truck and horse trailer pull in right behind me. It's a beautiful, warm day—almost hot for the coast. Sixty-five, maybe. All the horses are in their paddocks.

"Here she comes!" I shout.

Sophia, who was cleaning the stall that will be her mare's, comes out and claps her hands together. "She's here."

The driver parks under the big redwood in the driveway. Meg and Dillon lean their muck-rakes against the wall and we all crowd around as he gets out and comes to open the trailer door.

"Have any trouble?" Sophia asks.

"Not a bit, but she sure needs a good home. That's one pitiful-looking horse."

"She's got one now," Sophia says.

Sophia opens the top half of the trailer door and speaks softly to the mare inside. Her rump is dusty brown and smeared with a crust of dried poop down her right hip. The horse doesn't even lift her head when Sophia and Meg pull the bolts and let the ramp down.

We all look at each other. The mare reminds me of the pictures of starving children in Africa—skin and bones except for her bloated belly. They always show those children with flies around their weepy eyes. This mare's eyes look like that—wet from a white discharge. Her breathing is wheezy like I used to sound before I outgrew my asthma. If she weren't so sick, she'd look made to order for Sophia—stocky and not very tall. Her feet are huge, hairy, and caked with mud and poop, but even the long hair can't cover her overgrown hooves. It must have been painful to stand for the six hours it took to drive from Galt, which is way over by Sacramento.

"Did you know what she looked like?" I ask.

"No. I just told them to send me the one that needed the most help. Looks like they took me at my word." Sophia steps up into the trailer and strokes the mare's swollen side. "It's okay, sweetie," she whispers as she unties the lead and tries to back her out.

Dillon told me Sophia's family owns the biggest inn on the coast. "She has lots of money and saving horses is her thing."

The minute Dillon saw the condition the mare was in, she went to her truck for her cell phone.

"I called the vet," she says when she comes back. "She'll be here within the hour."

"Thanks," Sophia says. "I know I said send me the neediest, but I had no idea any horse could be in this condition and still be alive." She tries again to back her out of the trailer.

"She's spent eight months out of every year of her life in a stall not much bigger than that trailer, she probably feels safe in there," Dillon says.

Sophia lifts the mare's head and strokes her face. Her head is so big that it looks out of proportion to her body. "What kind of horse is she?" I ask.

"A Belgian draft horse mix," Dillon says.

Sophia puts her hands against the mare's chest and pushes gently. Step by painful step, the mare backs out of the trailer.

"Good luck with her," says the driver.

Sophia nods grimly.

The first thing she needs is her hooves trimmed. Meg, who ran off to the arena, returns with a hoof pick, a pair of nippers, and a rasp for filing.

Dillon is the only one with the know-how to trim hooves properly.

"Do you think she'd like to stand in the sun or would her stall make her feel safer?" Sophia asks Dillon.

"Let's get her some water and a little hay, then we'll try trimming them in the sun. She hasn't had much of that on her back."

The mare ignores the hay. After she drinks her fill of water, Dillon walks her over to a paddock fence and loops her lead over the top board. She leaves lots of slack for the mare to bring her head up, but she doesn't. There's not enough spirit left in her.

I brought carrots but am afraid the effort of chewing one might finish her off. I go to the arena for a soft brush. When I get back, Dillon is standing with her back to the mare's head. She lifts the mare's left front hoof and begins to pick out the mud and muck packed inside.

Dillon moves around the beaten-down horse, cleaning and scraping one hoof at a time. When she's done with that, she circles her again, trimming each hoof with the nipper. She holds the mare's leg between her knees, taking a small amount off each toe of the hoof, eyeballs how it rests on the ground, then takes off a little more. She starts at the heel on one side and works her way around to the other side.

"How do you know when you've cut enough off?" I ask. I've brushed the mare from stem to stern and sprayed her mane and tail with the avocado stuff they use to get tangles out.

"There's a ring in the toe area. When it's a light pink color, I've taken enough off."

Joanne, the vet, arrives. She opens her black bag and takes out a stethoscope, a cable, and an iPod.

"What's she doing?" I whisper to Dillon.

"Joanne is almost completely deaf. She'll record the mare's heartbeat and listen to her lungs, then play it back on her iPod at a volume she can hear."

After listening to her heart, which she says is strong, and her lungs, which aren't, she prescribes antibiotics. "She's running a bit of a temperature and has pneumonia," she says. "Sterilize everything you used on her and keep her away from the other horses." She's smiling about something as she moves her hands over the mare's neck and sides. "Congratulations," she says to Sophia. "You saved two lives."

"What?" we all say at the same time.

"She's very pregnant."

"Are you sure?" Sophia says, then laughs. "Sorry. You *are* the doctor."

"I thought they only gave away the ones they'd used up.

Why did they let you have her, then?" I ask Sophia.

"Maybe they didn't know, or maybe she's from one of the barns they've shut down." Sophia kisses the mare's nose. "Ever since the news broke that taking hormone replacements was upping the breast cancer rates, women have stopped taking them. The pharmaceutical company that produces Premarin has closed down hundreds of their barns and is selling the horses off to slaughterhouses." To the mare, she says, "This time, my love, no one is going to take your baby away." She puts her forehead against the mare's for a moment, then her head snaps up. "Oh, Dillon, you didn't bargain for two horses. Are you okay with this?"

"Are you kidding? I'm thrilled. Just think what this means. You'll have a foal that is a clean slate. Not an abused wreck of a horse."

Sophia's smile nearly splits her face. "Come on, sweetheart." She unties her mare and leads her toward her stall. "You are eating for two."

"What are you going to call her?" I ask.

Sophia stops. She stands with her back to us for a moment, then looks straight up past the towering tops of the redwoods at the rich blue sky. "Free at Last," she says.

17

SATURDAY, JUNE 10

The Belmont Stakes—the third jewel in the Triple Crown—is today. So is my first riding lesson.

I wake this morning to Dad and Sondra arguing again. All I wanted was for Dad to be together enough to come watch me ride. It's a vicious circle: They fight because he drinks, and he drinks because they fight. I lie in bed and stare up at the ceiling wishing with all my might that things could be like they were before the war.

My ceiling is pine with lots of knotholes—like black stars. Stars form constellations. I know a few, like Orion, the Pleiades, and the Big and Little Dipper. I try to connect some of the knotholes to form a horse constellation of my own. I focus so hard on finding a horse up there that I stop hearing them, then it dawns me that I can pretend the ceiling is heaven and that Mom is there. I wish on the largest of my little black stars that Mom will hear me and make them stop.

By the time I come down for breakfast the air in the kitchen is icy. Sondra's at the sink with her back to me and Dad's parked in front of the fridge with the door open. He must have been sitting there like that for a while, 'cause his beer bottles have warmed up enough to start to sweat.

"Whatcha doing?"

I startle him.

"Nothing." He closes the door.

I open the fridge to get carrots and the orange juice out. "I'll be home about two thirty, okay?"

"What for?"

"To watch the Belmont."

He shakes his head. "I've kind of lost interest, haven't you?"

"Yeah. I don't want to watch horses race anymore either."

At least Barbaro is better. I've been tracking his progress on the Internet at one of the horseracing sites. Everyone is feeling good about his chances. They are planning to change his cast this week and it seems like the whole country is tuned in to news about him. I've wondered about the fascination, and have decided it's because he seems so heroic and brave. Like Sophia's Free, animals just do what we ask them to do. Barbaro didn't choose to be a racehorse any more than Dad chose to go to war. They were both sent to do a dangerous job. Maybe that's why Dad feels such a kinship with him—like they are in this battle together.

The good news about Barbaro didn't keep Dad from getting drunk again yesterday. By the time I got home to tell him about my riding lesson it was already too late but I still made the mistake of asking him if he would come watch. He started in about how dangerous horses can be, and demanded to know Dillon's qualifications, how long she'd been teaching, did they provide helmets, have insurance, yada, yada. I ended up wishing I'd never mentioned it and hoped he'd forget by morning.

When Sondra came down from putting Jeffy to bed, I went up to play on the computer. Even with my door closed, I could still hear the ebb and flow of their voices, especially Sondra's asking him to please not drink anymore. She finally gave up and made her escape about an hour later. She came in and stood behind me for a moment with her hands on my shoulders, not saying anything. It made me edgy and I was just about to say—what?—when she kissed the top of my head, then left and softly closed the door.

About eleven, I went downstairs for some juice. Daddy had tumbled out of his chair and was sprawled out on the carpet in front of the TV. After all the nights we've listened to him fighting the war in his sleep, I was afraid to try and wake him. I went back upstairs and knocked on Sondra's door.

"Daddy's passed out on the floor."

"I know."

"Will you help me get him up?"

She shook her head. "What for?"

"He might get cold, or wake up and have to go to the bathroom."

"If he does he does, Hannah. Throw his bedspread over him." She started to close the door, then said, "I can't try any harder than I'm trying. I hope you know that."

I got the afghan Momma knitted from the upstairs hall closet, covered him with that, turned off the TV, and kinda left it to her to watch over him for the night.

"How do you want your eggs?" Sondra asks. She doesn't look at me.

I shrug, and after a minute she turns and says, "Can you answer me?"

"I don't care. Any way."

"I want you to babysit today," she says.

"It's Saturday."

"I *need* you to babysit."

"I have to work." I look pleadingly at Dad. Sondra wasn't there when I told him about the riding lesson and I don't want to remind him by telling her now.

"Work. Really? Or play with those horses? Where's all the money you're making?"

"It's not fair to ask her to give up her Saturdays," Dad says. "I can watch Jeffy."

Sondra looks at me, then at Dad. "I have to get out of here. I need a day to myself. Is that too much to ask?"

Dad's voice is soft. "I know you do, honey. You work hard all week, but I'm here and I'll watch the baby. It's not fair to ask Hannah to give up her job."

"She's not working there. She's hanging out. Now that school's over she can go every day if it's so important to her, just not today."

"Saturday is the day I'm needed most. They take all the horses out to . . ." I almost say *play*. "They work the horses on Saturdays." My lesson is at one. "I can be a little late. Can't you do whatever you have to do this morning?"

"Am I chopped liver?" Dad snaps. "I said I'd watch him."

From the living room, Jeffy starts to cry. I get up.

"No," Sondra says. "Let your hero father go." I can tell she regrets using the word *hero*, and she tries to cover. "Go ahead," she says to him, then turns to face the kitchen window.

Dad has taken the swinging door off the kitchen, so

he doesn't have to bash his way in and out. He wheels his chair into the living room.

Sondra bows her head and makes a muffled, choked-off sound in her throat, then raises her fists and slams them down on the counter. One of the eggs she hasn't cracked open begins to roll. She doesn't even look at it when it goes over the edge and smashes on the floor. She starts to cry.

"Please don't cry, Sondra." I get paper towels and begin to wipe up the egg.

She doesn't look at me. "Do you really want to leave the baby with him? Do you?"

I don't, but I want out of here so bad, I can taste it. "He'll be fine."

"What if he starts drinking as soon as we leave?"

"He won't if he's responsible for Jeffy."

"Are you sure?"

I'm not at all sure. "Yes," I say.

Dad rolls in with Jeffy sitting in his lap. When Jeffy sees me, he holds his arms up. I take and hug him. I wish I could tell him what Dad used to be like—that he was the safest person in the world to be with.

Sondra takes the frying pan off the burner. Tears still swim in her eyes as she takes Jeffy from me, grabs his diaper bag, and leaves the house.

Daddy stares at the slammed door with melted eyes. "I don't know how to fix this," he says.

I hate every minute I'm home, but now I feel totally selfish for wanting out of here as much as Sondra does. Then I look at the shell of my dad slumped in his wheelchair. He's more trapped than any of us.

18

THE SAME DAY

It's awful, but I'm relieved that Dad doesn't mention my lesson. I leave the house without a word.

It's too cold and foggy to be outside, but the lesson would be in the arena even if it were sunny—nowhere to run in there and nothing to spook them. Dillon never takes unnecessary chances. On the day I told her I definitely wanted to learn to ride, she said, "You have to know, it's not a case of if you'll get thrown, it's a case of when."

I act okay with that, but I'm not really. Between Dad's stories and Meg telling me about getting bucked off Super Dee twice, breaking her pelvis the second time, I'm nervous about riding. Meg said she was so scared that it took her two years to get up the nerve to ride him again. Dillon taught them both Parelli, which helped Super Dee get over his fear of ropes and whips and helped Meg get her confidence back. Still, I thought about Dillon's warning and have decided that even if I only try it one time, I have to do it. For as long as I can remember, riding a horse has been my fantasy.

Dillon only gives lessons on Indy, who is just as left-brained as Bobby but is more introverted. I am brushing him and bribing him to adore me with carrots.

Before I actually get on Indy, we go through all the games as a warm-up. It will give Indy a chance to use up any stored energy so he doesn't get too spunky with me on his back.

Dillon says when I do Parelli, I move around too much. "Point in the direction you want him to go, then stand still until you want him back."

I practice asking him to trot clockwise, canter clockwise, then change and trot and canter the other direction. Next we do Sideways, which makes him use the left side of his brain because he has to think about his feet. Even though I line him up wrong, Indy does it right anyway, blinking and chewing, which means he's thinking, as he moves down the wall from one end of the arena to the other with me walking perpendicular to him.

When Dillon finally says let's tack up, my heart lurches. This is it. I give Indy a cookie and get him to hook on and follow me. I snake toward Dillon, turning right, then left with Indy's head so near my shoulder, I can smell the cookie on his breath.

Dillon is inflating the pad that goes under the saddle. The arena doors open and Meg comes in with Super Dee and behind her is Sophia leading Jack and Free. "Mind if we watch?" Meg says.

I shake my head. I'm afraid if I speak my voice will shake.

Sophia loans me her gloves and is helping me adjust the helmet when I hear the dogs across the street barking. The arena doors are still open, but even before I look out, I know it's Dad.

I expect to see the Dial-A-Ride van pulling away, but instead Dad's just turning off the bike path. The dogs from across the street are loose again today. They run across the road, barking and snapping at his wheels. Dad pushes harder and, because the stables are downhill from the road, he's going pretty fast by the time he reaches the bottom of the driveway, so fast he nearly sails through Super Dee's open stall door. He stops himself by grabbing the door frame.

Dillon shouts at the dogs and they retreat.

"It's my dad," I say, as if they didn't already know.

Dillon and Meg smile, but I can't. The butterflies in my stomach have turned to stones. I don't know what to expect. He may be drunk, and if he is and starts in on Dillon about insurance and helmets and her qualifications, I may never be allowed back here. He turns his chair and I wave.

"Am I too late?"

"No. I was just getting ready."

"Dial-A-Ride never showed."

My guess is he got impatient and left before they had a chance. I walk over and hug him and am relieved that he doesn't smell of liquor. "You mean you wheeled here all the way from home? It's uphill."

"About the only choice I had if I was going to get here in time."

He's still breathing hard, but otherwise seems okay. I walk around and start to push him toward the arena. Dillon waits for us at the door and shakes hands with my dad when I introduce them.

"I've heard a lot about you," Dad says.

"And I about you."

She's being polite. I haven't talked about Dad at all, not since the day we met, except to tell her that he came back missing a leg.

"He wheeled here all the way from home," I say to her, then turn to Dad. "I've already groomed Indy and warmed him up."

There's a row of five white plastic lawn chairs that sit with their backs to the extra saddles and blankets. I push Dad's wheelchair through the shallow layer of dirt and park him at the end of the row of chairs, then close the doors behind us.

I introduce Meg and Sophia, who wave from the center of the arena, where Super Dee and Jack trot around them.

Dillon puts a western saddle on Indy so I'll have the saddle horn to hold on to in case I feel tippy, and just his halter and a rope for reins. No bridle. Indy hates the bit and I'm going to learn to start, stop, back up, and go sideways with just my legs. At least that's the plan. I give Indy the next to last chunk of carrot, saving the last big piece as a thank you if it goes well.

Dillon does my helmet strap and we look each other in the eyes. She's reading me like she does the horses. "You'll do just fine," she says.

I go up the two steps of the mounting block. Dillon signals Indy. He moves forward and stands so that the left stirrup is level with my knees. I hold on to Indy's mane and reins, put my left foot in the stirrup, stand in it, and swing my right leg over his back. It feels just like I've always imagined it would—except higher. I turn and grin at Dad, then give the royal wave by rotating a cupped hand like the Queen of England.

Meg and Sophia have called in Dee and Jack. The horses hook on and follow them over to stand near the doors. Dee walks the closest to Dad's wheelchair. He could step over my father as easily as he could over one of the barrels. "That's Super Dee, Dad. Remember I told you? He's a grandson of Seattle Slew."

Dad nods. He has a white-knuckled grip on his armrests and it shocks me to realize that he's afraid of the horses. But why not? He was a kid the last time he was near a horse, and his only memories of them are of being kicked and nearly killed. Now he's defenseless and completely vulnerable there in his wheelchair with huge horses walking around him. How would he have known; how would either of us have known how near the surface his fear of horses really is?

I look back at him and smile as Dillon leads Indy toward the middle of the arena. I sink into the saddle and feel the way Indy is moving beneath me. I try to concentrate on lowering and raising my hips in time with his.

When we are in the center of the ring, Dillon leads Indy in a tight clockwise circle. "Press your right calf into his side and don't put any pressure on his left side. Good."

My saddle slips a little to the right, which makes me feel like I'm tipping over, but I don't say anything.

We stop and she starts circling him the other direction. "Now apply the pressure with your left calf."

The saddle slips back to center and a little to the left.

"That's it."

She walks us to the wall and lines Indy up like we are going to play the Sideways Game. His head faces the wall, his rump the center of the arena.

"Now, as he moves, his right hip will drop. When his hip

drops, apply pressure with your right leg. When it comes up again, release. Okay?"

I nod.

We start to move and I lean to the right.

"No. Don't lean. Just press his side with your leg. That's it."

I glance over at Dad. Both hands are gripping his armrests, and his body is rigid. I'm glad when we start back the other way and I can't see him watching me.

"Now, to back him up, put your insoles against his stomach and wiggle your ankles."

Meg is sitting on one of the barrels near the row of chairs. Super Dee is standing beside her. She's rubbing his ear. Sophia is brushing Jack.

"Okay," Dillon says. "Walk him."

"How do I do that?"

"Up your energy. Tighten your cheeks."

I'm not sure what up my energy means, but I kind of squeeze the cheeks of my butt together and Indy starts to walk. "How do I stop him?" I think to ask.

"Relax in the saddle and say whoa."

We head for the far wall of the arena. "And how do I turn him?"

"Look the way you want to go."

I do and Indy turns, walks over to a barrel, and begins to lick it.

"Back him up."

I wiggle my ankles, but this time he ignores me. I lean to the side, away from the barrel, and try to pull his head away with the rope. But the saddle slides and suddenly I'm hanging off Indy's side, both feet in the stirrups, my head about three feet off the ground. I grab for the saddle horn and get a fistful of mane.

"Jesus. Hannah!" I hear Dad shout.

Indy turns his head and looks at me but doesn't move. I see the women coming toward me, walking fast and talking soothingly to Indy. Meg reaches me first and grabs Indy's halter. A second later Dillon's arm goes around my waist. My right foot has gone through the stirrup. If Indy takes off, I'll be ripped out of Dillon's arms and dragged around the arena. Sophia tries to work my foot back out of the stirrup, but I wore hiking boots and I can't bend my ankle. She picks at the double bow I made and after a minute, pulls my boot off and feeds my foot back out of the stirrup. I kick off the left stirrup and Dillon eases me to the ground.

"I should have told you it felt loose," I say, then remember Dad and look over to tell him I'm okay.

He'd tried to wheel toward us, but got stuck in the sand. He's gulping air.

"Oh my God. Your dad," Meg says.

Heart attack is what the others probably think, but I

know he's having a panic attack and will hyperventilate but might not remember what to do. I scramble to my feet and start across the arena.

Everyone left their horses to help me. Super Dee is standing right where Meg left him, but Jack is walking toward Dad.

I don't want to make it worse by running, but with Dad's fear and Jack's hatred of men, my own heart thunders in my chest.

Dad remembers to breathe his own carbon dioxide and cups his hands over his nose and mouth; when Jack stops right beside his wheelchair, his eyes dart to his right, then his head slowly turns. He stiffens and drops his hands to his wheels as if he could wheel himself out of danger.

I'm afraid Jack can smell my father's fear. "Don't move, Daddy," I whisper.

Dillon, Meg, Sophia, and Indy join me as we move like a wall toward Jack. When we are a few feet away, Dillon holds up her hand and we stop. "It's okay," she says. "Look at his ears."

Jack's ears are up, not pinned, and one is turned toward my dad, which Dillon has told me is a sign of respect. He lowers his head and smells the wheelchair, my dad's shoulder, then puts his nose against the back of my father's neck. I know how that feels—soft, warm, and moist.

Daddy looks at me. I can tell he's not sure what Jack's going to do.

I smile at him.

He slowly turns his head so that his cheek is against Jack's muzzle, then reaches up and strokes Jack's face.

Dillon smiles. "Can you beat that?" she says.

I fish in my pocket for the Ziploc with the last chunk of carrot and hand it to Dad. He holds it out for Jack, who takes it gently with his old yellow teeth.

Dad looks at me; tears swim in his eyes.

I push my bike as Dad and I head home down Simpson. He's talking and laughing. *Laughing.* I haven't seen him laugh since he got home from Iraq.

"You rode like a pro," Dad says. "I remember my first time on a horse. I was sailing through the air five seconds after swinging my leg over the saddle." He smiles at the memory.

I know he's thinking about Nevada. "I didn't feel like a pro," I say, and suddenly think of all the things Daddy has lost: Momma, his leg, his job, his dignity, his pride, his joy. I stop my bike.

Dad wheels another yard, then turns and looks at me. "What's up?"

I shrug.

"So how does this Parelli stuff work?" he asks, but his

eyes are so sad-looking, like he knows I'm feeling sorry for him.

I can't answer and shake my head.

"It's been a long time, hasn't it, honey?" He holds his hand out to me.

I nod. "It feels like forever."

"I'm sorry. I'll try harder."

"This is the most wonderful day I can remember in such a long time." I put my kickstand down, go and squat beside his chair for a hug. I feel desperate to hang on and not let go. It reminds me of the day Momma died. It took a nurse and an orderly to pry me loose once I had my arms around her.

"They say a good soldier makes a bad civilian," he whispers against my hair. "But it shouldn't make a bad father."

"You're not."

"I will try harder, Hannah Banana. I promise. Starting today, we'll have more days like this one."

Sondra meets us at the door. "Good God, Jeff, where have you been? I was just about to call the sheriff." She's wiping her hands on a dishtowel, so I know she's exaggerating.

"I'm sorry. I should have left you a note."

Sondra looks at me. "Is he okay?"

"Sure. He came to watch my riding lesson."

Dad is grinning at her and she finally notices the change in him. "What?"

"You should have seen her."

I have my hand on Dad's shoulder and he reaches around and pats it.

Sondra's face is a topo map of emotions. She wants to stay mad at Dad and she scowls, but I imagine there's a part of her that longs for this change in him to be a turning point. Her eyes soften and she tries to smile.

"The amazing thing is how the horses are trained. It's so gentle and humane. Sure not the way I learned to break a horse. The way we did it was violent, with constant whippings, and it took weeks. The idea was to show 'em who was boss; hurt him before he could hurt you. Everything we did was to break a horse's spirit ..." His voice trails off.

"What did you . . . ?" I start to ask, but the veins in his forehead are standing out like mole trails. "Daddy?"

"We did to the horses what they did to us in boot camp," he says. "They degraded us until we were emotionally empty ..." His eyes grow dark. "Then they built a new mentality on the slate they'd cleaned and here I am." He spread his arms.

"Stop, Jeff," Sondra says. "Please don't bring all that stuff up now. You were feeling better than you've felt in months."

Dad ignores her. "Here's some irony for you." He wheels to the refrigerator and gets out a beer. "One of the ways we broke the horses was to tie a leg up, so the poor thing had one less to stand on. How's that for what goes around comes around?" His laugh is bitter and angry.

Sondra and I watch him drain his beer, crush the can in his fist, toss it toward the recycle bucket by the door and miss. He gets another beer and wheels into the living room.

"He was so happy," I say.

"Nice while it lasted." Her voice is as flat as Kansas.

19

SATURDAY, JULY 8

Over the last two and a half months Free's been gaining weight and her pneumonia has gone away, but still the first thing I think is she is dying when I turn into the driveway to the stables and see the vet's truck parked under the redwoods. Her stall door is open and it's lit up like a ball field by the floodlight that's hanging from a ceiling hook.

I drop my bike and run toward the stall. "What's wrong?"

Dillon smiles and puts her finger to her lips. "Free's having her foal. I noticed her udders filling a couple days ago, so my guess is she started labor about dawn. As many times as the poor thing has been pregnant, it shouldn't take long."

Sophia grins at me when she and Meg step aside so I can fit into the stall with them. Joanne, the vet, is there.

Her long auburn hair is pulled up in a ponytail. I know she is deaf, but this is the first time I've seen that she wears hearing aids in both ears.

Joanne doesn't just ignore me like most adults would; she says—as though my presence mattered, "Hi, Hannah. You're just in time."

Free is lying on her side, which glistens with sweat. Her tail is wrapped with white gauze and flicks up and down. A couple of times, she paws the air with her left front foot, then lies back in the straw. Nobody does anything; we just stand and watch and wait. I have to remind myself to breathe. Every time she moves, I think this is it.

I'm not sure how long we have watched her rear end when suddenly, like a fire hose, out comes this flood of cloudy, yellowish liquid. Joanne looks at her watch: "Ten thirty-four," she says. Dillon writes down the time. "Should only take another fifteen minutes or so."

Free sits up, then struggles to her feet. We edge toward the doors to give her room. She bobs and shakes her head. Her mane is a tangle of straw and she moves her feet from side to side before lowering her head to lick the fluid off her bedding. Last year, watching her do that would have made me gag, but I've helped Sondra change Dad's bandage on his stump, and clean up after he's gotten sick enough times that I'm fine.

Joanne looks at her watch. "We should start to see the birth sac soon."

No one says a word. I'm scared for Free and her foal, probably more than the others, who've been through this before. I try to imagine how a whole baby horse is going to fit through that small opening, and that reminds me of when I was little and sat staring at the flue of our wood-stove wondering how Santa was going to make it down the long thin stovepipe. My hands are sweating and I'm afraid I may start to giggle.

"Here it comes," Joanne says.

We see a white sac emerging. Inside is the tip of one tiny hoof, then a second hoof.

"Come on, sweetie," Joanne whispers. Her hands are raised like if it shoots out, she'll catch it.

I cross my fingers, feel silly, uncross them, then cross them again. My heart is ricocheting around in my chest.

Free pulls her stomach in. The membrane covering the foal's feet pokes out farther until we can see its knees.

"Let's see that baby's nose," Dillon says.

Sophia has a viselike grip on my wrist, turning my hand red with trapped blood.

"There's the nose," Sophia says. "Thank God." She lets go of my wrist and covers her mouth with her hands.

My hand tingles. "Why is that good?" I whisper.

"It means the foal is positioned exactly right—feet first

133

with its head parallel to its legs—like its diving into life. Any other way could be fatal to mare and foal," Dillon says.

Free drops to her knees and lies down again. Her stomach heaves in and out. With each contraction, more of the foal shows. It's the color of a foggy night—black sky through the whitish sac.

Free pushes three more times until only the baby's hips and hind legs are still inside her. There's one more contraction, and its hips and hind legs slip free and the baby, all wet and gooey, slides out and flops onto the soft hay-covered floor.

"She's a filly," Joanne says.

Dillon puts her arm around my shoulders. "How cool is that?"

"Oh my God," I whisper. My whole body is shaking. "She's so beautiful. And tiny."

The foal is still in the membrane, which sinks against her nostrils when she tries to breathe. Joanne peels it away and the foal takes her first full breath. "They both need to rest for a few minutes," Joanne says, and moves the foal close beside Free. The umbilical cord is still attached and I can see blood moving through it.

After about ten minutes, Free gets up, snapping the cord. Joanne ties it off with sterilized fishing line, then dips the baby's short umbilical in an iodine solution.

"Free should start to clean her," Sophia says.

We wait.

After a moment, Free looks over her shoulder at her baby, then turns and starts to eat her oats.

"Premarin mares are so used to their foals being dragged away after birth that they have learned to ignore them," Joanne says.

Joanne moves the filly closer to her mom, then guides Free's head around until her nose touches her baby. She sniffs her, licks once, then again. I think my heart will melt when Free begins to clean her foal and talk to it, making low little whickering sounds.

The filly tries to get her long, rubbery legs to work enough to stand up. Her legs look like soft black pretzels as she tries to get up without tangling them. The third time she makes it to her feet, only to fall over again. The urge to help her is almost more than I can stand.

Sophia is stroking Free's cheek and praising her when the after-birth plops out looking like a big, bloody jelly-fish.

"Good," Joanne says. "It's totally intact."

"Is that important?" I ask.

"If it had ruptured, there could be infection."

It takes the little filly about an hour to finally get all four of her legs straightened under her, though they are splayed for balance. She wobbles toward her mother and pushes her nose against her mother's side. Joanne guides her little head toward a nipple. The foal latches on.

Dillon's fist pumps the air. We high-five, but tears come so unexpectedly, I turn away. My mother's hazy face pops into my mind. I'm having this amazing morning and the only person I want to share it with has been dead for over five and a half years.

"Have you thought of a name for her, Sophia?" Dillon asks.

Sophia's forehead is against Free's. She looks up and smiles. "Well, *el regalo* is Spanish for the gift. Let's call her Regalita."

20

THURSDAY, AUGUST 31

The reports on Barbaro are pretty good. Every other day or so I check timwoolleyracing.com and print out the report for Dad. On Sunday it said there is still no sign of infection. The joint looks fused and the bone that broke in so many places is almost ready to have the cast removed.

I am just about to log off when I see the word *laminitis* a couple of paragraphs down. Chill bumps rise on my arms.

"The colt's left hind foot has laminitis . . ."

For a moment, I was relieved because I didn't think they were talking about Barbaro. It said "the colt." But he still is, of course. He's not even three and a half. He'll be called a colt until he's four—if he lives that long. Laminitis is the hoof infection that finally killed Secretariat.

Sondra thinks Daddy has reached a plateau. He drinks a

lot at night but then he sleeps, so I only print out the good news about Barbaro.

I didn't start school until I was six and a half. Dad told me it was because Mom was getting better after her first bout with breast cancer and wanted to spend as much time as she could teaching me all the things she thought were important, just in case she wasn't around later. I don't remember everything about that year we had together, just moments, like snapshots.

Fort Bragg schools start the last week in August and I'm now in the seventh grade. I thought I'd like it better, but I don't. For one thing, Rega, my nickname for Regalita, is seven weeks old and all I want to do is be at the stables to watch her grow. On the upside, because of that year with Mom, I'm about the oldest kid in my class. Not that it matters. I don't feel any smarter

Sondra says she'll drive me to school today, since she's taking Dad to physical therapy—which doesn't seem to be helping. He's been home for four months and he's still not used to the difference in his weight with a leg missing. Neither prosthesis fits right, they are painful to wear, and he feels tippy when he's on his crutches. At home, he stays in his wheelchair.

There's the usual uproar to get ready: find the car keys, then load Dad's wheelchair and his "peg" leg into the trunk, add Jeffy's diaper bag and his stroller. Dad says it's fitting that all the men in the family get wheeled around and the women do the pushing. "In case we don't whip al-Qaeda and the Taliban, our girls will be well trained," he tells Jeffy.

"Don't count on that," Sondra says, as if Jeffy had a clue what Dad was talking about.

I put Dad's wheelchair in the trunk, then go back for Jeffy and buckle him into his car seat. He smiles at me when I find his plastic horse under the seat. "Horsy," I say. I want *horse* to be his first word, so I've been drilling him in secret.

He kisses the horse's head, then holds it out for me to kiss. I know Sondra is getting tired of us, so moments like this with Jeffy cause a pain that starts in the pit of my stomach and spreads up through my chest. I give the horse a loud smooch, then kiss Jeffy's warm little forehead and close my eyes against the hollowness and fear I feel.

"Hannah, do you have your books and a coat?" Sondra's in the doorway with her hand on Dad's back, bracing him so he doesn't fall over sideways.

"Yes and yes." I open Dad's door, then go around and get in the backseat beside Jeffy. If I could just hug him and never let go.

"It's Thursday, did you put the trash and recycling cans out?"

Geez. "Yes."

Dad's jumpy today. He's gotten worse over the last couple of months about riding anywhere in the car. Sondra's asked him about it, but he says he doesn't know why. I think it's pretty obvious; he lost his leg in a roadside bomb explosion. If that could happen in a Humvee, then it's no wonder he doesn't feel exactly cocooned in our Honda. Sondra knows that too, she's just trying to get him to talk about it so he doesn't keep it bottled up. A doctor at the VA suggested she do that. I think if he doesn't want to talk about it, we shouldn't try to make him.

Him being nervous makes Sondra edgy too. She backs out of the driveway and looks one way but not the other. We all jump when a horn blasts, then turn to see this white SUV coming from our left. It has to swerve to miss us.

"I'm sorry," she says. "Are you two all right?" she asks me.

"We're fine."

Dad doesn't say anything and I try to quiet Jeffy, who started to cry when the horn blared. Another inch or two and that car would have hit us—and on Jeffy's side.

We make it out onto the road. The speed limit on Sequoia Street is thirty, but no one goes that slow except old people and Sondra. With morning commuters trying to get to work, it's only a couple of minutes before we have a line of traffic behind us and the closest one is right on our rear bumper.

"Do you see them," Daddy says suddenly.

Sondra's grip on the wheel is already white-knuckled. "See who?"

"The children." He points to the school bus stop ahead of us on the right. Seven kids are waiting by a row of mailboxes. The school bus is behind us in the growing line of traffic.

"I see them, Jeff," Sondra snaps. "I'm sorry about before, but I am watching the road."

"Don't throw them anything," Daddy yells. "Don't throw that candy." He bats at me in the backseat, then whacks Sondra's arm. "Run," he screams out the window. "Get away." He claws at the door looking for the handle.

The kids I ride to school with every day, including Lacy, the girl from my math class, run a few yards, then stop and look back and start to laugh.

"Daddy, stop." I grab for his collar.

Jeffy is screaming and Sondra pulls over to the side of the road near a pair of garbage cans.

"Are you crazy, soldier?" Daddy shouts. All the veins in his neck are showing and his face is red. "You're gonna get us killed."

He jerks away from me, opens his door, and rolls out of the car. He tries to get up and run on his stump and one leg, but pitches over and tumbles into the ditch at the side of the road. "Run!" he screams at the children.

They do.

Drivers, who had been honking at us, slow down, then stop to watch this one-legged man claw his way through the shrubbery.

Sondra puts her head against her hands on the steering wheel.

"I'll get him," I tell her, and start to crawl past Jeffy so that I'm not getting out into the traffic.

The kids begin to seep back toward the bus stop. They point at my dad and laugh. An old Ford pickup pulls up and parks in front of us. A big bald man with a long gray ponytail gets out. He reminds me of pictures of my grandfather. There's a small, tattered American flag attached to his antenna and a faded Support Our Troops yellow ribbon on his tailgate. He starts after my father before I can squeeze past Jeffy and out the door.

Daddy is on his belly, pulling himself under a fence with his elbows.

"Soldier!" the man shouts. "Return to your unit."

Daddy stops. He's on one knee and his stump. He rolls himself over and sits up.

I grab his crutches and follow the man around the end of the fence.

I can tell that Daddy's mind is coming back to us. He looks up. Tears roll down his cheeks. "They're all dead, sir."

The man kneels, puts his hands in my father's armpits, and lifts him to stand on his one leg. I hand him the crutches. "I'm sorry, son," the man says. "Was it an IED?"

"Yes, sir," Daddy says. "We were throwing candy to those kids when the trash can blew. Killed 'em all, Bill and Moss and Shorty—the children . . ."

"Well, you're home now, soldier, and your family is waiting for you right over there. And I bet this here's your daughter." He puts a hand on my shoulder.

"Hi, Daddy." I hug him.

"Hi, Hannah Banana," he whispers.

I look at the man through a blur of tears. "Thank you."

"This boy needs help, you hear me?"

"Yes, sir."

"He's got PTSD. Know what that is?" We're walking back to the car with Dad.

"No, sir."

"Posttraumatic Stress Disorder. He's reliving all the crap that happened to him over there and he needs help coping with it. You tell your momma to call the VA—today. You hear?"

I nod and look at Daddy.

The man helps him into the car, then steps back and salutes my father. "Thank you for your sacrifice, son."

I watch him cross in front of our car, drive his big fist into the yellow ribbon on his tailgate, rub his knuckles, and get into his truck.

Cars pass us for the longest time, their drivers staring.

"I'm sorry," Daddy says after a minute or two. He puts his hand on Sondra's arm. She doesn't pull away or anything, but she's sitting board straight, looking at me in the rearview mirror, her eyes dry.

I don't know how she can be unaffected. I got a knot in my chest the size of a hay bale when that man saluted my dad.

Sondra moves her arm out from under Daddy's hand, looks over her left shoulder to check the traffic, waves a thank you to the car that lets her in, then pulls out and drives down the road.

I look back at the wad of kids. Lacy is standing a little apart from the rest of them with the expression of shock still on her face.

Math is fifth period. When I come in, Lacy is in a desk near the rear of the room.

"There she is," Lacy says to Melissa, who's sitting in front of her. They both watch me all the way to my desk.

I try not to care, but I don't have any real friends since Madison moved to Oregon. It's my fault. I haven't tried to make a new friend since Daddy got home. Friends do things together: spend the night at each other's house, go to the movies. I never know how Daddy will do at night, so I don't want to have kids over. And I'd rather go to the stables than to a movie.

After class, they catch up with me in the hall. "So, is your dad crazy?" Lacy snickers and elbows Melissa.

"No. He was in the Iraq war and has flashbacks." I keep walking.

"My dad says that war's illegal and we have no business being there," Melissa says.

I stop. "Your dad's right." I turn. "But that didn't stop them from sending my dad over there."

"Did he kill a lot of innocent people?"

I ball my fists and lean my face close to hers. "My father was an innocent person, but he still got sent to a war where they blew his leg off and killed all his friends."

21

SATURDAY, SEPTEMBER 2

Dillon says she has time this weekend to give me another riding lesson. I don't tell Dad this time. I want to keep home and the stables separate. For a while, anyway.

My lesson is at two, but I fix myself a sandwich and leave the house at eleven so I can watch Rega for a while. She's lying in the paddock, asleep in the sun, with Free standing guard. Free, who knows I always have carrots, nickers when she sees me, waking Rega. They both come to the fence, but Rega gets behind her mom and peeks at me from under Free's tail. It make her look like she's wearing a huge wig with bangs so long, they cover one eye.

Rega used to pretend to graze, copying her mom, but now she has a lot of her baby teeth and is grazing more and nursing less. She's dark gray, but Dillon says when she sheds her baby coat, she'll be black. She has lots of whiskers, and long, silky black hair hanging from her fetlocks—just above her hooves. It's called feathering and it's because she's part draft horse. She's the most beautiful thing I've ever seen.

"You're early." Dillon is leading Jack across to his paddock. "Come to watch our baby girl?"

"I hate not being here every day. She grows so much in a week."

"She's a weed, all right, and Free turned out to be a wonderful mother when she finally got the chance."

I hold my hand out to Rega, who stretches her neck to sniff it. Her whiskers tickle my fingers.

I give Jack his share of the carrots and rub his ears. "Barbaro has laminitis."

Dillon's lips compress and she shakes her head. "That's not good. They don't beat that very often."

After playing Parelli games to let Indy burn off some energy, Dillon saddles him for me, making doubly sure his cinch is tight.

"How do you feel?" she asks when I'm in the saddle.

"Good," I say, but I'm not. This is the first lesson since I slid off Indy's back. I didn't think it had bothered me, but now I'm scared.

"You look tense."

"I guess I am a little."

"Your choices are to get off or stay on."

I was so sure I didn't want Dad here and now I wish he was parked there at the end of the row of plastic chairs, watching me—watching out for me.

"You know Indy swallowed his instinct when your saddle slipped?"

"He did?"

"A saddle slipping feels like something is about to rip at a horse's stomach. Most would have started to buck and kick."

Indy turns to look at me. I pat his neck.

Dillon nods. "Let's start with getting you seated correctly."

I tuck my blue glass necklace into my T-shirt, then I sit up very straight and square my shoulders.

She shakes her head. "You want to find your balance point. You're right up on your crotch. Roll back on your cheeks." She shows me by bowing her back a little. "If you're in the right position you can reach around and put the flat of your hand on his rump.

"Good. Now drape your legs around him. Don't grip with your knees and don't brace on your stirrups. That's it. Drapey legs. You want the weight in your seat."

Dillon is straddling a barrel, showing me what I should look like in the saddle. It makes me want to giggle, especially since, so far, Indy and I haven't taken a step.

"Pull your feet back until only your toes and the balls of your feet are in the stirrups. Now do this." She starts to move her feet up and down by lifting and lowering her heels. "It's called pedaling. You want to pedal in rhythm with his hind legs."

Dillon gets off her barrel and crooks her finger at Indy. When he is close enough, she takes his halter rope from me and starts to lead him around. "Can you feel his right hip up, left hip up? Match his rhythm with your feet. Stay fluid." She stops. "You're opposing his gait. Start again. No, wait. Lie forward on his back and let your arms dangle on either side of his neck."

I do as she says with the saddle horn jammed into my stomach and my nose in his mane.

"Now you are on all fours like he is. Match the gait of his hind legs with your feet." We start to move again. "That's it. Now swim with your arms in time to the rhythm of his front legs."

I feel like an idiot, but I begin dog-paddling with my arms and pedaling with my feet.

"Fantastic," Dillon says. "Now pedal and swim sitting up but, this time, move your arms only in your mind." She drapes Indy's halter rope over his head. I take it and click for him to start walking.

"Oh, my gosh. This is totally cool." It feels like we are fused together.

"You look beautiful up there."

I bite my lip. "Thanks."

"You're the lead in this dance, Hannah. When he feels you in harmony with him, he can feel when you change something and he can think about what you want him to do."

We've reached the back wall of the arena. I pull his lead to turn him and lean the direction I want him to go.

"I don't think so," Dillon says.

"What?"

"If you want him to turn, don't pull him around. Look where you want to go with all your eyes."

"I don't remember what that means."

"Imagine that you have eyes on both shoulders, one in your belly button, eyes on your hips and eyes on your knees. Turn all your eyes and he will turn. He can turn on a dime if you are turning on a dime."

I think about what she's said, then try, and Indy turns as if he's read my mind and, without Dillon saying anything, I up my energy and he starts to trot.

"You're too bouncy. Your butt's coming out of the saddle."

I relax and Indy stops.

"Give me a thumbs-up."

I do, though I'm not sure why since I wasn't doing it right.

"Now turn that thumb upside down, stick it under your right cheek, and hold on to the saddle with your fingers. This time when you trot don't let your bum lose contact with your thumb."

It works. I grin at Dillon.

It's not until I get off Indy and put my arms around his neck that I realize how protected I felt this time and believe that he protected me the last time too.

As I brush him, I can still feel the sway and rhythm of his gait. It reminds me of when I was little and had been fishing with my dad. As soon as we were back in port I wanted him to swing me up onto the dock so I could close my eyes and feel it rocking like the sea beneath my feet.

22

FRIDAY, OCTOBER 27

The phone rings early. Sondra calls me to pick up.

"Hannah." Dillon's voice is flat. "I think you need to come on up to the stables."

"What's wrong? Is Rega all right?"

"She's fine. It's Jack."

When I get there, he's lying in his paddock near the fence where I first touched him.

"He fell yesterday but managed to get himself up," Dillon says. "I'm afraid he's not going to succeed this time." She puts an arm around my shoulders. "I'm sorry, Hannah. I know, besides Rega, he's your favorite."

"What can we do?"

She shakes her head. "Put him down."

It hasn't rained since April, and what's left of the grass is dry. For some reason I wish it was spring. "Can I go in with him?"

"I don't think you'd better. He keeps kicking trying to get up."

Just then he does, sending up clouds of dust like spirits.

"I called you first, then Meg. She's on her way," Dillon says.

I sit at the edge of the driveway with the fence between us, reach through and stroke his neck. His skin twitches against my palm. "I'm so sorry, Jack." I close my eyes against the tears that well up and see my dad, wounded and scared in Iraq, not able to stand.

"You've changed my life. I want you to know that." I look up at Dillon. "Can't we try to help him up?"

"What about tomorrow, Hannah?"

Dust billows as Meg comes down the driveway. Super Dee comes to his stall door and whinnies when he sees her, but she jumps from her truck and comes toward us, her eyes red and swollen from crying. She goes into the paddock and sits on the ground near Jack's head. He moves so his nose rests against her leg.

"Oh, Jack." She leans and puts her forehead against his.

"Joanne's on her way," Dillon says.

Meg nods. "Thank you."

"There's still time to change your mind."

"No," Meg says sharply.

I look at her, then at Dillon, who shrugs. "I told her she

could save the vet bill and the expense of burying him if she'd let me call Jason."

"Who's Jason?"

"The pig farmer."

"What?" I put my hand on Jack's neck again.

"If he's put down with chemicals, he has to be buried. If we shoot him, his body serves a purpose."

"You'd shoot him and feed him to pigs?" I know Dillon's not the sentimental type, but I can't believe she would even suggest this.

"Once he's gone there's just an empty shell left. It's his spirit that stays with you."

"I can't," Meg says. "I just can't."

"Okay." Dillon nods. "We'll bury him over under those trees then." She points to a clump of redwoods in the westernmost paddock.

Meg and I sit with Jack while we wait for Joanne. She fans his face to keep flies from landing near his eyes, and I stroke his neck.

"Why'd you buy Jack?"

"I went to a local auction with a completely different horse in mind but when I saw him he was so beautiful ..." She runs her finger down his longest scar. "In spite of these, so I asked about him. The guy who owned him told me he was mean and no one could ride him, but when I walked up to his stall, he didn't pin his ears, he started to tremble. He wasn't mean, he was terrified, and getting him away from that man became more important than owning a horse I could ride."

"But you used to ride him."

"Eventually, but it took a long time."

The backhoe operator arrives. Dillon shows him where to dig the hole and he starts right in. The noise makes Jack try to get up again.

"For heaven's sake, go tell that fool to wait until he's dead," Meg says.

The driver is a huge man, bigger even than Daddy used to be, with great big hands black with oil and dirt. He turns off the backhoe when I wave my arms.

Joanne pulls in. When Meg sees her coming toward them with her black bag she begins to sob. Jack lifts his head and looks at Joanne, then puts it down again.

"Hey there old boy." Joanne drops to her knees beside him and strokes his face. "He seems pretty calm," she says to Meg, "but may I give him a tranquilizer first?"

I know she's asking because it costs more than just the shot to put him down.

"Yes, please," Meg says.

Joanne takes two small bottles and two syringes from her bag. "We'll use the sodium pentathlon first," Joanne says. She fills the first syringe, looks at me, then at Meg.

Meg takes a deep breath, then nods and puts her hand

beside Jack's eye like a blinder. Joanne rubs a spot on his neck, then pushes the needle in. The backs of my knees tingle and I look away when the point pierces his skin.

One leg moves when he feels the prick of the needle, but he doesn't struggle and after a few minutes, he kind of sighs.

"When you're ready," Joanne says. She's holding the second hypodermic. A drop of the poison, as clear as water, glistens on tip of the needle.

Meg turns and puts her cheek against Jack's for a moment, kisses him, then looks up at me. "Do you want to say good-bye, Hannah?"

I'm crying too hard to answer. I sink down beside him and put my hand against his cheek just like I did that first day. Jack has been my best friend here, my first horse.

"I'll always love you," I whisper.

Joanne finds the vein in his neck and pushes the needle through his old skin.

In just a moment, his side stops moving and the light in his eyes fades and goes out.

Dillon sits with Meg and they have their arms around each other. Meg sobs against her shoulder, which upsets me more. Jack wasn't mine, so I don't feel like I'm entitled to hurt as much as I do. I wish Dillon had let me sit with him until Meg got there.

It's Joanne who comes over and puts her arm around

my shoulders. "I'm sorry for your loss, Hannah. I know just how you feel." She hugs me, and her arms are as strong as Dad's.

Meg reaches out, catches my hand, and pulls me down to sit with them.

"I'm just glad it was quick and peaceful," I say.

I've never seen anything die before, but I do read the obituaries every week in our local paper. I read them to see how long past the age my mother died that other people get to live. I think of Momma now and how she suffered. Seeing how easy this was for Jack, I think it shouldn't have to be so hard for humans.

"He's been my horse for twenty-five years," Meg says. "He was five when I saved him from that awful man. I remember his smile when he told me—after we signed the bill of sale—that I'd paid four hundred more than the kill buyer had offered."

"What's a kill buyer?" I ask

"Someone who buys unwanted horses for the slaughterhouses." Dillon gets up. "We'll need rope," she says, and walks off toward the barn.

A few minutes later the backhoe driver starts the engine and begins to dig the hole.

"I'll go help Dillon." I stand up too. "I really loved him."

"I know, Hannah. He loved you too."

Dillon is still looking for a rope. There are lots of leads

hanging on hooks, but no really strong rope. "Where do most of the horses people eat come from?"

"Pets that people are tired of, or can no longer afford and can't sell. Some horses are stolen, old Premarin mares and their foals, ponies used for pony rides." She looks around the shed and sighs. "Let's try the arena."

The backhoe driver has a huge hole dug.

"What about racehorses?"

"Them too. Thousands are killed every year. They get injured or used up or, like Super Dee, just never quite make the mark."

I help her take the blankets off the chest in the arena. There's a huge coil of rope inside.

Meg and Dillon tie Jack's legs together, put a rope around his neck, and pull his head in line with his feet to keep it from dragging on the ground. The backhoe man drives over and hoists him like a sack of potatoes.

The others all follow him to his grave, but I don't want to watch them put the dirt over Jack. I go to look at Rega. She and Free are in their stall, where she stands bumped up against her mother. I reach my arm over the door. I want to feel her little muzzle against my palm, but she's not ready to trust me yet.

Seeing Rega and Free together makes me think about Momma again and what I'd give to have her to lean against right now. Dillon, Meg, and Joanne are standing side by side on the rim of Jack's grave, their arms around each other. I decide being alone here isn't really what I want either. I start toward them just as the backhoe lifts Jack's body high enough to swing it into the hole.

There's a wild rosebush growing on the side of the stables where we keep the wheelbarrows. I break off four flowers, one for each of us, then run to join the others. I pull the petals from my bloodred rose and let them float down into the hole like tears from a broken heart.

"You're early," Dad says when I get home. He's pulled up to the picture window that looks out at the Hare Creek canyon behind our house.

"They were all going for a trail ride, so I thought I'd get some homework done," I lie.

I want to tell him what's happened, so he'll hug me and let me cry, but that's not an option anymore.

"Good girl," he says without looking at me.

"Did you eat?"

"Yeah." He tilts his head back and drains the beer he's drinking.

I go upstairs, crawl into bed, and stare at the black stars on my ceiling.

23

THURSDAY, NOVEMBER 23

I f we are going to be a family, we need to act like one."
Sondra's mashing the potatoes with the force of a jack-
hammer.

Dad had another of his reliving-the-war nights, but
Sondra still wants us all to go to her parents' house for
Thanksgiving.

"He just needs to stop thinking about all the stuff that
happened over there," she says.

"Don't you think he would if he could?"

She looks at me like I'm a just a kid, what do I know.

"He's only been home for seven months." I see Dad
coming out of his room. "Cut him some slack," I whisper.

Dad wheels into the kitchen and gets another beer from
the fridge.

"Jeff, we're leaving in a few minutes, please don't drink
any more."

He's wearing his camouflage uniform and his dog tags, but not his Purple Heart. He's had a six-pack of beer already and it's not even one o'clock.

"Maybe I'm just trying to lubricate myself for this ordeal." He pops the tab, puts the can between his thighs, and wheels back to the living room.

What happened to Dad, happened exactly a year ago. "Why won't you let Dad and me stay home? Your mother will be happier if it's just you and Jeffy anyway."

"Thanksgiving is about family. We are going as a family."

"Yeah, well, pretending we are won't make us one."

"Just start loading the car, okay?"

Sondra's made a green bean casserole and the mashed potatoes and is bringing two pies—pumpkin and mince-meat, which she bought at the Laurel Street Deli. I know she's trying to make Thanksgiving a nice holiday again instead of the anniversary of what happened to Dad and his friends, but it's too soon. I wrap the casserole in a towel to keep it warm and make the first trip out to the car.

It's not like I don't want to go. Her parents live in a big house in the rich section of town. It has a big yard with a nice garden and a row of old cherry trees along the side they share with their neighbors. Sondra grew up in that house, so her mother sees living where we live as a giant step down.

Sondra's father is nice and seems to like me, but her mother is just polite, like I'm someone whose name she can't remember. She's gets all ga-ga over Jeffy—but then, he's her real grandson. I'll always be Sondra's husband's kid. That's okay by me; I'm not that crazy about her either.

Mr. and Mrs. Lutz are at the picture window that faces the street when we drive up. Mrs. Lutz has her hand on her husband's arm. She looks nervous, as if a carload of criminals has just pulled up out front. She forces a smile, waves, and heads for the door. She's down the walkway, has the car door open, and is cooing and unbuckling Jeffy before I even get my seat belt undone.

"Mom." Sondra taps her own cheekbone to remind her mother that she has two curls Scotch-taped to the side of her face. Mrs. Lutz pulls the tape off. "Who are you hiding from?" she asks Dad. "Dressed in camouflage like that."

"The enemy," Daddy says, and smiles at her. "Guess it didn't work."

Mr. Lutz is standing on the porch. He salutes my dad, then comes down the walkway to shake his hand. He pats my shoulder. "You're growing like a weed, Hannah."

I never know what to say when adults make statements like that. "Yes, sir. I guess so."

"Don't sir me. I'm your grandfather. I've told you before, call me Roger."

Roger gets Dad's crutches from the backseat and helps

him stand and balance himself. I get his wheelchair from the trunk.

Mr. Lutz—Roger—has one earlobe that is longer than the other—a lot longer, as if he'd hung a horseshoe off it. Because of that he looks like one person from his left side and some other person from the right. I like looking at his different sides. He also has a bunion on his right foot and has cut a hole in his shoe for it. He's wearing white socks and black shoes, so his bunion sticks out like the white middle of a roasted marshmallow. I like this about him— his don't-give-a-hoot attitude.

I get on one side of Dad and Mr. Lutz gets on the other, just in case he tips, and together we get him up the steps to the front porch.

"I don't know why you don't use your prosthesis," Mr. Lutz says.

"It doesn't fit and it hurts like hell."

"Shoulda healed by now. How long's it been?"

Dad's face goes slack. "A year," he says.

I can't believe Mr. Lutz asked that. Maybe he doesn't remember that it was last Thanksgiving when Dad lost his leg. Sondra gives her dad a sharp look, which he totally misses.

"Have you told the docs?" Roger says. "They can order you a new one. A buddy of mine from Nam went through five—"

"Dad," Sondra says. "Enough, okay?"

Once Daddy's inside and settled into his chair, Mrs. Lutz goes to the kitchen and comes out carrying a tray with iced tea, sparkling cider, and other assorted non-alcoholic drinks.

"No thanks," Dad says when she reaches him. "I'll take a beer if you have one, or a bourbon. On the rocks."

"Sure thing," Mr. Lutz says, again ignoring Sondra, who is behind Dad shaking her head.

"Why not wait until we are closer to eating, Jeff. It's too early to start drinking," Sondra says. Her fingers squeeze his shoulder.

"Who's starting? I'm already numb and I'm trying to stay that way."

"That's right," Mr. Lutz says. "It's Thanksgiving and the war hero can have a drink if he wants it."

Sondra sighs. "Hannah's been taking riding lessons," she says to no one in particular.

"What kind?" Mrs. Lutz asks, but she's watching Daddy, her lips in a tight thin line.

"Horseback," Sondra and I say at the same time.

"Do you think that's a good idea? They're so dangerous."

"They're not if they are trained correctly," I say.

"Mom had a horse when she was young," Sondra says.

"Dan was a pony, not a horse."

"They eat ponies, you know?" I say.

Mrs. Lutz looks at me like I'm too bizarre to be permitted in the house with such normal people. "Who eats ponies?"

"The Japanese and the French and the Belgiums."

"Belgians, dear. Not Belgiums."

Whatever.

"I've got the game on," Mr. Lutz tells Dad. "Who do you want to see in the playoffs?"

Sondra crooks her finger at me. "Let's go help Mom in the kitchen, Hannah. Shall we?"

I shrug. I'm pretty sure today is not going to end well; I might as well help get the ball rolling.

"I don't know, who's playing?" Dad says.

"Dallas and Tampa Bay."

Dad has his head down. When Mr. Lutz hands him the tall glass of bourbon, he wraps his hands around it like he was overboard and someone just threw him a rope. "If you've seen one game, you've seen them all," he says, then takes two long gulps and closes his eyes.

"Will you set the table, Hannah?" Mrs. Lutz points to the counter where she has laid out everything. She chucks Jeffy under his chin, then gives him a big wet smooch on the cheek. Jeffy's walking now, but I suspect Sondra's afraid to put him down. The house is full of fragile little knick-knacky things.

I gather up the silverware and the napkins.

"How's he doing?" Mrs. Lutz whispers before I even leave the kitchen.

None of your business. It's not like she's asking 'cause she cares about Dad.

". . . another bad night," I hear Sondra say.

"I sure hate to see you going through the nightmare I went through with your father."

I come back for the plates.

"Be careful with those," Mrs. Lutz says. "They were my mother's and they are irreplaceable."

When she thinks I'm out of earshot, she adds, "You don't have to stay, you know. You and this sweet, sweet baby—yes you are—can move into the garage apartment any day."

"You didn't leave Dad, why would I leave Jeff?"

"I didn't have a job and had nowhere else to go. You have both."

"The one thing you are leaving out, Mom, is that I love Jeff."

I'm standing on the far side of the china cabinet, listening. There's a mirror on the wall opposite me. I glance at my reflection and don't even recognize myself. I look like a skinny, flat-chested old woman—brow all wrinkled and sad eyes.

"You'll find out, dear. Sometimes that isn't enough.

What happened to him in Iraq and your father in Vietnam unleashes something in them that's almost impossible to get back in the box."

God, I wish Dad and I had stayed home. I hate being here and am dying to say the worst thing I can think of to Sondra's mother, but nothing comes to mind.

They stop talking when I come into the kitchen again. Mrs. Lutz smiles at me—the phony.

"... he needs to get help," she says when I leave with the tray of water glasses.

"He's going to the VA shrink, but it doesn't seem to be helping."

"Those quacks. Do you think if they were good enough to have a real practice they'd work for the government?"

"We can't afford a psychiatrist, Mom. My insurance isn't that good."

"Well, all I can say is, take it as long as you can, then get out."

I feel myself start to shake. The glasses that are touching start to clink together before I get them safely to the table. From where I'm standing I can see the back of my dad's head. Mr. Lutz is ticking off football statistics.

My hands still shake when I put the first one of her fancy china plates at the head of the table. The dining room chair has been pulled away so Dad's wheelchair will fit. The plate has a gold loopy scroll along the edge and roses. The center is maroon trimmed in gold with roses, tulips, and other flowers. I turn it over: *H&C Bavaria, Heinrich & Co. Ivory Body Supreme.* I lift it above my head and let it go. It crashes to the hardwood floor and shatters into a million pieces.

From the living room, Daddy shouts something. By the time I get there, Mr. Lutz has him pinned to the floor. A table is on its side and the lamp that was on it is broken. Sondra and Mrs. Lutz run up beside me.

"The noise set him off," Mr. Lutz says.

"Daddy. I'm sorry."

"Where did that shot come from?" he shouts. "Moss? Shorty? Oh God. Oh God. My leg!" he screams. "Where is my leg?" His eyes are wild and he tries to twist free of the hold Mr. Lutz has on him. "Let me go. I gotta find my leg."

I drop to my knees and crawl toward them. "I'm sorry. Daddy. I made the noise. It's not the war."

"Hannah. Thank God." He crushes me in his arms. "Thank God you're safe." He starts to sob. "All the other children are dead."

24

SATURDAY, DECEMBER 9

We've had rain every day for a week, but this morning it's clear and freezing. There's ice on the road in the parts shaded by redwoods. Where the sun shines through and hits the pavement, steam rises, which makes the sunlight blinding. I stop when I come out of the trees. The paddocks look like a fairyland. The grass is covered with frost, the fencing is wet and black, and steam rises from the drying wood and the roofs of the stables. I imagine I can hear horses' hooves and their neighing and expect to see them come riding toward me through the mist.

On the north side of Sequoia there's a pull-out where people who want to ride their horses along the trails through Jackson State Forest park their trailers. There are two parked there this morning. They're empty and I'm thinking they got an early start, before I see two more parked in front of the stables. There aren't any horses in these trailers either, but there is a whole group of people gathered around the picnic table by the arena.

Free and Rega are in a paddock. Rega gallops toward me, pulls up short, then runs back to her mother, kicking up her heels, like she's showing off. No matter what's happening at home, I always feel better when I see her.

I take the bag of carrots from my pocket to lure Free over so Rega will follow. I give Free a chunk and hold my hand out to Rega with a piece for her. She steps forward on her little hooves like a toe-dancer, takes it, then dodges away, kicking and leaping.

"What's happening over there?" I ask Free, who tosses her head.

An angry voice rises above the other conversations.

"The S.O.B. should be shot."

"What happens to him is in God's hands," someone says. "It's up to us to save the horses."

I walk up behind Meg. "What's going on?" I whisper.

"Dillon's organizing a rescue."

"What kind of rescue?"

"Starving horses."

"Oh. Why all the trailers?"

"There are thirty-six of them."

"Hey Hannah," Dillon says. "I'm glad you're here. Have you got a few hours to spare?"

"Sure."

"Will you finish feeding the horses and muck-raking? I didn't quite finish Indy's stall."

"But . . . I want to go on the rescue."

"I don't think that's a good idea, Hannah."

People were heading up the driveway, back to their trailers.

"I'll finish the stalls," Meg said. "I really don't want to see one more mistreated horse. Dee was enough."

Dillon studies me for a moment. "This is going to be ugly, Hannah."

I just look at her.

"Okay. You can ride with me."

At the bottom of Simpson, the caravan of horse trailers turns north. "Where are we going, anyway?" I ask.

She shrugs. "Somewhere near Westport."

Westport is about twenty-five miles north of Fort Bragg. About five miles out of town, I start to see the Ten-Mile sand dunes off to the left. There are more people with horse trailers waiting for us at a pull-out where people park to go hiking in the dunes. When they see us coming, a truck from Animal Control pulls out in front. I turn to watch as one by one the waiting trailers join at the end of our line. I'm sad for the horses, but excited about being a part of this.

A few miles north of Westport, we begin to slow and I see the Animal Control truck turn right. We're fourth in the line that turns to follow them up the narrow road to Haven Creek Ranch. Trees line both sides, making it so dark that Dillon's headlights come on. The road is rutted and we bounce through potholes full of muddy water.

We're about two miles in when Dillon groans.

There are deep, dark ravines on either side of the road with tree-covered hillsides so steep that no light gets through. She's looking at something, but I can't see anything. "What?" I say, and lean as far forward against my seat belt as I can to look out her window.

We slow, but still all I see is a ring of trees with big patches of bark missing. It's when she stops that I spot the pen full of horses—mud-caked, skin-covered skeletons. Chill bumps rise on my arms. "They ate tree bark?"

"They ate what they could reach."

Most of the horses have their heads down in total defeat. Only one looks up when we stop—the one eating manure. Dillon's mouth draws down. "The rescuers in the back of the line will get these."

I've never seen a horse in need of saving except Free. "How long have these horses been like this?"

Dillon shakes her head. "Reports have been coming in for months, but Animal Control is short-staffed, so there's been no one to check on them."

My stomach starts to knot. "How many checks would it take to see that horses penned in a cold, damp forest with nothing to eat need help?" I'm sick of the excuses people in charge have for not helping.

We follow the line of horse trailers up the hill in low gear. The road narrows and becomes a series of switchbacks until we break out of the trees into the sunlight. I look back and can see the ocean.

The higher we climb, the more scared I get. It's a sheer drop-off on Dillon's side, and that will be my side on the way back down. There are places where the rain has cut wide gullies across the road. The front tires fall in, roll up the other side, then the rear tires drop in followed by the two sets of trailer tires. I'm afraid if a trailer tire goes over the side, it will pull us over with it. Dillon's scared too. Her hands are wrapped around the steering wheel like vises.

"I'm afraid of heights," I say.

"Me too."

The hills are green and rolling with thick groves of bare oak trees in the ravines. "At least the horses up here have grazing land," I say.

Dillon doesn't answer, and around two more bends I see why. The rest of the horses are in paddocks up to their ankles in mud. Every blade of grass they could reach has been eaten, leaving a circle of bare ground around each pen. They have no cover from the rain, but there are two brand-new pieces of farm equipment under a lean-to. We park and get out, as do the other people who are here to help, and we all walk toward the pens silently.

These horses are in as bad shape as the others—maybe worse. They are skeletons too, with their hip bones and ribs clearly outlined beneath winter coats that are caked with mud and manure. Many of the horses have big patches of hair missing and just bare skin shows. "Is that mange or are they molting?" I ask.

"They have rain rot," Dillon says.

Joanne's truck pulls in at the end of the line of trailers. She just sits there looking out her windshield, then puts her head back and closes her eyes. She stays like that for a moment, then gets out and starts toward the first pen.

Apart from the others, on a little hillside, is a pen with three small horses in it. They look about five or six months old, but there's no mare with them, so they must have been weaned. The grass under my feet is still damp from last night's rain. I pull up clumps—as much as I can hold—and take it to the babies. I smell the fourth one before I see it dead in the pen, half buried in the mud.

I've often wondered what it must have been like for Daddy to have to kill someone in the war. I've never asked him, but now I think they must have trained him to hate the Iraqis. I hate the person who owns these horses enough to wish he was rotting there in the mud with the baby he let die.

The babies—two colts and a filly—watch me with half-closed eyes. Mud covers their hooves. I unlatch the gate with my elbow and step in. My own feet sink in the mud and when I try to take a step, it sucks my boot off.

I drop the fistfuls of grass I've brought, but they watch it fall with dull eyes.

In another pen, someone is filling the water trough. Nine or ten horses nip and nudge each other as they fight to find a gap in the crowd that got there first. I pull my boot out of the mud, put it on, and back out of the corral. The trough in this pen is empty too. There is only a soup of mud and green algae in the bottom. I turn on the spigot, not expecting it to work, but it sputters and spits, then gushes fresh water. I'm so angry; I don't know what to do. How hard would turning on a spigot have been? The babies suck their feet free of the mud and crowd around the trough, where they drink and drink.

I stand at the fence and watch them. The tiny filly has three-inch-long hair, which is full of lice. She looks up at me with runny black eyes, then puts her muzzle through the bars of the pen. I give her the back of my hand to smell, then press a finger to the little white butterfly-shaped patch of hair on her forehead.

The carrots! There are nine pieces of carrots in my coat pocket. When the others see me take the Ziploc out, they push forward and twist their necks trying to reach through the rails. The filly comes in alongside them and I give her the first piece. Her upper lip quivers as it touches the carrot. When they've eaten them all, they push against the fence trying to find something else to eat in my empty hands. I'm standing in dense grass, so I lean and pull up handfuls and hold it out to them, then get on my knees to pull up more and hand it through the bars. By the time Dillon touches my shoulder I'm sobbing and throwing wads of grass to the babies.

"Hannah." She kneels beside me.

"They're dying."

"No, sweetie, they'll be okay."

"Can we take them?"

"Someone in the group is taking these yearlings."

"Yearlings? They don't even look old enough to be weanlings."

"They've been starved."

"What will happen to them?" The one who'd let me touch her has her muzzle through the bars again.

"Most are being transported to a ranch in Ukiah. If they can prove neglect, they'll be permanently taken away from the owner."

"*If* they can! I saw someone taking pictures. How much proof do they need?"

"It has to play out in the courts."

"Then what?"

"They'll be auctioned off."

"I want to buy this one." I put my hand against the filly's muzzle. "How much will she cost?"

Dillon shakes her head. "I don't know, but don't get your heart set on her, Hannah. The young ones will be easy to find homes for." She puts her arm around my shoulder. I want to shake her off, but I think better of it. Dillon's awfully nice to me and she doesn't have to be.

"Sophia called and told me to pick the worst one and bring it back with us. She's in the trailer already."

"Please, can't we take this baby too?"

"No, we can't, but ask your father when you get home and see what he says. Maybe you can buy her at the auction."

The mention of Dad kind of brings me up short and I look at Dillon. She's never treated me like a kid, so it surprises and hurts me that she pulled the ask-your-father thing when she knows as well as I do that we can't afford to buy a horse.

I keep looking back at the little filly as we walk away, and she's watching me. There's a brown mare in our trailer, but I resent her for being the chosen one. Why couldn't Sophia have said to bring a baby back?

I notice that two of the mare's hooves are wrapped in duct tape, but I get in without asking why.

Dillon starts the engine and we pull out and start carefully down the road she's calling "cardiac hill." The drop-off is worse than I imagined it would be. I talk because I'm afraid to look down.

"Why'd that guy get so many horses if he wasn't going to take care of them?"

"Who knows." Dillon's watching the road like a hawk. "They are all from good bloodlines, so some people thought he might be laundering drug money by buying and selling horses. I'm not sure that makes as much sense as the idea that he is a horse hoarder."

"What's that mean?"

"Do you remember a few years back when that old woman on Turner Road got killed during a storm?" she says without looking at me.

"No."

"The top of a redwood tree went right through the trailer she lived in and killed her in her bed. When they found her, her trailer, an abandoned car, a shed, and numerous cages were all full of cats. There were dozens and dozens of them. I can't remember how many there . . ." Dillon pauses. We've come to the narrowest part of the road. She stops, rolls down her window, and pulls her side mirror in flat against her door. "Why don't you get out and walk across this stretch?"

"Thanks, but I'm okay."

"It's not that. You can watch the trailer tires for me. If

the road is undercut at all, it might not hold the trailer now that we have a horse in it."

When I open my door my stomach sinks. It doesn't look any wider than the length of my mud-caked boot. I slide out, step sideways with my back to the side of truck, close my door, then slide back toward the hood.

"How's it look?" Dillon asks.

"There's this much room." I hold my hands about six inches apart.

"Does it look undercut?"

"No," I say, but I can't leave the middle of the road to look over the side. My knees are weak and I feel dizzy.

Dillon begins inching toward me. I glance over my shoulder, then begin to back up. Her side of the truck is hugging the sheer side of the cliff. I hold my breath. I was worried about the empty trailer dropping a wheel over the edge on the way up; now I'm afraid that the horse will lose her balance, fall against the wall of the trailer, and that will be that.

I get back in when she's past the really bad part.

"So what about the woman with the cats?"

"She was a cat hoarder," Dillon says. "She probably started out rescuing them, then it just escalated. Pretty soon, she thinks she's saving their lives and that no one else will take them. Who knows, but when they found them they were wild and starving. It was a nightmare."

I think about this but don't believe that is what the owner of the horses was doing. He was buying horses, not rescuing them. "How much does it cost to keep a horse?"

"A lot."

"No, really."

"I don't know right off-hand. Just the hundred pounds of hay a week is more than some people can afford, then there is the cost of boarding if you don't have a place of your own, vet bills; the list is endless."

I sit back and look down at the ocean. "Are that mare's hooves falling off?"

"Sorry?"

"What's the duct tape for?"

"She has hoof abscesses. Joanne packed them with something that creates heat so that the abscesses will break open."

"What causes those?"

"The bacteria in the mud they were standing in."

"Do they hurt?"

"I'll say. And that poor thing had them on two feet. If it was just on one she could take some of the pressure off."

"So why the duct tape?"

"One of the women rescuers had a package of diapers with her. Joanne used a couple to wrap her hooves, then used the duct tape to hold them in place. Once they break open, we'll keep them clean and diapered until the holes heal."

When we get back to the stables, Sophia is waiting for us. She and Dillon open the trailer door. On the floor is a writhing mass of what looks like spaghetti.

"Worms," Dillon says before I can even get the question out.

Sophia backs the poor mare out. On her rump, someone had spray-painted the number 9.

"Good job," Sophia says as she runs her hand over the bony, cow-hipped horse. "Nine is my favorite number."

25

THURSDAY, DECEMBER 14

I'm in science when the announcement comes over the speaker in the classroom for me to come to the office.

"Your mother called," the counselor says when I go to the desk.

It always makes my stomach flutter when someone says that, as if all this time Momma has just been away and now she's back and looking for me. I guess I look at her blankly.

"From the bank," she says.

"Okay."

"She needs you to come over there."

"Right now?"

The woman nods, sadly, like she knows what this is about but isn't going to tell me. Doesn't matter. I've already guessed it has something to do with Dad. If Jeffy was sick at the sitter's, Sondra would have just left work, not called me.

"I've sent for someone to drive you," the counselor says.

I don't know what I'm going to find when I get there, so I don't want anyone from school with me. "I'd rather walk."

"Someone has to drive you over. It will be about five minutes. Why don't you wait there." She points to one of the chairs lined against the wall.

Not much sense in arguing, so I shrug and sit down. The hand on the clock clicks off another minute. "May I run to the restroom first?"

"Of course."

I go out of the office, around the corner, and down the hall. The middle school is attached to the Fort Bragg Senior Center. If I go through their building, out the door into the parking lot, they won't be able to see me from the office.

Sondra's bank is at the other end of town, but Fort Bragg is only about two miles long end to end. I start off slowly so as not to draw attention to myself, cut down a side street in case whoever is supposed to drive me tries to find me, then start to jog.

When I get to the bank I go in from the employee parking lot side of the building. It's not a door many customers use, so no one is looking in my direction. Sondra's on her stool behind the counter. She has a tissue held to her nose and her closed sign is up. One of the other tellers is standing beside her; he's patting her shoulder. The two loan officers are on the other side of the lobby standing at the windows that overlook the other parking lot. The bank manager is in his office doorway, also looking out the windows, his arms crossed over his big stomach.

I might as well have had the school band with me. When I reach the center of the lobby everyone turns to look at me. I have a moment to wonder what's going on before I see Dad's head skim past the windows.

The manager comes toward me, takes my arm, and walks me back outside. "If you can calm him down and get him to go home, I won't call the police. Otherwise, I have to."

"What's he doing here?"

The manager shakes his head. "I'm not sure. He came in shouting that your mother was having an affair with Ronald."

Ronald was the one comforting Sondra. He's a nice man, but really young—eighteen or nineteen, maybe. Sondra's at least thirty.

"I'll talk to him."

"I can't allow this to happen again, Hannah," the manager says. "I know he's been in the war and he's got a lot of stuff going on around that, but I can't have him coming in here threatening people and scaring the customers. You can understand that, can't you?"

"Yes, sir." If he fires Sondra, we'll be in big trouble. "He won't do it again. I promise."

The manager compresses his lips and nods.

Rather than go through the lobby and out the front doors with everyone watching me, I go around the bank and meet Daddy coming back along the sidewalk. His head is down and he's pushing the wheels of his chair like he's in a race. He's not aware of anything but his anger, so he doesn't see me, or if he does, he doesn't recognize that it's me. I have to step off into a bed of geraniums to keep from getting run over. I make a grab for a handlebar when he passes me, which kind of spins him.

"What the . . . ?" He whips the chair around. His face is murderous, narrow-eyed and tight-jawed. It slackens a bit when he sees it's me. "She's running around with that little snot-nosed kid, Hannah."

"What makes you think that?"

"Where do you think she goes Friday nights after work?"

"They all go to the Coast Hotel for drinks."

"That's just a cover. She goes to be with him."

"You're going to get her fired, Dad. Then what?"

"I don't give a rat's ass about that."

"Well, you'd better. She's not dating that guy; she's trying to spend less time with us. And you know why; 'cause you're drunk all the time. You can't blame her. You're my dad and I sometimes wish I didn't have to be around you either."

Daddy's eyes are red-rimmed, like he's been crying. It kills me to say something mean to him, but he's scaring me.

"What if she leaves me for that guy?"

"If she leaves it won't be because she's in love with some nineteen-year-old gay guy."

"He's gay?"

"Well, yeah. Are you blind?"

Dad slumps deeper into his chair, his hands palms up on his legs.

"Come on, Daddy. Let's go home." I go around behind him and push him toward the Dial-A-Ride bus that is now waiting in the parking lot. When Sondra gets home—if she comes home—I'll fill her in on what I've told Dad in case Ronald isn't gay.

26

SATURDAY, DECEMBER 16

Since I don't have to pay for my riding lessons, I have about forty-five dollars saved from babysitting. I hitch a ride to town with Sondra this morning, though I'm not sure why she's going in on a Saturday.

"How will you get home?" We're creeping down Sequoia Street. I could ride my bike faster than she's driving.

"Walk. It's only about three miles."

"Suit yourself."

I've been watching Sondra for the last few days. It's as if a switch has been thrown. She's quit reminding me to get off the computer and clean my room, and she's quit telling Dad that he's had enough to drink already. "Are we ever going to decorate our tree?" She bought it before the bank thing and it's been leaning against the living room wall for five days now.

She doesn't look at me. "I was thinking of just going to

187

my mother's for Christmas. She's got a beautiful tree all decorated and a load of presents for Jeffy, and for you."

"We've always had a tree, even when Daddy wasn't here. And it's Jeffy and Dad's first Christmas together."

Her jaw tightens but for a moment she doesn't say anything. "What do you think will be different about Christmas morning, Hannah? Nothing, that's what. Thankfully, Jeffy's too young to know the difference."

"I'll know the difference!" I shout.

"Then decorate the bloody thing yourself," she snaps.

I feel numb, as if I've been locked out of my own heart. *Okay*, I think to myself. *Okay. That's how it is.* But somewhere deep inside I feel sure she's finally finished with us.

The Spunky Skunk is a toy store on Main Street right in the middle of town. I know what I'm looking for and head straight to the back of the store into the room that used to be floor-to-ceiling stuffed animals. There are a few there, but nothing like they used to have.

"May I help you," the clerk says.

"I'm just looking, but what happened to all your stuffed animals?"

She points up. All along the top of the display cases for the entire length of the store are stuffed animals jammed onto pegs, like they've been skewered.

She must have seen the that's-weird look on my face,

because she says, "We needed the back room for other things."

"Not like those, anyway. I'm looking for Beanie Babies."

"We only have a few left. They're in the case by the register."

"Do you have Barbaro?"

"I've never seen one of him. We used to have Derby 132 the Horse, but they are long gone."

"Okay. Thank you anyway."

"We have lots of plastic models of horses."

"No, thanks."

As long as I'm in town, I go by the kitchen gadget store and buy Sondra a little tool that makes zest out of lemon skins. It was the cheapest thing they have that looks nice, and it has a bright green handle, which is Sondra's favorite color.

I go next door to the Cheshire Bookstore to try to find something for Dad, but end up with a card and gift certificate. He used to read all the time, but he doesn't do anything but watch TV now.

Disappointed over not finding Beanie Baby Barbaro for Jeffy, I start walking home.

Another storm is coming; a cold wind blows in my face, which makes me miss my long hair and the feel of wind lifting it like a horse's mane. In my mind, I imagine Rega when she's grown and riding her along the beach into the approaching storm. I give her full rein as we race through the waves. I'm imagining that when a picture of Dad pops into my head. He's sitting in his wheelchair on the crest of a sand dune watching us. He's not waving, not smiling, and then not there at all.

"She's cutting out," Dad says when I come in from shopping. He's sitting in his wheelchair watching cartoons on TV.

I look at the TV as if what he said had something to do with what's on the screen. "Huh?"

"Sondra. She's leaving."

"Aren't you going to try to stop her? You act like you don't care."

"If it were me, I'd leave me too.

"That's bull. You love her and she loves you."

"Love can only carry so much before self-preservation takes over."

I run up the stairs. Her bedroom door is open. Jeffy is on the floor in the middle of the pile of sheets she stripped from the bed. He smiles at me and puts his arms out. "Up, Banna. Up."

Horsy wasn't his first word. *Banna* was. I lift and hug him. His breath smells of Cheerios. I press my cheek to his and twist back and forth. I want to take him and run.

"What are you doing?" I ask Sondra.

"Just what it looks like, Hannah. I have to get out of here."

Clothes are everywhere. Two suitcases are open on top

of the mattress. Bare hangers still swing and jangle in the closet.

"Are you leaving because of me?"

Tears come to her eyes and roll down her cheeks. "You've made staying this long bearable." She hugs me quickly, then lets go. "I just didn't bargain for this. I fell in love and married a whole man. There's too little left of him."

I want to hate her for leaving us, but I can't. "Don't you care what happens to him—to us?"

"Of course I do."

Jeffy kisses my cheek. It's his new thing—kisses with big smacky sounds. "What about Jeffy?"

"What about him?"

"When will we get to see him? You can't just take him . . ." My voice cracks. "And disappear."

She wipes her eyes. "I've already talked to my lawyer. As unstable as your father is, I don't have to let him ever see Jeffy again, so don't tell me what I can't do."

"I didn't mean it like that. I mean morally. He's my little brother." My voice catches on the lump in my throat. "I love him."

She closes her eyes. "I know you do. He'll be at my mother's. Come over anytime."

"Is that where you're going?"

"It's the only place I have *to* go, but I told your dad that I got an apartment in town. I don't want him coming over and wheeling up and down the sidewalk in front of my parents' house. I'll get a restraining order if I have to."

"He only did that 'cause he thought you were in love with someone else." I look at her. "Are you?"

She shakes her head. "No, and what happened at the bank doesn't matter anymore."

I hear a horn beep and go to the window. The town's only taxi is in the driveway.

She stands up. "Take the baby and let me finish."

When I come back to sit with Dad and wait, he's still watching cartoons. He even smiles at some of their antics, like he's completely out of touch with what's happening.

I hug Jeffy tight against my chest. He puts his head against my shoulder, sticks a thumb in his mouth, and holds on to one of my earlobes with his other hand. Dad glances over smiling, sees us there, and turns away. "It will be okay, Hannah." His voice is croaky. "We'll manage like we always have."

I hate you, I think.

The taxi beeps again.

A couple more minutes go by before Sondra comes down the stairs, passes by without a word, headed for the garage with her suitcases. When she comes back, she looks at us for a moment, then holds her hands out for me to give her Jeffy. I get up and walk with her to the door, where I hand him over.

She looks back at Daddy. "I'll be in touch, Jeff."

He stares at the TV and doesn't answer. I follow her outside.

"Maybe he'll get better and you'll be able to come back."

"Maybe," she says. She leans and puts Jeffy in his car seat, which is strapped into the backseat of the cab.

"Sondra."

"Yes?" She looks at me.

"I really always liked you, you know."

"I really always liked you too, Hannah."

When she straightens, she hugs me. "You really did make these months since he came home bearable." She goes around and gets in the back beside Jeffy, then leans across him and looks up at me. "Come by anytime, okay? I want him to have you as his big sister."

I nod, afraid to say anything for fear that I will beg her to stay, or worse, to take me with her.

I watch until the cab pulls out on Sequoia and slowly drives away before I turn and head back to the house. As I get closer, I hear a sound like a dog's been hit by a car. I start to run. Inside, Daddy's chair is on its side and he's lying on the floor, his leg drawn up, his arms over his head.

I get on my knees and stroke his back. "Shhhh, Daddy. It'll be okay."

"Jenny," he cries. "Jenny."

Jenny was my mother's name.

27

THE FIRST MONTH OF THE
NEW YEAR, 2007

In the two and a half weeks since Sondra left and took Jeffy, I've quit going to the stables. I feel like I'm about the only thing keeping Daddy harnessed to the real world and I'm afraid to leave him alone more than necessary. He's started sitting guard at night. If he sleeps at all it must be during the day, because all night long I hear him downstairs rolling from window to window, door to door, checking and rechecking the locks, assembling, cleaning, and reassembling his AK-47. It may make him feel safer, but I feel like his prisoner. I'm afraid to get up and go to the bathroom at night, afraid he'll hear the floor creaking and fire through the ceiling.

The tree dried out and was shedding, so the day before Christmas I dragged it out, leaned it against the woodpile, then swept up the needles and put them in the woodstove.

Dad never said a word and Christmas passed like any other day.

The day after Christmas, I told Dad I was going to the stables, then rode my bike to town to deliver Jeffy's Beanie Baby Barbaro, which I found on Amazon, and Sondra's lemon zester. Sondra didn't ask about Dad and I didn't tell her how scary he was acting. I almost told Dillon when she called to see if I was okay. Instead I lied and told her I'd been busy. If I tell her what's going on, she may call Child Protective Services and they might take me away from him.

School has started again and for the last three days Dad has been waiting for my bus in the trees near the end of our driveway. The first time I saw him out there, I thought maybe he was getting the mail. I looked back as we passed and saw him roll out into the road and wave his arms over his head. I jumped up to get off at the next bus stop, which is about a hundred yards east of our house.

"Where do you think you're going?" Mrs. Laurie said.

"I have to get off here. My . . . my dad's sick."

"I can't let you off where you have to cross the road."

"You have to. It's an emergency."

She must have been able to tell by the look on my face that I wasn't kidding. She left the red flashing lights on, put out the bus's stop signs, pulled a handheld sign from behind her seat, and got off ahead of me. She stood in the middle of the road holding the sign while I crossed.

"Thank you," I said, and started to run back down Simpson.

I was out of breath when I reached him. "What's the matter? Why are you out here?"

He seemed surprised I asked. "Making sure you're safe."

Safe! I looked at him so tempted to say, yeah from everyone but you, but his eyes were so tortured, he reminded me of that little filly I left behind at Haven Creek. His mind has him penned up. I can't believe it's been less than a year since I stood at the stable fence missing him and thinking how much my life sucked without him.

"Let's go, Dad. Everything's all right." I wheeled him back to our fortress where he could draw the blinds and lock all the windows and doors.

When I get on the school bus this afternoon, our usual driver isn't there. "Where's Mrs. Laurie?"

"Out sick."

Good, I think. This driver doesn't know where I live, so I can just get off with the Grether kids without Mrs. Laurie making her usual big deal of stopping, getting out, and standing in the road with her stop sign and watching me with her sad eyes. I hate that she pities me.

When the bus stops, I get up with the Grether kids.

"Where do you think you're going?" the driver says.

"This is my stop."

Paul Grether looks at me and snickers.

"No it ain't," says the driver. "You live on the north side. I got it all right here." She holds up a clipboard. "Mrs. Laurie told me about you."

"If that's true, then you know I have to get out here."

"I'm not Mrs. Laurie. I ain't making no special stop just for you, and you're not crossing the road alone."

"I'm thir . . . fourteen. I can cross the road alone."

"Not on my watch." She pulls the door closed and the bus starts to roll. I look back. Dad has wheeled out of the trees onto the bike path and is trying to follow us.

I go to the window and wave to let him know I'm okay and will be right back, but I can't tell if he sees me.

Nine minutes later, when the bus stops opposite our house, Dad is rolling back and forth at the end of the driveway.

When the brakes squeal, he looks up. He hasn't shaved in a week and his hair is wild-looking, but I expect it is the expression of torment on his face that most shocks the driver. "Is that your dad?"

"Yes."

She opens the door for me. "I'm sorry."

"Yeah. Me too."

"Where have you been?" Dad screams at her. "I'll have your job for this."

The same kids who'd been at the bus stop the day he rolled out on the ground and tried to chase them away from the trash cans are at the windows watching—Lacy among them. At least she's not laughing.

The driver slams the door, grinds the gears, and pulls away in a black cloud of diesel smoke.

Weekends aren't much better. Every other Saturday is Dad's day to visit Jeffy.

When we pull up in front of the Lutzes' in the Dial-A-Ride van, I hear Jeffy screaming, "Daddy and Banna. Daddy and Banna," at the top of his fifteen-month-old lungs. Mrs. Lutz opens the door and he comes marching out onto the porch with his elbows up and swinging from side to side. Mr. Lutz must have told him Daddy was a soldier. He has to stop marching to get down the steps, then he runs into Dad's arms. Nothing makes my father as happy, or as sad, as our allotted hour with Jeffy.

If the weather is nice, the routine's the same. Dad puts Jeffy in his lap and whizzes up and down the sidewalk, Jeffy laughing with his chubby little arms flung out like he's flying. Then they play cowboy, Dad bouncing him on his remaining knee. Watching nearly breaks my heart. Jeffy will never know what Dad was like whole.

If it's rainy, we have to get Dad up the steps and into the house. There he watches me play on the floor with Jeffy while Mrs. Lutz stands guard with her arms crossed over her big fat boobs watching Dad like he's Jack the Ripper. Sondra's never here when we are.

We get an hour, but Mrs. Lutz makes us feel about as welcome as gum on her shoe. If we're inside, Dad usually lasts about thirty minutes, then we go to wait on the curb for Dial-A-Ride to take us home. I don't see Mr. Lutz when we're there, but sometimes I hear him walking around upstairs. I'm pretty sure Sondra's mother won't let him come down. He might start talking to Daddy, and encourage us to stay.

Before we leave, Dad hugs Jeffy with his eyes squeezed shut. It only lasts a few moments before Jeffy starts to squirm and wants down, but always long enough for me to wish I never had to watch it again.

Dad comes home so depressed it scares me. He skips the beer and goes right for the bourbon. There's no way I can go to the stables after one of these visits.

To make things worse, Barbaro isn't doing well and it's all over the news and in the paper. The foot he broke in the Preakness is pretty much healed, though they fused the joint, so it looks awful when he walks. It's the laminitic foot that's the problem. A couple days ago they put a cast on it, but yesterday they took it back off. The website described removing part of the hoof and the infected tissue like it's an in-grown toenail, but Dad, who hasn't gotten over Saturday's visit with Jeffy, wags his finger at me and pronounces Barbaro a goner—as if all that bourbon has given him a special insight.

Friday's report on Barbaro is better and this isn't Dad's weekend to see Jeffy, so I decide to go to the stables—at least for a little while.

"We've missed you," Dillon says.

"Dad's been sick." It's not a big lie.

Rega looks like she's doubled in size in the last two weeks. She hesitates when I call to her, but Free comes clomping over on her big hairy hooves, so Rega comes too.

"It's about time our little she-devil learned to wear a halter. You want to try and put it on her?" Dillon takes one off the peg by their door and adjusts it.

"Put a halter on her? I can't even catch her."

"You should know by now. You don't catch her, you let her catch you."

"Right," I say. She means get Rega to follow what she's afraid of. That will be me when I'm in the paddock with her.

Except for the day Jack died, this is my first time in a paddock with any of the horses, much less with the one I love even-steven with Jeffy, but as soon as I'm inside, Rega races away, kicking and prancing. I don't move until she stops and looks at me, then I turn my back on her, walk over, and start to brush Free. Out of the corner of my eye, I see her start toward us. When I look at her, she stops. "You're a big sissy," I tell her.

She cuts sideways, kicks her legs up, and races off again. She stops at the far fence-line. I walk toward her until her big knobby knees bend, ready to dash away again, then I turn and walk back toward Free. She starts after me but I don't look directly at her. I just keep walking, holding the halter behind my back until she's so close I can feel her warm breath on my hands. After a few moments I feel her bristly nose against my hand. I walk over to Free and start stroking her face, ignoring Rega when she comes to stand by her mom. I even lean over her to reach the middle of Free's back and massage her withers. The halter is hanging off my wrist and touches Rega's face. When I bring the hand with the halter down Free's side, I continue over to Rega and along her back like they're a unit. The halter drags along her side. I stroke her face and around her nose, slipping the noseband over her muzzle.

"Remember to press her ears back, then pull them under the strap," Dillon says. She's watching me from the gate. "Very good," she says when I have it on her.

I feel around inside the Ziploc for a chunk of carrot without taking the bag out of my pocket. When I give Rega her reward, her soft lips move against my palm.

I think I would die if all the time I was allowed with Rega was an hour every two weeks, like Dad and I have with Jeffy.

28

MONDAY, JANUARY 29

I get on the bus and see Mrs. Laurie has the *Press Democrat* open. The headline reads: Barbaro: Champion captured nation's heart but couldn't overcome injury.

My heart starts to pound. I don't understand. Dad and I watch the news every night and the vet has been hopeful. There's nothing I can do. I have to wait until the bus gets opposite my house.

When Lacy comes up the steps and sees the headline, she stops. "He's dead?" I hear her ask Mrs. Laurie.

"Yes. Isn't it a shame? That poor horse."

The front door is locked and I don't carry a key. Dad's always home. I knock and call for him to let me in, but there's no answer. I put my school books on the bench by the front door and start around the house looking in the windows. The drapes are all pulled, so I can't see in. At the back, there's an outside staircase to the second floor. I know the door at the top is locked. It's never unlocked, but about halfway up the stairs, there's a place where my shoulders are even with the deck that runs the length of our two bedrooms. I crawl up on the banister, step up on the narrow edge of the roof that sticks out beyond the deck, and walk sideways, holding on to the railing, around the deck to the peak, never once looking down. The sliding glass door to my bedroom is always open.

"Dad?" I call from the top of the stairs. The living room is empty. The TV is on, tuned to CNN. He knows about Barbaro. I feel the hair rise on the back of my neck.

"Daddy, where are you?"

There's no answer.

The bathroom door is closed. I tap lightly. "Daddy?" When he doesn't answer, I begin to pound on the door before I think to try the knob. It's not locked and it's empty.

I cross to his bedroom, then back to the kitchen and out the back door, into the yard. "Oh God. Daddy, where are you?"

I hear something, but my heart is thundering in my chest, so maybe that's what I'm hearing. I listen, trying to quiet my breathing. The garage. I come down the side of the house and press my ear to the wooden wall. I don't hear the car running or anything, but something makes me afraid to open the doors. I go back into the house and to the door in the kitchen that opens to the garage.

Even the bright light from the kitchen doesn't pierce the darkness enough for me to see inside. I reach for the light switch.

"Don't," my father hisses from somewhere in the blackness.

"Why?" My eyes begin to adjust and I can see him in his wheelchair near the rear bumper, a shotgun across the armrests.

"They're out there," he whispers.

"Who's out there?"

"Insurgents, for Christ's sake, who do you think?"

"There's no one there, Daddy. You're home in your own garage."

He doesn't answer, but I hear him pull back the hammers on the shotgun.

"Daddy." My voice trembles. "Can I turn on the light and show you?"

"You'd better be right, soldier."

I step back into the kitchen and reach around until my hand is on the light switch. If he fires, all he'll hit is the door instead of me. At least I hope so. I flip the switch, flooding the garage with fluorescent light.

For a moment, there's just the ticking of the clock on the kitchen wall.

"Hannah?"

"I'm here." I peek around, then step out where he can see me. "Put the gun down, Daddy, okay?"

He lowers the shotgun and slowly releases first one hammer, then the next. "They killed him."

"Who'd they kill?"

"Barbaro."

"I know, Daddy. I saw the paper."

"They gave up on him, just like they did on your mother, like Sondra did on me and you."

"It's not the same thing, Daddy. He couldn't get better; neither could Momma. You said so."

"Well, neither can I, Hannah Banana. Neither can I." He hangs his head.

I'm suddenly furious. "That's bull!" I shout at him. "And stop calling me Hannah Banana. I'm not a little girl anymore. You're not even letting me be a kid. There's a big difference between someone giving up on you, which is their problem, and giving up on yourself. Don't compare yourself to that brave horse. You've stopped trying; he never did." I flip the light off, go into the kitchen, and slam the door. With my back against the wood, I listen for the cocking of the hammers again. *What have I done?* Tears stream down my face. I never told him about Secretariat's huge heart. I should have. I still don't move and after a long few minutes, I feel the doorknob turn against the small of my back. I step away and turn to face it.

"I didn't mean it," I say when he pulls it open. My hands are raised, as if I expect to be shot, but I don't realize it until tears fill Daddy's eyes and roll down his cheeks.

"Please put your hands down, Hannah. I'm not so far gone that I would ever hurt you."

February 3 is Dad's Saturday with Jeffy, but he doesn't want to go. I call Mrs. Lutz and cancel our visit. I hate the relief in her voice. I fix Dad some breakfast, which he doesn't eat, and offer to help him get dressed. "Later," he says, so I leave even though I'll worry all day.

The day after Rega was born, she was afraid of all of us, as if everything her mother had been through with humans had gotten passed on. Now when she sees me, she runs to the fence on her long spindly legs and pokes her little black face through the boards for me to kiss. I feel sick with love for her.

Today Super Dee is in the paddock next to Rega and Free's. I have apples and carrots, and he comes over for his share. Rega gets as close to him as she dares and makes little lip-smacking sounds so he'll know she's a baby.

"Hey, Hannah. How are things going?" Dillon is mucking Bobby's stall.

"I'm sorry. Dad's . . . Dad's been . . ." I start to cry.

She leans the rake against the stall door, puts an arm around my shoulder, and guides me toward the picnic table. Rega follows right beside me on her side of the fence until she can't go any farther.

"I don't know what to do. I'm afraid he's going to kill himself or something."

"Sit down," Dillon says.

I sit on the table with my feet on the bench. Bobby is tied up at the wash stand. Dillon was getting ready to bathe him. He looks over his shoulder at me and lets his tongue loll out.

"You're not the same kid who came here eleven months ago, but I thought as long as your stepmother was there, you'd be okay. This has to stop. You're thirteen, for heaven's sake."

"Fourteen in a couple of weeks."

"Whatever. You can't take full responsibility for a man as sick as your father."

"There's no one to help us. Sondra's mother says if the VA therapist was any good, she wouldn't be working for the government, but what choice do we have?"

"There are other alternatives."

"Not Protective Services. If they took me away, he'd kill himself. I'm sure of it."

"Maybe just a visit from them would shock him enough to make him get some real help."

"But if that didn't work, it's not like they would just shrug and walk away. I can't take that chance."

"Look, I have a friend who's a therapist; she might be some help. Would you like me to call her?"

When I nod, she unclips her cell phone from her belt and punches in a number. She smoothes my hair while it rings. It feels nice, like something Momma used to do when I'd been crying.

"Hey, Julia. It's Dillon. Do you remember when you said you owed me one? Yeah. Well, I'd like to call in that favor."

Dillon hangs up and smiles at me. "I taught her Parelli and helped her with a horse she rescued. She'll see you tomorrow, if you're willing."

"On Sunday?"

"Sure. What better day to turn your life around?"

"And she likes horses?"

"It's more than that. You'll find out."

29

SUNDAY, FEBRUARY 4

I tell Dad I'm going to the stables and turn my bike east on Simpson, in case he's watching, wait a few minutes, then whiz by headed for the highway. My appointment with Dillon's friend is at ten thirty. I've never been to a therapist even though after Mom died, the doctors suggested Dad take me. "We'll tough it out," he'd said. "Just like we always have."

Julia's office is in her house. She lives at Todd's Point, overlooking the ocean. I don't pay much attention to the sea anymore, but from her house I can see the waves hit and explode against the cliffs. It's a day too rough for fishing.

Julia and four dogs come out to meet me when I ride up. There's a cat the size of a pumpkin in the window facing the driveway. Though this has the feel of a visit to a neighbor, I'm nervous and not sure what to expect. Maybe I'll have to lie on a couch like in the movies, but I'm pretty sure

I'm going to have to tell her all about Dad and Sondra and me and Jeffy. I'm afraid the second I start, I'll break down again like I did with Dillon. When we shake hands, mine is damp with sweat even as cold as it is today.

"I have a pitcher of water poured, but if you'd prefer, I can get you a cola or something."

"No ma'am. Thanks. I don't want anything."

The dogs push through the door ahead of me.

Her office has a separate entrance from the rest of the house. It's paneled in redwood with lots of framed degrees on the wall and a packed to overflowing bookcase along one side. The pitcher of water with lemon slices floating in it is on a little side table. Two blue leather recliners face each other. One of them has a box of Kleenex next to it, so I guess that's the one I'm supposed to sit in. If I start to cry they're in easy reach.

"First things first, Hannah." She hands me a telephone book for my lap. "I need you to fill out this form." She gives me a single piece of paper and a pen, then pours herself a glass of water. "You sure?" She tips the pitcher toward my glass.

"Yes ma'am. I'm sure."

While I put down my name and address, Daddy's name, and our ages, there is only the sound of the big dog's panting and the sweep of his tail back and forth on the hardwood floor. I finish filling in the form and hand it to her.

She reads it over, then puts it on the table.

"Let me get a little background first, then you can tell me why you've come."

I suspect that Dillon has told her some stuff, but I tell her about Momma dying and how Dad and I love horses. I take a breath and tell her how he lost his leg and won't use his prosthesis and about Sondra leaving. I mention Barbaro dying and Dad's flashbacks to the war. She takes notes.

"He's been going to the VA shrink . . . sorry . . . psychologist, but all she tells him is that he has an adjustment disorder, then okays another prescription refill. Dad says the VA solution for his problem is a pharmaceutical lobotomy."

"Do you know what that means?"

"Yeah. It's like in the movie *One Flew Over the Cuckoo's Nest*. Doctors took out part of Jack Nicholson's brain and he wasn't crazy anymore. He wasn't anything—just a walking vegetable."

"It was a very common surgery for schizophrenia forty or fifty years ago."

"Daddy's not crazy. The war caused this."

"I know. It sounds like a classic case of posttraumatic stress disorder. Do you know what that is?"

I think of the nice man who helped us on trash day. "Kind of. It keeps him from forgetting what happened to him over there."

"He'll never be able to forget what happened, but he can learn to live his life in spite of those memories. Right now they're keeping him from doing that. PTSD is an anxiety disorder that occurs after someone has been through something horrible and terrifying. That's what traumatic means. The person feels they have no control over what happens to them, and that creates confusion and anger and the vivid flashbacks, all of which can get worse without help. Is he drinking and taking drugs?"

"Drinking mostly. Lots. Beer all day; bourbon at night."

"It sounds as if he's trying to cope by staying numb. How much is he drinking?"

"A six-pack or two of beer, then he starts on the bourbon and goes through a half bottle or more at night, and there are the pain pills."

"Is he sleeping?"

"Not since Sondra left. He guards the house all night. He must sleep when I'm at school, but I don't know for sure."

"But you say he loves horses?"

"I don't even know that for sure. I thought he did. We used to like to watch horse races, but since what happened to Barbaro, we don't do that anymore." I pet the dog that comes in and sits beside me. "He hasn't ridden since he was a kid."

"Your dad sounds as if he might be a good candidate for both kinds of therapies I do. Did Dillon tell you about either of them?"

I shake my head.

"The one I think we'd start with is equine-assisted psychotherapy."

"What's that?" *Equine.* "Something with horses?"

"Exactly."

I almost grin, as if she'd told a joke. As much as I love horses, this sounds a little woo-woo. Dad will call it New Age crapola when I tell him I want him to do psychotherapy with a horse. I swallow the urge to laugh, and ask, "How can a horse help my dad?"

"Well, it may not, but psychologists have been having success with programs to help veterans recover from their emotional and physical war wounds by putting them to work with animals since the air force first tried it in the 1940s."

Sixty-seven years. I straighten a bit in my recliner. "Including horses?"

"Especially horses."

"How's it work?" I say, and hope my tone of voice didn't give away the fight going on in my head between hoping it's true and thinking it's bunk.

"You're around horses a lot, how do they make you feel?"

"I was scared at first."

"And now?"

I shrug. "I'm not afraid anymore. I like them and I think

they like me." I smile. "It may just be the apples and carrots I bring them."

She smiles too. "But at first you were scared. What's changed?"

"I got to know them and we learned to trust each other."

"Uh-huh. And how does having them trust you make you feel?"

"Good, I guess."

"Anything else?"

Tears suddenly swim in my eyes. "Not so alone."

Julia leans over, pulls a tissue from the box next to my chair, and hands it to me. "Anything else?"

"I don't feel so helpless with them. They're big and powerful and yet they do whatever I ask them to do. They see me as a person, not as a kid. Dillon says I'm part of their herd."

"Do you think your dad feels helpless?"

"I know he does, and he thinks he'll never get better, but I'm not sure being around horses is the answer. He's lost his connection to them."

"Do you know why?"

"He got hurt a bunch of times when he was breaking wild mustangs, and because of that he never had the kind of relationship that I have. Maybe he just liked the idea of horses and never really liked the horses themselves."

"The horses that hurt your dad were just trying to protect themselves. It's such a shame that the old way of breaking a horse always resulted in the horse fearing people and vice versa." The largest of her dogs is sitting beside her chair. Julia rubs his ear.

"A horse has three needs for self-preservation: mind, body, and spirit. Isn't it the same for us? Isn't that what's wrong with your dad? Basic training broke his spirit, the war broke his body, and his mind isn't letting him heal."

"He said kind of the same thing. He broke the spirits of horses and the war broke his."

"With the right care, horses heal. Maybe your dad will recognize that possibility in himself. Does that make sense?"

I nod. "There was this one time with Jack."

"Who's Jack?"

"An old horse at the stables. He hated men 'cause he was abused, but he was nice to my dad, and Dad . . ." My voice shakes. "Whatever happened between them made my dad happy for the first time since he got home from the war."

"Do you think Jack sensed some connection with your dad? Recognized someone else who needs physical and emotional healing?"

"How could he?"

"Well, Hannah, PTSD isn't limited to war veterans, or for that matter, to humans. Don't you think the violence

Jack experienced was similar to your dad's?"

"I never thought of that."

"Few people do. We think our emotional and physical distresses are separate from those of other animals. They're not."

"But how could Jack have felt differently about Dad than he did about other men?"

"You've never had a pet, have you?"

"No."

"People with pets know how easily their animals sense their moods. Horses, because they are prey animals, are especially good at reading our emotional state. For their own protection they have to be able to read our intentions and emotions in our body language, then they mirror it back to us. They don't lie. They have no hidden agenda. All they do is focus on the safety or threat in our intentions. But because they are large and powerful animals, they create a natural opportunity to empower us, help us overcome fear and develop confidence. My hope is that working with them will show your father the part of himself he no longer believes in."

I look at my hands knotted in my lap and want so much to believe this is possible.

"You've used Parelli with horses, so you know working with them is all about communication and leadership. It sounds as if your dad can't do one and doesn't believe he can be the other—be a father anymore. He hasn't learned that all he's missing is a leg."

I put my head down and close my eyes. Tears roll out and drip on my jeans. I hook my necklace with my index finger and pull my chunk of glass out from under my shirt. When I look up, Julia is watching me.

"Do you think you can talk him into trying?"

"I don't know. If I ask him to do it for me, he might agree. He's going through a lot of guilt over Sondra and how we're living. He'll say it's B.S. though."

Two more cats wander in and one rubs against my leg, then jumps up on my lap.

"You okay with cats?"

"I've never had one, but I like them."

The cat makes a circle and lies down.

"Tell me about your necklace."

I open my hand and look at it. It's just a piece of cobalt blue bottle glass from Glass Beach, which used to be the city dump. People backed up to the edge of the cliff and pushed their trash over the side. Over the years, the sea washed it in and out, until the broken pieces of glass became rounded. Cobalt is the hardest color to find.

"Right after we found out my mom's cancer was back, she took me to Glass Beach. She used to make things out of the pieces of glass she found there. 'I turn trash into treasure,' she used to say. She was so excited when I found this piece." I pull my collar away from my neck and drop it back inside my shirt. "She said it was the biggest and best she'd ever seen. After she died, Daddy had a jeweler wire it in gold so I could wear it. I never take it off."

"It's kind of like having your mother with you all the time, isn't it?"

"I guess. I like to think it brings me good luck."

"I'm sure it does."

She stands, so I guess my time is up.

Julia waves good-bye to me from her deck; her dogs and two of the three cats stand with her. Seeing them all together makes me feel like the last horse on the track. I walk back and stand with my head bowed. I can't think of anything to say.

She steps down and puts her arms around me.

"Please help my dad. Please help us."

"I'm going to try, Hannah."

I put my arms around her, then think I shouldn't and let her go.

"You know abused, hurt horses need a different understanding. So do abused, hurt humans. Get him to come once and I'll do the rest."

30

THE SAME DAY

Julia's house is a street away from the new Pomo Bluffs
park. I decide to go sit and watch the ocean for a while
before I go home. Huge rollers are coming in, driven by a
storm at sea that is headed our way. I sit on a bench and
watch a small fishing boat bob in the rising surf just off
the jetty. I imagine it's Dad and me in the *Hannah Gale*.
We are waiting to catch a wave in just the right way that it
will launch us through the channel and not cast us over the
breakwater onto the rocks. It's all timing and skill. Daddy
had that. It was as if he was a part of the boat. Dillon told
me when I was riding Indy to feel the whole horse. That's
what she meant. Become part of the horse's skin like Dad
was part of the *Hannah Gale*'s planking.

I can hear the shower running when I come in from
Julia's. It must be a pretty good day if Dad is showering.

Maybe we can go up to the stables together. He hasn't seen Rega yet.

It's nearly two and I haven't eaten since breakfast, but when I come into the kitchen I get a chill. It's not anything I can name specifically, but something feels wrong. Dad usually puts his dirty dishes in the sink, but they are on the counter along with a half-finished glass of milk, which has been there so long that the beads of condensation have formed a puddle on the counter. I glance at the recycle bin I emptied this morning. There are no crushed beer cans. Instead of relief this scares me. I run on tiptoes to the bathroom door, but when I knock there's no answer.

"Daddy, I'm home."

Nothing.

I crack the door, expecting steam to roll out. Instead, the air feels cold. I push the door all the way open. Daddy is on the floor of the shower. His stool is on its side. However long he's been there, the hot water must have run out long ago, because the spray of water beating down on him is freezing.

"Daddy!" I turn the heater on and the water off.

He's shivering and his lips are blue, but he's conscious.

"Hannah?"

"It's me." I cover him with one of his big bath towels, but it doesn't hide his stump, the skin of which is gathered together like the end of a sausage. The sight of it always makes the backs of my knees tingle.

"I'm so cold."

"How long have you been in here?" I get him to sit up and put another towel around his shoulders.

"I don't know. Hours, I think."

"What happened?"

"I missed the stool and hit my head when I fell." He reaches and touches the red knot on the side of his head.

"I don't know if I can get you up by myself."

We had a handrail installed months ago. I lift his icy hand and fold his fingers over it. "Hold on, okay?"

He closes his eyes and nods, but his hand slips off.

"I'm going to call 911."

"No," he snaps.

I wouldn't really. I'd flag a stranger down on the road before I'd take a chance on some moonlighting social worker seeing this house and the way we live.

"Then hang on to the railing and help me." I put his hand back on the railing. Wheeling himself everywhere has made his grip like steel. He holds on this time.

"Pull yourself up enough for me to get the stool under your butt, okay?"

Daddy brings his right knee up, gets his foot flat on the shower floor, then pulls himself up. I put the stool under him and he sits down, but not before the towel slips off his legs. He grabs it and covers himself again. I quickly turn away and adjust the heater. I know having me see him naked is the worst part of this for him.

"I'm sorry, Hannah."

"For what?" I act like I didn't see him.

"You shouldn't have to be taking care of me. I should be taking care of you."

"You will again," I say.

I order us delivery pizza for dinner. Dad has a beer before it arrives and one with it, then stops.

We're watching *Cold Case*. "How's that little filly doing?" he asks during a commercial.

"She's so cute. I'm totally in love with her."

"Is what's her name—the owner, going to keep her?"

That startles me because I've just assumed she would, but what if . . . ? "Sophia'd never sell Rega," I say, but I'm suddenly scared to death I'm wrong.

We don't talk for a while. I sit thinking about Rega and Julia and how I'm going to go about asking Dad to see her. A commercial comes on for a Presidents' Day sale at Mervyns. I was born on George Washington's birthday. "My birthday's coming up, you know?"

Dad seems a little jolted by this, enough so I think that he's forgotten it's in a couple of weeks. "I haven't decided what I'm getting you yet," he says.

"I know what I want."

"That filly?"

"No. Well, yeah, of course, but we can't afford the stable fees. No, it's something else."

"Am I supposed to guess?"

"No, I'll tell you if you promise that you'll give it to me."

"How can I do that if I don't know what it is?"

"Just say yes."

"I'll say maybe. That's the best I can do."

I take a deep breath. "I went to see a therapist today . . ."

His head snaps around. "You what? Why?"

"Because we need help and I want you to go see her too."

"Absolutely not. I'm not going to see another damn shrink. I'm going twice a week now and it isn't helping."

"This one is different."

"The answer is no, Hannah."

"It's with horses." I put Julia's business card on the coffee table.

Daddy looks at it, then at me, and grins. I realize he's having the same reaction that I had. "No really. She does equine-assisted psychotherapy."

He snorts. "What a load of bull I bet that is."

I stare at the TV screen and feel my body stiffen. After a minute, I get up and go to the kitchen, get the bourbon down from the cupboard, his favorite glass from the drain board, pitch in some ice, and pour the brown liquor over the cubes.

"What's that?" he asks when I slam it down in front of him.

"I don't want you sitting here pretending that you are the father I had before the war." My voice shakes. "If I'm going to be the adult in this family, the only one trying to find a way for you to get better, I'd rather not have the lie of a normal night." I cross the room and start up the stairs. Before I make it to the top, I hear the glass shatter against the brick wall behind the woodstove.

31

MONDAY, FEBRUARY 19

I'm coming down the driveway from the school bus stop when I hear a twig snap. Dad wheels out from behind a Doug fir.

He'd promised to stop this. "What are you doing out here?"

"Waiting for you." He puts his hands up. "Not where anyone could see me. I won't embarrass you again."

"Whatever." I keep walking. He wheels along behind me.

"I called your shrink today."

"Yeah. And?" I say over my shoulder.

"We have an appointment for Saturday at noon."

I turn. "With the horses?"

"With the horses."

"Oh, Daddy. That's wonderful." I hug his neck.

He undoes my arms and holds me away. "I'm going to try, Hannah. Okay? I can't promise anything."

"All I'm asking is that you try." I get behind him and start to push him along the driveway. "What made you change your mind?"

"I remembered what you said when I called from Walter Reed on your last birthday. You said my coming home was the best birthday present ever. Instead, I made this year hell for you, and for Sondra. Maybe February twenty-second will be sort of a birthday for me too."

Today is Saturday the twenty-fourth. I'm fourteen years and two days old. Dad had Harvest Market deliver a birthday cake on Thursday, but we didn't do anything else to celebrate. He stayed sober and we watched *Seabiscuit*, my other favorite horse movie. Today I get my real birthday present.

I call Dial-A-Ride early. They don't usually go that far out of town, but we're good customers and I think the driver agreed to take us because he likes my dad—or feels sorry for him—maybe both. He gets here at eleven thirty on the dot. While the driver gets Dad and his wheelchair loaded, I run back to the house for his crutches.

"What are those for?" Dad's uptight about this.

"With all the rain we've had, you might not be able to wheel where we need to go."

When he shrugs, I suspect he left them behind on purpose.

I look out the window toward the ocean as we ride. Dad looks out the opposite side. We turn inland after we cross Pudding Creek. Right away we start to pass houses with pastures for yards. They seem to have either horses, llamas, or goats, and finally, farther out, cattle.

The Seaview Stables are in the rolling hills northeast of Fort Bragg. I've never been this far inland before and it's beautiful. The round grassy hills are dotted with clumps of trees and it feels ten degrees warmer up here than at our house in the forest. When we pull in I can see the ocean even though it's three or four miles away.

For a February day, it's sunny and warm. I start shedding layers as soon as I get out of the van. After the driver gets Dad unloaded, I help him off with his jacket. We make a big pile of clothing on a picnic table.

A woman is walking toward me. "It's Jeff, isn't it?" she says, and shakes Dad's hand. "And you're Hannah?"

"Yes ma'am." I like that she spoke to Dad first. Most people talk to me, instead of him, as if being in a wheelchair has crippled his mind too.

"I'm Heather, Julia's assistant." She shakes my hand. "Nice to meet you both."

"You too," Dad says, but he's backed his chair up and is looking through the horse barn. Stalls line both sides instead of just one, like Redwood Springs. A horse's head sticks out of nearly every one of them.

"Julia's around here somewhere," Heather says.

"She's in the far corral," I say. "I saw her when we drove up."

"That's where we'll be doing the session." She takes a clipboard from the table. "First, Jeff—is it okay if I call you Jeff?"

Dad doesn't answer. I don't think he's being rude; he's just not listening.

"Mr. Gale, I need you to sign this liability release."

"Hannah will fill it out." Dad rolls over to the entrance of the barn.

I fill out the form and take it to Dad to sign.

He scribbles his name and hands it back to me. "I wish I'd had a beer."

"We're around this way, Mr. Gale," Heather says.

I think she's gone from calling him Jeff to Mr. Gale because he's not acting friendly at all.

I walk around behind his chair to help push him through the soft, thick grass.

"Don't," Dad says. He grabs his wheels and with quick turns, follows Heather.

I wonder what Dad found so riveting and look down the row of stalls. I thought he was looking at the horses, but there's a corral on the far side of the barn. It's right next to the one we are going to use. A woman is standing with her arms hooked over the railing watching her daughter take a riding lesson. From the back she looks a little like Sondra. The little girl looks tiny on the horse's back, like a peanut in a helmet. A smile almost comes, until I realize what Daddy must be feeling. He's going to roll into a corral to sit belly-level with two horses, two attractive women, and me watching while next door, a child about seven is doing what my dad can't do—all within view of a woman who looks like Sondra. I feel so sorry for him that I want to run tell him he doesn't have to do this, but instead I get his crutches and follow him toward the corral.

Behind each stall is an outdoor pen. All of the horses come out to watch us pass. Daddy doesn't even look at them. His head is down as he muscles his way through the mud and clumps of grass.

"Hello, Jeff," Julia says when he rolls to a stop. "It's a beautiful day, isn't it?" She shakes Dad's hand and mine, then holds open the gate to the corral.

Both horses are with Heather on the far side eating the little bit of grass that grows within their reach. Dad doesn't move. He's looking at the thin sliver of ocean that can be seen through the trees. He turns after a moment and pushes himself through the dirt to the center of the ring.

One of the horses is a brown, slightly lame gelding and the other is white like Jack, except she's a mare. She comes right over and starts sniffing Dad and the wheelchair.

Dad looks calm but his hands are wrapped tightly around his wheels, his fingers woven through the spokes.

"How are you feeling, Jeff?" Julia asks.

"Fine."

I prop his crutches against the fence and climb up to sit on the top rail.

"This is Gus," Julia introduces the brown gelding, who keeps his head up and his ears forward. "And this is Babe." The white horse is right behind Daddy smelling his hair.

Dad leans his head away.

"Jeff." Julia's voice is soft. "What are you feeling?"

"I don't know. Nothing."

"You look tense. I want you to try to relax. Take deep breaths."

Julia gets between Babe and Dad. "When you feel comfortable enough, I'd like you to close your eyes and tell me what you smell."

When Daddy closes his eyes, I close mine and take a deep breath. I smell the wet dirt and horse manure and the cattle across the road. The air is warm with smells. I open my eyes and see that Heather has moved Babe around in front of Dad so the horse's face is inches from his.

"Nothing," Dad says. "I don't smell anything." He opens his eyes and is startled to see how close Babe is. He leans back in his chair.

"What do you think Babe is doing?" Julia asks.

"Smelling me." His tone is sarcastic, like isn't it obvious.

"Dad, you promised to try," I say.

"I am trying."

"No you're not. You're shutting them out."

"What's this supposed to accomplish? What's the big deal about sitting here letting a horse sniff me?"

"Forget it. You're acting like a jerk." I jump down, which since I was facing them means I land inside the corral, spooking Gus, who runs to the far side of the ring.

Heather holds her arms out and leans to look at his butt. Gus stops and turns to face her. He's been Parelli trained.

"Hannah, your dad has to do this in his own time," Julia says. She puts a finger to her lips, then says to Dad, "Both these horses were abused, Jeff. Getting close enough to smell you helps Babe build up some trust."

"Okay," Dad says. He's watching Gus. "Where do you want to start?"

"Pick one horse," Julia says.

"This white one."

"Why the white one?"

"I don't know. You said to pick one."

"She looks like Jack," I tell Julia.

"The horse at Redwood Springs." Julia walks over and reaches through the fence for a bucket of brushes.

"Yeah. He was white like Babe."

Dad turns to me. "What do you mean *was*?"

"He died four months ago."

"Four months. Why didn't you tell me?"

"I don't know. So much was going wrong, then Sondra left and Barbaro . . . There was never a right time."

Dad's hands are palms up in his lap. He stares at them. "What do you want me to do?" he says.

Julia crooks a finger at Babe. "I want you to close your eyes and just touch her. Let's start with that."

When Babe is standing close enough for Dad to reach her, Julia takes his hand and places it on Babe's neck. Daddy strokes her a couple of times.

"Open your eyes."

Babe's face is next to Dad's right shoulder. Her head is down and her eyelids are half closed as if she might fall asleep.

"What do you see in her eyes?" Julia asks.

"She looks sleepy," Dad says.

"Is there any emotion there?"

"Can you give me a goal here?" Daddy says.

"How about the first step to putting you back in touch with what's missing from your life."

"That's a tall order. What *isn't* missing?"

"Hannah . . ."

"Except Hannah."

"I started to say Hannah told me you were a cowboy once."

Dad touches the side of Babe's face. "*Boy* is the operative word. It was a very long time ago and just for one summer."

"How do you think Babe is feeling?"

"She's relaxed."

"What does that tell you?"

"That she's not afraid of me."

"And?"

"If animals can smell fear, then I must not be afraid of her either." Dad touches the soft skin between her front legs with the back of his hand, then her neck again. Julia hands him a brush and he begins to brush her chest and neck as high up as he can reach.

Gus walks over and stands opposite Babe. Gus is so tall that Dad would only have to duck his head to wheel under his belly. If my six-foot-two father was nervous around horses when he could stand up, I wonder how vulnerable he must feel now. I slip off the railing and sit on the ground by the gate so my view is more like his.

Julia gets Dad's crutches. "I could help you stand if you'd like to," she says.

"Yeah. Okay." Babe has lowered her head until her nose is nearly touching Daddy's knee. His hand is flat against her forehead and his eyes are soft like I've seen him look at Jeffy.

No one says anything, or moves. It's the woman clapping for her daughter at the end of her lesson who breaks the spell. Heather steps forward to help Dad stand on his right leg, and Julia holds first one crutch then the other out to him. He gets balanced by leaning his stomach against Babe, then lets Julia take away the crutch under his right arm. That leaves his hand free to brush Babe.

He brushes her for a few minutes before laying his arm across her back.

Babe brings her head around so Dad is in the space between her neck and her body.

"She's giving you a horse hug, Daddy."

"I almost feel forgiven," Dad says to Julia.

"Forgiven for what?" She strokes Babe's neck.

"For the way I treated horses when I was a kid. The lead trainer put me in charge of the sacking out."

"What does that mean?" I ask.

"It's a gentle way of getting a horse used to things that might scare them," Julia says.

That's what the beach ball, tarp, and bubble wrap are for at the stables.

Dad looks at Julia. "The way we did it wasn't gentle, but I was fourteen and didn't know any better." He begins to brush Babe again. "I tied yearlings to a post and threw things at them."

My stomach turns. "But why?"

"The idea was to get them used to surprises, a plastic

235

bag blowing across the trail, a car horn, loud music, the saddle blanket. It was to keep them from spooking when something unexpected happened."

"But you can do that by having them follow what they're afraid of, or just touch them with it a few times. What did you throw?"

"Anything and everything: I hit them in the face with my shirt, threw tin cans, a plastic trash can lid, a hubcap. I traumatized them."

I try not to imagine Rega tied and tortured, or think Dad should have known better. Julia, Heather, and Dad are all looking at me—waiting. He's held on to this guilt for twenty years. I remember what Julia said about how, for their own protection, horses read our intentions in our body language. Babe's head is down. She's at peace with my father. "I'm with Babe on this one, Dad."

Julia gives me an almost undetectable nod, then touches his arm. "You've chosen the right horse to grant you forgiveness. Babe was a rescue. So was Gus. They were used for trail rides. Both got leg injuries and weren't worth anything, so their owners were selling them for dog food. Gus belongs to a friend and Babe is mine."

"Gus seems more standoffish," I say.

"He is. He was more severely mistreated. He hasn't learned to trust us yet, but he's better than he was."

Julia gives Dad his other crutch and rolls his wheelchair

up behind him, but Dad doesn't sit down. Instead he runs his hand along the curve of Babe's back, then looks toward the hills to the east. I think I can see in Dad's eyes how much he wants to saddle this horse and ride into those hills.

"I hope you'll come back again, Jeff," Julia says.

"I'd like that."

"Wait." I jump up. "Wait here. I have carrots in my coat pocket."

I'm on my way back with the Ziploc full of carrots when I see a girl about my age leading a horse out of one of the stalls. Her back is to me and she's wearing a helmet, but something about the way she walks looks familiar.

Dad is still standing beside Babe. He has his forehead against hers and he is scratching her ears. I hand him carrots to give her while I feed some to Gus. The two horses push their muzzles against our palms.

The girl is leading her horse into the riding ring that the little girl is just leaving. They pass each other. "Hi Mandy," the older girls says. I recognize her voice. It's Lacy. She glances in our direction, but really doesn't see us. Four people, two horses. Who we are doesn't seem to register. I watch her put a foot in a stirrup, then have to jump along on one foot as the horse swings around trying to keep her from getting mounted. I smile to myself. I could sure teach her a thing or two about handling that horse.

"Do you know her?" Dad says.

"Yeah. I know her."

The instructor has to hold the horse still for her to get on. When she's in the saddle she looks in our direction again. This time she recognizes me, blinks in astonishment, starts to wave, but doesn't.

"I'm sorry about Jack, Hannah." We're standing back to back feeding the last of the carrots to Gus and Babe.

"Me too, Dad. I really loved him."

"It's worse that you felt you had to protect me from knowing."

"It's been a rough few months." I wad up the empty Ziploc and put it into my pocket, then turn to face my dad. For the first time in nearly a year, I am looking up at him. He wraps his free arm around me and pulls my head to his chest.

32

THE LAST WEEK OF FEBRUARY

After how well Daddy did with the horses yesterday, I kind of wanted to hang with him this morning. He's in a pretty good mood, though his missing leg is itching. The doctor told him that being able to feel his phantom leg would pass in time, but Dad says sometimes it feels so real, it's hard to believe he can't get up and walk on it.

"I'm going to the stables," I say when he wheels into the kitchen. "Want to go with me?"

"No, you need a break from me. I think I'll go to physical therapy."

"Really?" The last time he went was in December shortly before Sondra left us. "That'd be great, Daddy." I slide half the eggs I've scrambled onto his plate.

"I'm going to work on getting better, Hannah."

I've heard that before, but this time, and after yesterday, I think maybe he means it.

Sophia now has three healthy horses. The one we brought back from Westport has slowly gotten better and gained nearly two hundred pounds. She's not very pretty, but she's sweet, especially considering what she went through. Sophia hasn't officially named her, but she's called her "such a sweet thing" so many times, that's what we call her.

Every time I see Sweet-thing, I can't help wondering what happened to the filly we left behind. Dillon told me the horses were all being taken to an auction in Ukiah, the county seat, so I guess I'll never know.

When I get to the stables, they've got the horses, including Sweet-thing, running at liberty in the arena. Free and Rega are in the pasture. When I stop, Rega, who was stretched out in the sun, gets up and bounds over. Though Free is part Belgian draft, Dillon thinks Rega might have a little Thoroughbred in her. She's long-legged and doesn't have her mother's heavy head and thick body.

"Hey Hannah, we've been waiting for you," Sophia hollers. "I have more than I can handle here, how about fetching Free and Rega. We thought we might start teaching that filly some manners."

"Really?"

"Sure. If we're ever going to find her a home, we've got to make her more appealing."

My stomach lurches. "You'd sell her?" The pain spreads to my chest.

"I don't know yet," Sophia says. She must have heard the emotion in my voice, because she adds, "I don't even care about riding, sweetie. She needs someone who will enjoy her."

I feel like a zombie as I get a halter and lead for Free and go into the paddock with them. Rega races from the road all the way down to meet me, her tail flying. She whizzes past, then turns, trots up behind me, and butts me between my shoulder blades.

"Don't," I snap, and throw my arm across my eyes to stop the tears.

She butts me again, then takes my sleeve in her teeth and pulls. I look into her dark eyes, then put my forehead against hers.

Free comes up beside me and breathes against my neck. I put her halter and lead on and open the gate. Rega will follow.

Everyone expects me to play Parelli games with Rega, but I'm sick thinking about what I'd do if Sophia decides to sell her, and I just can't. I sit on the saddles and watch Rega run with Free, Bobby, Dee, and Sweet-thing.

Dillon and the others look at me once in a while, but they don't ask what's wrong. Sophia plays Parelli with Free, and Rega entertains herself by dragging the blue tarp around the arena and putting her nose against the big ball, then running from it, kicking and bucking. She's so cute that I get up, cut through the kitchen, get my bike, and go home.

When Lacy gets on the bus Monday morning, she glances at me, starts down the aisle, then changes her mind and sits near the front.

In math class, she takes the desk behind mine. "I'm sorry for what I said about your dad."

"It's okay."

"What were you doing at Seaview?"

I don't want to risk telling her the truth. "My birthday was last week and Dad's talking about getting me a horse."

"Julia's not thinking about selling Babe, is she?"

"No. We . . ." I've got myself all twisted up in a lie. I turn to face her. "Julia thinks being around horses will help my dad want to walk again. That's why we were there." I'm ready to tell her where to get off, but she doesn't even smile.

"I love horses," she says.

"I do too."

"How long have you been riding?"

"Not very long. What about you?"

"Since I was eight. Maybe we could go together one day."

"Was that your horse I saw you on?"

Lacy nods. "But I'm thinking about getting a new one. She's too hard to handle."

The classroom door flies open and Melissa runs in.

The bell rings.

After class, Lacy catches up to me in the hall. "Want to have lunch with us?"

Melissa grins like this is a great huge joke.

"Sure." I smile sweetly at Melissa.

"Do you have a horse?" I ask Melissa. It's a warm day and we're at one of the picnic tables along the outside wall of the cafeteria.

"Melissa doesn't ride," Lacy says. "She's afraid of horses." Lacy's tone is mocking. If I want Melissa to like me too, this is my chance.

"I used to be, but since I've learned how to train them by the Parelli method, I'm not anymore."

"What's Parelli?" Lacy says.

"Maybe you can come by the stables one day to watch. It would help with your horse."

The phone rings early Friday morning. I run from the living room to the kitchen and catch it on the second ring.

"Hi, Hannah. It's Sophia."

"Hi," I whisper. Dad's still asleep.

"Are you free tomorrow? I need some help."

"Sure. With what?"

"The auction of the Haven Creek horses is in Ukiah and I'm taking Sweet-thing over. I'd love some company. Want to come?"

"I thought you were going to keep her."

"I never planned to. Everyone who could afford to take one of the sick horses did, but not to keep—to heal. The owner has been forced to relinquish ownership of all but four . . ."

I think of the little filly. "Do you know which four?"

"I don't, but if he's found guilty of animal cruelty—and how could he not—they will take the rest too. Unfortunately, his trial has been postponed, but Sweet-thing is one of the ones he's given up, so she'll be sold."

"Why don't you buy her?"

"My interest is in helping save lives. I don't need or want to keep them."

"What about Free . . ." I take a deep breath. "And Rega?"

"Well, Free is different, and we'll wait to see about Rega."

Chill bumps spread up my arms and I can't find my voice.

"Hannah? Are you still there?"

"Yes."

"We need to leave pretty early to get to the fairgrounds by eight. Can you be ready by six fifteen?"

"I'll be ready."

Dad is in the doorway when I hang up. "Who was that?"

"Sophia. She wants me to go with her to Ukiah tomorrow. They're auctioning off the horses from Haven Creek."

"That should be exciting."

244

"I guess."

"What's the matter?"

"She might sell Rega someday."

Dad looks at me. "Sometimes, no matter how much you love something, you can't hold on to it."

"I don't want to learn one of life's lessons here." I brush past him and run for the front door, but when I'm outside, I don't know where to go. It's a school day. The bus will be by in a few minutes. I don't care. I get my bike and head up Sequoia toward the stables.

It's so early that no one has been around to open the tops of the stall doors, but the horses nicker and whinny when they hear my brakes squeal. I go straight to Rega and Free's stall, unlatch the top of the door, and swing it open. Rega scrambles to her feet. I open the bottom half, step inside, and throw my arms around her neck. She holds still and hooks her head over my shoulder.

"She has to keep you. She has to."

Rega moves her lips against the side of my head. I'm leaning into her horse kisses when I hear a car turn into the driveway. I'm still not allowed in a stall with a horse—even Rega and Free—so for a second I feel caught. I look out, afraid it's Dillon. It's Dial-A-Ride.

I close the stall door behind me—top and bottom—and walk over to meet Dad. The driver opens the side of the van and lowers Daddy in his wheelchair.

"I'm sorry," I say when he's on the ground.

"I'm the sorry one. I'm never really there when you need me, am I?"

"Yes you are."

"Mr. Gale," John, the driver, says. "I have another pickup."

"Sure," Dad says. "We'll walk back."

"I've missed the bus," I say.

"The other customer is out Mitchell Creek. I could swing back and take you to school," John says. "No extra charge."

"That's nice of you, John," Dad says, "but how about you load me back in this thing. Hannah and I are going to town for breakfast, then she can go to school."

"Really?"

"Really."

"The Home Style Cafe? Like you and Mom and I used to?"

Dad gives me a sad smile. "We'll tip a chair up for her."

"What does that mean?"

"Save her a seat."

My hand goes to my necklace and I smile at Dad. "Yeah. She'll be there; I know she will."

33

SATURDAY, MARCH 3

Sophia pulls into the driveway a little early. I hear her truck and open the front door.

"Sorry, I wasn't sure how long it would take me to load our girl, but don't rush."

"Do you want to come in?" I say, hoping she won't.

"No thanks." She looks at her watch. "On second thought, you don't have any coffee going, do you? I drove off and left my mug by the sink."

"I think Dad's making some. Let me warn him in case he's not dressed."

I leave the door ajar, and race straight to the bathroom, grab Dad's comb, and run to the kitchen. "Sophia's coming in for coffee." I run water over the comb and slick down his wild hair.

"Damn. Why did you ask her in?" He didn't lower his voice and I wonder if she heard him.

"I was being polite," I whisper. "She wanted to know if there was any coffee made."

"Never mind, Hannah," I hear her call from the front porch. "We need to get going."

"Okay," I shout. "She heard you." I hit his shoulder with the dishtowel.

We're waiting at the end of our driveway for a couple of cars to pass. "Were you feeling okay on Thursday?" Sophia says. "One minute you were there and the next you were gone."

"Yeah. I just had other stuff to do."

She nods and pulls out. Even pulling the horse trailer, she drives faster than Sondra used to.

"How's your dad doing?"

"Better."

"That's good."

"Yeah."

It's been three weeks since the therapy session with Julia and though there's been no real change, he hasn't gotten worse. That's the same as better as far as I'm concerned. When I asked him about seeing her again, he said he will when he's ready.

We're taking Highway 20 to Willits, which is thirty-three curvy miles. It's slow going with the horse trailer and we have to pull over at nearly every turnout to let cars pass us. "I probably should have taken 128 and 253," Sophia says.

I have nothing to say one way or the other. I've never been on either, or to Willits or Ukiah, for that matter.

We ride for a while without talking. I expect she doesn't know what to talk to me about, and I don't have much of anything to say to her. We're strangers really, with only Free and Rega as a bond, but I get uncomfortable with the silence first. "How'd you get started helping horses?"

"It's a long story."

I shrug. "It's a long drive."

"I'm an only child and when I was eight my parents got divorced. Back then custody was always awarded to the mother unless she was a serial killer or something. I adored my father and wanted to live with him, but we only got to see each other on Tuesdays and alternate Saturdays."

"That sounds familiar. Dad and I only get to see Jeffy every other Saturday." I don't tell her that it's getting harder and harder to get him to go at all. Sondra's mother makes our visits so miserable.

She glances at me. "Then you know how unfair it feels."

"Yeah, I do."

"Anyway, by the time their divorce was final, my parents hated each other and I became like a chunk of taffy pulled back and forth between them. Dad bought me anything I wanted and Mom never told me no. I guess I read *Black Beauty* or something and got it in my head I wanted a horse. The very next week, Dad surprised me with a palomino pony. I named her Annie."

There's another line of cars behind us, so Sophia pulls over to let them pass. Even when we're back on the road, a minute or so passes without her saying anything.

She finally takes a deep breath. "I can't tell you how much I loved that horse. She was the only honest thing in my life. I was convinced my parents were just using me to hurt each other, but not Annie. I knew she loved me."

I wait, but it seems she's not going to finish. "How long did you have her?"

"A year maybe."

"What happened to her?"

"I don't know." A tear forms and rolls down the side of her face.

I look out my window. We're at the top of the Coast Ranges, just before starting down into Willits. There are beautiful green hills as far as I can see. "I'm sorry," I say. "I shouldn't have made you talk about her."

"It's okay. It's the not knowing what became of her that hurts the most."

Sophia pulls off to let the traffic pass us again. "It's gorgeous up here, isn't it?"

I nod.

"Something scared Annie one day and she bucked me off. She didn't mean to and I wasn't hurt, but my mother saw the bruise on my butt and threatened to take my father to court and make it so he couldn't see me again. He got rid of Annie and three months later he was killed in a head-on collision with a logging truck. For years—maybe even to this day—I blamed my mother for the loss of them both. He was killed on a Tuesday when he would have been at my riding lesson with me." She looks over her shoulder, then pulls back out on the highway.

"Every horse I save is for Annie—and my dad."

Ukiah is another fourteen miles south of Willits. We've gone about five miles south when I see a sign for Ridgewood Ranch. Sophia must have seen me look at it.

"That's where Seabiscuit was from," she says. "Do you know who he was?"

"Of course I do. He lived *there*?"

"Yes ma'am, he did. He's buried there, as I recall. A church group owns the property now and they put a nice statue of him by the school, and hung all kinds of pictures and memorabilia on the walls of the cafeteria."

"That is so cool. Maybe Dad and I can come over someday."

She smiles like I'm cute, or maybe it's some other kind of smile; I can't tell because she doesn't actually look at me.

Ukiah is the biggest town in the county, though that's not saying much. The fairgrounds are at the junky north end of town, near all the fast-food places and tacky strip malls. Rows of horse trailers are lined up. Sophia parks at the end of a row and we get out. Sweet-thing's hooves have healed and she's gained another hundred pounds. Sophia gave her a bath and sprayed her coat with Avocado Sheen before she picked me up. Last week Meg shaved all the horses, leaving the hair a little longer where their saddles go and to form designs on their rumps. Super Dee has a shooting star on one hip and a four-leaf clover on the other. Sweet-thing has a heart with a jagged line down the center like it's been broken. She whinnies as Sophia backs her out of the trailer. Her head is up, ears forward, nostrils wide open to the smells. Now that I know about Annie, I don't understand how Sophia can be sure someone kind will get her—that the cracked heart on her hip isn't an omen of more heartbreak to come. I'm glad she can't know that the person she's learned to trust is letting a stranger buy her.

Maybe Sophia thinks the same thing. "It will be okay," she whispers to Sweet-thing, but tears roll out and cling to the mascara in her bottom lashes.

"I don't understand why you don't keep her."

"Right now, I don't either, but I have to make room for the next one."

"What next one?"

"The next dying horse." She leads the way; Sweet-thing and I follow her into the fairgrounds.

There are four corrals, each with seven or eight horses in them. As we weave our way through the crowd, I slow at each one looking for the little filly. I see a small, reddish brown horse among the larger horses in the last pen and leave Sophia for a better look. The horses are so much healthier than they were in December, and I'm thinking I might not recognize her. But there she is, watching me like she did three months ago. She's grown a little taller and has filled out, but I know it's her by the white butterfly on her forehead. I step up to the side of the steel-tube fencing and put my hand out like I did that day at Haven Creek. She comes forward and presses her nose against my palm. My heart swells to the point I think I may choke on it. "You remember me."

"She'll sell in a flash."

I turn. An old man is at my elbow. His cowboy hat is too big for his head and it causes his ears to flare under the weight. "How do you know?"

"Ain't nobody here knows more 'bout horses than me."

"How much do you think they'll want for her?"

"Whatever the market will bear. She's young and clearly don't need no gentling," the man says.

I'm rubbing the filly's left ear.

"If I was in the market—and I ain't—I'd go eight hundred, maybe a thousand." He grins, then sees the look on my face and tries to cheer me up. "You never know. Lots of nice horses here. Maybe she'll go cheap."

The horses in the next corral move in a nervous group away from the gate as someone opens it and leads Sweet-thing in. I see Sophia pause for a moment, lower her head, then turn and walk away.

The number nine is on a piece of duct tape attached to Sweet-thing's halter. It's the same number she had spray-painted on her rump at Haven Creek. I remember that it is Sophia's favorite. My little filly's number is fourteen— my age.

There is a shrill noise from a microphone, which star-tles the horses. Somewhere a voice booms across the fair-grounds, "Ladies and gentlemen, the auction has started. Qualified buyers have thirty minutes."

Along one side of each corral, clipboards—one for each horse—have been attached to the fence with twist ties. People push forward looking for the number of the horse they want to buy.

"Bids go up in five-dollar increments," the announcer says.

I find number fourteen's clipboard. Someone has already written seventy-five dollars down and next to that is the number 45. I look at the clipboards on either side. Bidder 45 has bid on those horses too.

Two women are standing beside me. "Who is number forty-five?" one of them says.

"Something's fishy. He's going down the row bidding on every one of them and nothing about him smacks of knowing jack about horses."

"I wonder if they checked him out?" the woman says to her friend.

I think of what Meg told me about kill buyers going to auctions to buy horses for the slaughterhouse. What if that's who he is? I break out of the circle of people around this corral and stand on tiptoes. It's a moment before I spot Sophia signing some papers at a table nearby. I run over and tap her shoulder. She's been crying. "I was looking for you," she says. "I'm ready to get out of here."

"I need a favor."

"Okay," she says, but starts toward the truck. When I don't move, she stops.

"Will you loan me some money?"

"Sure. How much do you need?"

"I don't know for sure."

"If it's for a hot dog, why don't you let me take you to lunch? I owe you that much."

"I'm not hungry."

"What then?"

"I want to buy one of the horses."

Sophia shakes her head like it's an automatic no. "I don't ..."

"Please. It's one of the babies. She remembers me from the rescue."

"Look, Hannah, the young ones are going to bring the highest price. It could be a thousand or more. Where are you going to get that kind of money?"

"She's only seventy-five right now."

"The bidding just started."

"The person who bid on her is bidding on a lot of the horses. I heard some ladies talking about how strange that is. He may be a kill buyer."

"There are no meat men here. This is a Humane Society auction."

"Please. Let's go back and see. Maybe nobody'll top his bid and we can wait 'til the last minute and get her for eighty or a hundred."

"Winning the bid is just the beginning, Hannah. Where are you going to keep her and how will you afford to feed her?"

I open my mouth to answer, but she puts her hand up.

"Where are you going to get the money for grain and vet bills?"

"I'll get a real job."

"You're fourteen," she says. "No one will hire you

until you're sixteen, and even then it will be at minimum wage."

"My mother had a little insurance. It's for my college, but I can pay you back out of that, then when I'm sixteen, I'll get a job and replace it."

She starts toward the truck again, then turns and looks at me. "I'll tell you what . . ." When she opens her purse, my stomach does a flip-flop, but she takes out her cell phone. "Call your dad. If he says yes, I'll loan you the money."

I take the phone. My heart is pounding. "Do I have to put in the area code?"

"Yes. We're roaming."

"Ten more minutes," the announcer says.

I'm not sure what to pray for as I punch in our number. Do I want him to be drunk or sober?

34

THE SAME DAY

The phone rings and rings, which always scares me. I think about pretending that he's answered and said yes, when he suddenly does answer.

"Dad. Remember that little filly I told you about?"

"Yeah. I guess." He isn't slurring his words.

"I want to buy her." I clutch my necklace.

"Buy her? That's ridiculous, Hannah."

"You don't even know how much she costs."

"I don't care how much she costs to buy, we can't afford to keep her."

"I'll get a job." My voice is shaking.

"You've got a job . . ." He stops. "Don't you?"

I close my eyes. "I don't actually get paid," I whisper.

He doesn't say anything for a minute or two. "We barely make it now. Two entire disability checks go just to pay the taxes on this place."

"Daddy, please. I'll eat less . . . and . . . maybe you could quit drinking so much. That costs a lot."

There is only silence at the other end. I can't even hear him breathing. "I'm sorry," he says, and the phone goes dead.

Sophia takes it from me, snaps it shut, and puts it in her purse.

"Sophia, please buy her?"

"No, Hannah. She'll have a home. I only save the desperate." She puts her hand on my shoulder but I jerk away and start to cry.

"That's it, folks." A bell rings. "The bidding has ended. If you have a winning bid, please line up in front of the cashier over there by the trailer. Once again, time is up, no more bids will be accepted."

A number of people step out of the crowd and start collecting the clipboards. I take off running toward the truck and am crying against the hood when I hear the locks pop up. Sophia opens my door, then goes around and gets in behind the wheel.

I hear someone shouting directions. A trailer is being backed up to a chute. I'm afraid it will be my filly and want to look away, but I can't. A gate opens at the other end and a grown horse trots through. It balks at the door of the trailer and tries to turn and go back the way it came. A man reaches through the bars and gives its butt a whack. It clomps up the ramp. I get in the truck and don't look again.

"I'm truly sorry, Hannah," Sophia says, and starts the engine.

"Whatever."

Sophia sits for a moment, then kills the motor and turns to me. "Don't give me that *whatever* teenage malarkey. I've spent my life and a great deal of money trying to save the few lives I could. There are thousands of horses and millions of animals who are abused and need homes. Because you got attached to one, you think the world should stop. Grow up, Hannah. My heart is broken too, you know."

I look down at my hands, open in my lap. The right one still shows the imprint of glass and wire. I'm thinking I hate her, when the first tear lands in my palm. She pulls me into her arms and hugs me. I hug her back.

There's only one person left to be mad at. I slam the front door and take the stairs two at a time.

"Hannah?" Dad calls.

I don't answer. He can't do a thing to stop me unless he puts his leg on.

"Hannah. I want to talk to you."

"Well, I don't want to talk to you," I shout from the top of the stairs.

"Surely, you understand we can't afford a horse."

I go to the railing. He's in his wheelchair at the bottom

of the stairs. "I do everything for you and you couldn't do this one thing for me?"

"What about Rega, Hannah? What are you going to do if Sophia decides to sell her? Are you going to blame me for that heartbreak too?"

The pain of hearing her name makes me feel stabbed. It's not that I've forgotten about Rega, it's just I have more time to plan for her. I look down at him and see grief in his eyes, see how it must have broken his heart to say no to me. "I'm sorry, Daddy."

"I am too, Hannah. I really am."

Today is Sunday, but I skip going to the stables. Sophia will be there and I'm not ready to be around her yet. I've lost the filly. I know that, but I don't care about all the adult reasons we can't have a horse. When it comes to Rega, I'm not leaving this up to any of them to decide. Sophia's right about one thing. I have to figure this out and be ready next time.

On Monday, I cut my last class and sneak through the senior center. To get to McDonald's I have to cross the new Noyo Bridge. It trembles as the traffic whooshes by. About midway across, I look down at the harbor and the restaurants Dad used to take Sondra and me to when they were first married—Silver's, Captain Flints, Chapter and Moon, and Sharon's by the Sea. Dad said she worked too hard to have to come home and cook for us. I haven't thought about those dinners in a long time. Dad told dumb jokes and Sondra would laugh to please him. I thought she was silly. Now that she's gone, I miss her.

McDonald's is on the next corner. I go to the counter and order some fries, then ask the girl if they're hiring.

She shrugs.

After a moment of her just looking at me, I ask, "Could I have an application?"

She shrugs again. "I'll get the manager."

A kid just a little older than I am comes toward the front counter, followed by the girl. "May I help you?" he says.

"I'd like to apply for a job."

"We don't start hiring again until the summer, but I'm happy to give you an application."

"That would be nice, thank you."

He smiles, leaves, and comes back in a minute with the application. He hands it toward me, but doesn't let go. "You're sixteen, right?"

"Yes," I say without blinking.

"There is a place on the second page for a parent's signature to that effect. Just have one or the other of them sign it—in front of a notary."

"I will. Thank you again."

There's a trash bin just outside the front door. I stand

near it to finish my fries, crumple the application, jam it into the greasy red cardboard cup, and throw them away.

The Surf Motel is between McDonald's and Harvest Market. I cross the street and walk down the motel driveway.

The story is the same, except the woman there knew my mother and knows how old I am.

I'm standing on the corner of the highway to Willits and Highway 1. It's about a two-mile walk home and I'm trying to decide whether or not to call Dial-A-Ride. I decide it's a waste of money, look to my left when the light changes, and catch a glimpse of the Hare Creek nursery about a half mile up the hill.

"Sorry," the woman who is watering the plants says. "We don't really need anyone right now."

I bite my lip. Sophia was right. No one's going to hire me. "Well, thank you anyway." There are doves cooing from a cage in the back. "I like that sound."

"It's funny, I don't even hear them anymore unless someone mentions them." She's studying me, and I think she might be reconsidering, so I pick a few dead leaves off some of the plants on the table. "You look familiar. Do I know you?"

"I don't think so." A pot has tipped over. I set it upright for her.

"I tell you what, let me find something to write on and if something opens up, I'll call you."

"Do I have to be sixteen?"

"Not necessarily. We're a family business."

I follow her back to a little office, where she searches through seed packets and catalogs for something to write my name on, then through a drawer full of junk for a pencil. She holds them up and grins at me when she manages to find both.

"Hannah Gale," I say. "Gale—as in a strong wind."

"And a phone . . ." Her head comes up. "Are you Jeff and Jenny Gale's daughter?"

"Yes ma'am."

"I went to high school with your parents. Your mom and I were in 4-H together." Her eyes get glassy. "I'm sorry about her passing and about your dad." She puts her hand out. "I'm Donna."

We shake hands. "Look, we just had someone quit and I figured I'd pick up his slack, but it's not like I don't have a million other things to do. The job would be watering, weeding, potting and re-potting plants, plucking dead leaves." She smiles.

"That would be wonderful."

"I can't remember. You're fourteen, aren't you?"

"Yes. I was fourteen last month."

"Well, Hannah Gale of the Fort Bragg Gales. You've

got yourself a job. I can't afford minimum wage. Would five dollars an hour be okay?"

I want to hug her, but I don't. "I get out of school at two thirty. I can be here by three. Is that okay?"

"Sure. We close at five and we're usually out of here by five thirty or six. This gonna be okay with your dad?"

I nod, then think about not being able to go to the stables anymore during the week, when she adds, "Are you available on Saturdays, for a full day?"

I don't hesitate. "Yes ma'am." *There's still Sunday.*

I start doing the math. Eight hours on Saturday, two or three hours a day during the week. That could work out to over twenty hours a week—as much as four hundred dollars a month! Rent for a stall at Redwood Springs Stables is two hundred a month, and that includes the hay. "Can I start tomorrow?"

"Works for me."

"Thank you." I pull my necklace out and hold the blue glass up for my new boss. "Mom gave this to me for luck. I needed a job and now I have one."

"Glass Beach?"

I nod and drop it back down the neck of my shirt.

"Cobalt blue is the rarest find," she says.

I fill out a tax form and take the papers she wants Dad to sign. After that she shows me where the faucets are, how to coil the hoses when I'm done, and tells me not to water the succulents. It's about three thirty when we finish and I ask to use her phone. I'm a person with a job. I call Dial-A-Ride.

Ten minutes later, the van pulls up in front of the nursery. John is driving. I grin up at him. "I got a job."

"Good for you," he says, then glances in his rearview mirror.

It's not until I get in that I see Dad sitting in the back in his wheelchair. He's been pretty good about going to physical therapy, so I figure that's where he's been.

"What are you doing here?" he says.

"I got a job. If Sophia decides to sell Rega, I'm going to be ready. You can't say no if I have enough money, right?" I take the seat across the aisle from him.

"We'll see, Hannah. It still depends on how much you need to maintain her."

I open my mouth to tell him how much I'll be making but think better of it. "Are you coming from physical therapy?"

"No. From seeing Julia."

"You're dating her?"

"No." He snorts like I'd meant that as a joke. "She offered to counsel me pro bono."

"What's that mean?"

"For free."

I glance at John, who's turned in his seat, smiling. He's been keeping Dad's secret.

"With the horses?"

"Sometimes. Other times we just talk."

"If it's not just with the horses, what's she saying that's different from the VA doctor?" Julia's blond and beautiful—prettier than Sondra.

"I've got one more pickup at Harvest," John says.

Dad nods, then says to me, "Well, she's not starting with my toilet training and whether my mother coddled me. We're trying prolonged exposure therapy."

"What's that?"

"Every session is a detailed retelling of . . . you know . . . what happened."

"Why is that a good idea? I thought you were trying to forget."

"I was, except I can't." Dad's eyes get that faraway look in them I've seen a hundred times since the day we picked him up in Palo Alto.

"Well, I don't see how going over and over it can help. Seems like you'd want to forget."

"It goes against your intuition, I know, but it seems to be helping. I'm already sleeping better and—I don't know if you've noticed—but I'm drinking less too."

I thought he'd cut back because of what I said when I

called from Ukiah. And I got so used to hearing Daddy roam the house at night that if he doesn't I wouldn't know. It stopped waking me. "I've noticed, and I'm glad, but I still don't get how going over and over it helps."

"She's trying to disconnect my memory of that day from the emotional trauma it continues to cause. It's called habituation." He glances out the window. "That's what sacking out is supposed to do to a horse. You get them accustomed to something by doing it again and again." He smiles his sad smile. "Julia's better at it than I was, and if it works I'll be able to leave the house on Thursdays when the trash cans are out."

He's trying to joke, so I laugh, and then I get it. That's what Parelli is all about and why I've gotten so used to Dad guarding us at night that I've stopped hearing him and why Donna doesn't hear the doves.

35

THE SAME DAY

I need to start riding my bike to school."

Dad and I are eating dinner that night in front of the TV off trays like we usually do. Tonight it's a roasted chicken from Harvest Market and the baked potatoes stuffed with broccoli and melted Velveeta cheese that I microwaved.

"I don't think so, Hannah. There's no bike path on Highway One." He takes another bite.

"It's only the one stretch that's bad, and most of it I can miss by cutting through parking lots. What if I promise to walk my bike across the Hare Creek bridge?"

He doesn't say anything for a few minutes and I think his first no was the end of it.

"Well?"

"Okay. You can ride your bike to school." He puts his fork down like there is something more he has to say, so I wait. He looks at me. "I'm trying to get myself together,

Hannah. God only knows I'm trying. The reason I didn't tell you about seeing Julia is because I didn't want you getting your hopes up. I can't disappoint you if you have no expectations."

"But I do, Daddy. I hope all the time."

He makes a sound like he's been punched.

"It's okay," I say quickly, and put my hand on his shoulder. "It's paying off. You are getting better." There's a can of beer on his tray. It's his second. Before Sondra left us it would have been his third or fourth bourbon chasing a six-pack of beer.

He sees me glance at it. "I had no right to tell you no. You go to school, work a job in the afternoons, then come home and cook for us ..." His voice trails off. He's looking at the picture on the mantel of him and Sondra in front of the lighthouse the day they got married. "Remember when the three of us used to go to dinner and watch the fishing boats come in?"

I nod, but he's not looking at me. "Eat, Daddy. It's getting cold."

"I put in a call to the guy who was interested in buying my boat."

"No." I slap the armrest.

"Think about it. If I sell the *Hannah Gale*, I could buy Rega for you and you could keep her in the style to which she's become accustomed." He tries to smile.

I get almost the same jolt out of the words *buy Rega* as I did sticking the safety pin in the light socket when I was little. I'm just about to tell him yes, when I realize he shaved this morning, his shirt is clean, and his hair is combed. There's a voice I hear sometimes that I think is Momma's. I hear it now: *Your prayer answered, what about his?* I can have Rega, but it will end Daddy's chance to ever fish again. I shake my head. "No, Daddy. I'll buy her myself someday. The *Hannah Gale* is your Rega. We'll have them both."

Daddy tries to say something, but his voice cracks. He blinks and tries again, gives up, squeezes his eyes shut, and pinches the bridge of his nose.

"Hey there Hannah, where have you been?" Dillon asks when I get off my bike on the following Sunday. She's carrying a water bucket in each hand.

For some reason I think she knows everything and I don't want her to, but I'm not sure why. "Did Sophia tell you about the auction?"

"A little. She said you overheard someone talking about a guy bidding on all the horses. Kind of odd."

"Is that all she said?"

"I think so." She puts one bucket down in front of Bobby's stall and carries the other into Indy's, empties it into his trough, then comes out and closes his door. "So where *have* you been?"

"I got a *real* job." It comes out sounding like I'm mad at her for not paying me to hang out here all these months.

"Well," she says, "I'm happy for you." She goes in to fill Bobby's trough. "We'll miss you."

My stomach knots. *Why am I being snotty to Dillon?* "I can still come on Sundays."

She shrugs. "You're always welcome." She hangs the pitchfork in the shed. "By the way, I've got something for you." She goes to her truck and reaches through the open window. "I finally finished this, you want it?" She hands me *Seabiscuit: An American Legend.*

"Yes, thanks. I've seen the movie a dozen times and we passed where he used to live on the way to the auction."

"Yeah. Ridgewood Ranch. Sophia told me."

I take the book and smile, but I'm not so sure Sophia didn't tell her everything. And I realize why I don't want her to know that I begged and cried for a horse I couldn't afford to buy—or keep. Of all of them, I want Dillon to believe I'm ready to own Rega.

Rega's been in her stall too long. I move Free to a paddock with Rega prancing and bouncing like a ball at the end of her lead. The minute I slip her halter and lead off and slip out the gate, she races to the other end, then back, her stubby tail flying. She does two more loops before she starts to graze beside her mom. I watch them for a few minutes, then go to muck their stall and fill their bin with hay. She needs more time to burn off that excess energy before I try to get her to focus on learning anything new.

When I finish the chores and come into the paddock with her halter and lead, she runs off. "You're rotten," I tell her. I know the drill: approach and retreat. I walk toward her. When she backs away, I stop and turn my back and start to walk away. I hear her come up behind me, but when I turn, she trots off. "It's up to you, you little monster." I pretend to give up and head for the gate. She whizzes past again, then trots up and stands facing me. I fit her halter over her black little face, then attach her lead and open the gate.

I have my hand on her withers as we walk toward the arena. She starts prancing, so I do too, trying to synchronize my hop in the air to hers. When we're inside I switch her lead for a twenty-two-foot lunge line. Everyone leaves their Carrot Sticks in the traffic cones; I pull one out and start toward the center of the arena. Rega grabs the cone with her teeth and swings it back and forth like a dog with a wet towel.

We start with the Friendly Game, which I've played with her before. I've gotten as good as Dillon at flicking the string across her back and neck, but Rega wants to stand next to me, like I'm her other mom. I tap her nose and use the Carrot Stick to back her up. Of course she doesn't budge, so I press it to her chest and push until she does, then release the pressure instantly. "You're such a good girl."

The one thing I haven't gotten her to do is to pass through the strips of plastic, which she is afraid of. They're opaque and she can't see what's on the other side. I lead her over to where the sheeting hangs from an iron beam like a sliced-up shower curtain, part it and walk through, then stand on the other side holding my end of the rope. I pull it tight until she resists. We stand there.

Dillon is watching from the kitchen door.

"Which game is this?"

"One of the Squeeze Games," she says. "The act of going through it is basically the squeeze from all sides and from over and under. You know, I think her daddy may have been a Friesian."

"What's that?" I keep the pressure on Rega.

"Just my favorite breed of horse. They're from Holland and always coal black. If she is, her tail will get long, thick, and wavy, and her mane will too." Dillon leans against the door frame. "Her ears are a little big for a pure Friesian, but everything else about her looks like the real thing."

"Will Sophia want more money for her?"

Rega takes a step forward and I instantly let the rope go slack.

"If and when she sells her, Sophia is only going to care about finding someone to give her a good home. Nothing else."

"Do you think I could do that?"

"Absolutely. If you were older."

"Other kids my age have horses." I've tightened the rope again with just the right amount of pressure so as not to pull on Rega but not let her back away either.

"And they have parents to foot the bill."

I look at her and she shakes her head. "I shouldn't have said that."

"My dad offered to sell his fishing boat last night and buy Rega for me."

"That's a wonderful offer. What did you say?"

Rega puts her nose against a sheet of plastic. I let the rope go slack again. *Nose, neck, maybe the feet.* The Parelli mantra. If a horse is brave enough to put his or her nose on something, then maybe the neck will follow, then maybe the feet.

"I told him no."

Dillon hops up onto the pile of blankets by the door. "Did you? Why?"

I put pressure on Rega again, but she bobs her head. I hold tight and when she takes another step toward me I let the rope sag between us. She's so close to coming through, her breath moves a strip of plastic.

"Dad doesn't believe he'll ever fish again. He only pretends he does for my sake. If I let him sell the *Hannah Gale*, he'll know I've given up on him too."

"Do you know why it's important for Rega to walk through that curtain?" Dillon says.

"Not really."

"It's all about trust and confidence. She has to learn you won't ever ask her to do something that will hurt her, but because she will pass through of her own accord, it will build her confidence."

Rega puts her nose between two of the strips of plastic, then her neck, then pulls back and rears. I hang on and release the pressure when she settles down again.

"You are doing the right thing for your dad. Just like Rega, you hold him in place until he makes a bit of progress, then you hold him in that new place."

I feel the burn of tears and close my eyes against them. When I open them again, Rega has pushed her little black head through two strips of plastic. She kicks up her heels and pops through on my side.

"Bingo," Dillon says. "Now ask her to do it again."

36

WEDNESDAY, JULY 4

July 4 isn't a good day for Dad. This Fourth we're home with all the windows closed waiting for the explosions that will start as soon as it's dark. Last year he was drunk and still had a full-blown flashback when someone drove by firing a gun in the air. This year Dad's determined to stay sober.

The CBS news is on, but I haven't been paying much attention. I don't like watching the news anymore.

Dad's in the kitchen getting only his second beer when the commercial ends and a story starts about the horses that pull the caissons at Arlington National Cemetery. Caissons carry the caskets of dead soldiers to their graves. I'm glad he's in the kitchen, but then they start talking about how they also use the horses for therapy. A picture of a man in a Marine Corps T-shirt and blue shorts comes on.

He's on horseback and he has a stub of leg a little shorter than Dad's.

"Daddy. Look at this."

"I'll be there in a sec."

"No, hurry."

Dad had turned down the sound and I can barely hear what the reporter is saying. I look for the remote, but he must have it with him in the kitchen. I get up and try to find the volume control on the TV itself. By the time I get the sound turned up, the story is nearly over. ". . . horses that usually pull caissons during military funerals at neighboring Arlington National Cemetery," the reporter says, "are helping soldiers such as Ramsey in their long struggle to learn to walk again, to regain strength, and to believe in their new limbs."

"What's up?" Dad rolls to his spot at the end of the sofa.

A commercial has started. I shake my head. "Nothing," I say, but in my mind, I see Jack standing behind Dad, his nose against his neck, and I remember the look on Daddy's face—that moment of peace, and at Julia's when he stood with his forehead against Babe's.

I can't get that story of the caisson horses out of my head. I went online to look for a place near us that might be doing the same thing, but the closest one I could find was in Petaluma, not far away but too far to get to on a regular basis. The next Sunday I ask Dillon: "Did you see the news on Wednesday?"

"I don't think so. Why?"

"They did a story about using horses to teach vets who are missing limbs how to walk again."

Dillon is washing Bobby, who is trying to munch my face. "I've heard of that . . ." she says, then releases the nozzle grip and looks at me. If we were in a cartoon, a lightbulb would come on above her head. "I can't believe I haven't thought of this before."

"What?"

"They do that kind of therapy at Ridgewood Ranch."

"Where Seabiscuit lived?"

"It's a new program, so I'm not sure they're certified yet, but it would be worth a call."

The minute I get home, I log on and Google *Ridgewood Ranch*. There's a history, but nothing about therapy with horses, and no phone number. I get offline and call Dillon's cell.

"Do you have a phone number for Ridgewood Ranch?"

I hear her flicking pages, like maybe a phone book, which I hadn't thought to look in myself. I copy down the number she gives me, thank her, then without stopping to think about what I'll say, dial it. There is a single ring. "This is Erin."

I hadn't expected anyone to answer. "Hi," I say lamely.

"Hi," Erin says.

"Do you work at Ridgewood Ranch?"

"I do. Who is this?"

"My name is Hannah Gale and my dad lost a leg in the war. Can you help him?"

For a moment, there's silence at the other end. "He'd be our first, Hannah. We've worked with hyperactive and autistic kids, Down syndrome, and MS patients, but so far we've never had an amputee. Do you think he'd mind being a guinea pig?"

"No. He won't mind," I say while trying to think of a way to even get him there.

"How about this Saturday. About nine."

"I work on Saturdays."

"Is there any time during the week?"

Since school let out, I've been working half a day, every day at the nursery. "Let me ask my boss, but I'll bet she'll give me Saturday off."

"Well then, Saturday it is, and if something happens just let me know. Is nine okay?"

"Could we make it a little later? We'll be coming from Fort Bragg and have to take a bus."

"We'll just see you when you get here. How's that? Do you know where we are?"

"Uh-huh."

"Okay, then. See you next Saturday."

"Erin, are any of the horses related to the Biscuit?"

"Only about half of them."

There's only one bus over to Willits and it leaves too early. The Skunk Train, which is mostly a ride for tourists, does go all the way to Willits, but it costs too much. I'm pretty bummed when I get to the nursery in the afternoon.

"You know," Donna says when I ask her about having Saturday off, if I can find a way to get there. "Mel goes to the plant wholesalers most Saturdays, maybe he'd be willing to give you a lift."

"Don't see why not," Mel says. "I'd enjoy the company and I can pick you back up on my way home."

I'm sitting on the sofa reading *Seabiscuit* again when Dad comes in from seeing Julia.

"Whatcha doing?" He heads for the fridge to get a beer.

"Reading *Seabiscuit*. Did you know that he never won any of the Triple Crown races?"

"He was never entered, was he?"

I shake my head. "But he could have. He beat War Admiral, who'd won all three that same year." I close the book. "Do you know what a sea biscuit is?"

"I do. It's a cracker sailors used to eat."

"I'd like to go see where he lived. Would you?"

"Yeah. Someday."

"How about Saturday? Donna's husband is going to Santa Rosa, and he'd drop us off and pick us back up in the afternoon."

Dad's recently started wearing reading glasses. He lowers his head and looks at me over the top of them. "What have you got up your sleeve?"

I shrug. "I just thought you'd like to get out of here for a day."

He opens his *Newsweek*. "Maybe some other time."

"He doesn't go all the time. Please."

"Hannah, stop. I've had a long day."

"No. We have to go this Saturday."

He takes his glasses off and rubs the dents in the bridge of his nose. "Why?"

I bite the inside of my lip. "They do horse therapy."

He shakes his head. "I've been doing that right here."

"It's not the same. This is physical therapy . . . to help you learn to walk again."

He glances at the umbrella stand full of prostheses, shoe ends up. My eyes follow his. "My stump is still too sensitive."

"That's 'cause you don't try. It's like going barefoot. It takes not wearing shoes to toughen your feet up enough not to have to wear shoes. Promise you'll think about it, okay?"

"We'll see."

About an hour later, my stomach starts to growl. I turn off the computer. From the railing I can see him sitting in his chair, his head bent. On the sofa beside him are two of his three prostheses. He is working on fitting the third over his stump.

He must hear me on the stairs, because he says, "How's riding a horse supposed to help me with this bloody thing?"

"The TV said it helps amputees regain their balance."

"The TV?"

"Yeah. I saw it first on the CBS news. About the horses at Arlington cemetery being used to help veterans learn to walk again."

"How'd you find the place in Willits?"

"Dillon told me about it."

"But you don't know how it helps?"

"We'll ask Erin when we get there."

37

SATURDAY, JULY 14

R idgewood Ranch is in a valley at the end of a road that winds down through lichen-covered oaks. The hills are golden from lack of rain.

Erin asked us to meet her in front of the cafeteria. "Can't miss it," she told me.

Mel drives right to the door. He's getting Dad's chair out of the back of the truck when an old white car pulls up behind us. There is a bale of hay in the trunk. A beautiful woman in her twenties gets out and waves. Her hair is long, blond, and curly. The breeze picks it up and lifts it like a mane.

I sometimes forget how young my father is. When I look at him, he's holding on to the door frame until Mel gets the chair open and behind his knees, but he's staring at Erin. There is something in his eyes that makes me feel like a gutted fish. He's a tall, handsome man—a man that someone like Erin might think is cute. He sits down heavily in his wheelchair and lowers his head for a moment.

"I'm Erin." She shakes my hand, then Dad's. "Whitney is on her way."

"Whitney?" I say.

"Sorry. I guess I haven't given you any details. Whitney is our physical therapist. I'm a therapeutic riding instructor."

Even though I asked the question, she's talking to Dad. I like that.

He smiles up at her, shyly, and I realize that his smile used to be bold. "Come on." Erin crooks a finger at us. "I'll give you the tour."

We take the road past where Mr. and Mrs. Howard, the owners of this ranch and Seabiscuit, lived. There's an old swimming pool and cabana on one side and a statue of the Biscuit in the yard in front of the Howards' house. The grass is thick and too tall to push a wheelchair through, so we don't go to read the plaque.

"Whitney called from the stables, so we'll walk down to meet her, if that's okay."

I like that she said walk. Lots of people avoid the word in front of Dad.

We head down a long narrow lane toward the stables.

Erin's on one side of him and I'm on the other carrying his crutches. The prosthesis he hates the least is lying across his lap.

"I asked Hannah how this is supposed to help, but she couldn't tell me or how the horses are chosen."

"Whitney will explain how the therapy works. The horses are chosen first for their friendly dispositions, then for their build and gait. We don't want them too wide or not wide enough. The way they walk needs to be very smooth, so we use gaited walkers—horses that are able to amble rather than trot. We have five horses in the program and two retirees—Woody and Sassy. Woody has gone blind and Sassy is his seeing-eye horse. They are in the lower pasture." She smiles at Dad. "We're really excited about our program, though I hope Hannah told you that we've never worked with an amputee before."

Dad looks up at me. "No, I can't say that she did."

Erin stops. "I don't for a moment want you to worry. Whitney has had experience with veterans, we've just never had a client here. We use these horses with children who have all manner of disabilities. I promise you there is no risk."

"I'm sure it will be fine," Dad says.

We've reached a stable. There is another woman there, saddling a big chestnut mare. "This is Whitney," Erin says. "Whitney, this is Hannah and Jeff Gale."

She's older than Erin, with long gray hair. There's something motherly about her, but her grip when she pumps my hand is like iron. "This is Ginger—a Tennessee Walker. Have you ridden before, Jeff?"

"Not since I was a kid."

"Dad was a cowboy in Nevada."

"That's cool," Erin says.

Whitney leads Ginger over, but it's not until they stop in front of us that I see that one of the stirrups is missing, replaced by something that looks like a pouch.

"Jeff is interested in how the therapy works," Erin says.

"As you well know, Jeff," Whitney says, "losing a limb throws one's balance off. How long ago did it happen?"

"Thanksgiving of '05."

Ginger has lowered her head and Dad is stroking her face.

"In the war?" Whitney asks.

Dad nods.

"I'm grateful to you and very sorry. It's a hideous thing, but," she says, smiles, and claps her hands together, "we have a gorgeous day and we're in a beautiful and peaceful place." She opens her arms to the surrounding hills. "Soak this place in, Mr. Gale." She takes a deep breath. "It's one of the few places left that can heal what ails us."

Dad gives me a look—like what have I gotten him into? He's not used to anyone being this cheery.

The four of us, and Ginger, have started walking.

Just outside the corral is a platform. One side has a steep wheelchair ramp and the other side has steps. Ginger grazes on the deep grass that grows around it while Whitney explains what to expect.

"So, Jeff, the idea behind this is that people and horses walk using the same circular motion in their hips. On a horse, your body will move as if you were walking. That's important because for a year and eight months, your mind has adjusted itself to that missing leg. It no longer recognizes the mechanics of walking. When you sit on a horse it kind of reteaches your mind how it feels to walk again."

I'm listening, but I'm also watching Dad. I can tell he's been doing therapy with Julia's horses. He's totally different around Ginger than when I watched him with Babe and Gus. She's right beside his chair and his hand is on her neck, but otherwise he's not paying any attention to her.

"Here are your options," Whitney says. "We can wheel you up the ramp or you can climb the stairs using your crutches and prosthesis. I would rather you not wear your leg when you ride—at least not this first time. My husband designed this pouch for your stump. I think it will make sitting in the saddle more comfortable and you'll feel more secure. Is that okay with you?"

Dad nods. "Just don't tell me to break a leg, okay?"

We all laugh, Whitney the loudest.

He's wearing chino shorts. His right leg is still big and muscular. What remains of his left leg is thinner and the gauzy white stump-cap shows past the hem of his shorts. He puts his prosthesis on to walk up the stairs, and uses his crutches for extra balance. It takes some time for him to climb the five steps. I go behind him with my hand flat against his back. Erin leads Ginger around to stand parallel to the platform. He'll have to stand on his prosthesis to put his right foot in the stirrup. He rests for a moment, his hand on the saddle horn, then smiles at me—a don't-you-worry smile.

Whitney and I get on either side of him, our hands out to catch him if he falls. Using his left crutch as a brace, he puts his full weight on his left leg and grimaces. When he nods he's ready, Erin takes the other crutch, then helps him find the stirrup with his right foot. When he's standing in the stirrup, he swings his prosthesis across the saddle, then pulls himself up until he is centered on Ginger's back. Whitney goes down the ramp and removes his artificial leg, then helps him fit his stump in the fleece-lined leather pouch. She adjusts it until it is exactly the right length. Erin is on the other side adjusting the stirrup.

"Now take a deep breath," Erin says. "Remember you are sitting on a big old cushion. Nothing personal, Ginger." She kisses Ginger's muzzle.

"Hannah, will you be a side-walker?" Whitney says.

"Sure." I swing under the platform railing and jump off into the grass. With Dad holding on to the saddle horn, Whitney on his left, and me on his right, Erin leads Ginger into the corral.

"One of the things you've lost being in the wheelchair is your core muscle strength, so you want to stretch up through the abdominal area and through the rib cage and lift everything up."

Daddy straightens in the saddle.

"And the most difficult challenge will be regaining your balance," Whitney says. "Riding a horse forces you to adjust your waist just to keep from falling off, which builds strength and balance in your body's core. Let your hips get into the horse's gait: up when her right hip is up, down when it's down. Concentrate on the rhythm. Good." She smiles. "You're doing great."

On Ginger's back, Dad's once again the giant he was when I was little. He smiles down at me and his eyes crinkle, and, though he doesn't say anything, I know he's grateful.

You're welcome, Daddy.

38

WEDNESDAY, AUGUST 22

I'm fourteen and a half today. I don't know why that seems important, but I'm standing with the fridge door open drinking orange juice out of the carton and thinking about how fast summer has gone. School starts next week.

The phone rings and I nearly jump out of my skin like I've been caught; Dad hates it when I drink out of the carton.

It's Dillon. "It's supposed to get hot today. We thought we'd take the horses to the beach. You wanna go?"

I think for a moment, *How weird*. It's a Wednesday, for one thing. They usually do fun stuff with the horses on weekends. It's also strange that yesterday Donna told me I didn't have to come to work today. I asked her why, worried I'd done something wrong, but she just said I should start taking a little time for myself before I have to go back to school.

Weird or not, I say yes.

"Would your dad like to go?" Dillon asks. "We're taking two trucks."

"Maybe. I'll ask him. What time are you leaving?"

"About ten."

"Who all are you taking?"

"Dee and Bobby. And Sophia's bringing her trailer for Free and Rega."

"Really? Rega too?"

"We wouldn't take Mom and leave baby home."

"Dad!" I shout, then race around the kitchen getting out the frying pan, bacon, and four eggs. I glance toward the living room. "Dad."

"What?" He wheels out of the den. Even though he's been riding to Willits with Mel every Saturday for therapy, he still spends most of his time in his wheelchair at home.

"Dillon called. They're taking the horses to the beach. Wanna come?"

"I don't know."

"Come on. It will be fun and you can meet Rega." That stops me. Rega's thirteen months old and Dad has never even seen her.

"Won't I be in the way?"

"Of course not. Please." I make prayer hands.

"Okay."

"Cool." I pick up the phone and call Dillon's cell. "Dad said yes. Can you pick us up on the way?"

I've just finished putting the dishes in the sink when I hear a horn honk from the road. "Dad. They're here," I shout.

"So am I," he says from the doorway. He's wearing chinos and his prosthesis.

I wolf whistle. "Nice leg."

He laughs. "Wish they still matched."

"Does it really matter anymore?"

"No, sweetie. It really doesn't."

It's pretty far to walk on a leg he's still not used to, so I wheel him down the driveway. It's Sophia's truck that's pulled off and waiting for us. Her passenger window is down. "I've got the most room," she says. "Dillon went on ahead."

Her truck has a backseat. I open the door and help Dad get in, then fold his wheelchair and put it in the back. I climb in next to Sophia.

She reaches between the seats and shakes hands with Dad. "It's nice to see you again, Mr. Gale."

"Call me Jeff. Please."

To me she says, "Long time no see, girl."

Because I've been working, I haven't seen her since the auction. "I know," I say. "Is Rega in the trailer?"

"She certainly is. She trotted right in. You've worked wonders with her."

"Thanks. I've been teaching her Parelli," I tell Dad.

Rega hears my voice and nickers.

"That's her."

Even though Fort Bragg is on the ocean, most of the beaches are small and in hard-to-get-to little coves. There's only one really long stretch of beach, and it runs the length of the Ten-Mile Dunes.

Dillon and Meg already have Dee and Bobby out of the trailer when we pull to the side of road and park behind them. There's a breeze and the horses are standing, heads high, ears up, nostrils flared. Sophia laughs. "You can tell this is the first time any of them have seen the ocean."

I turn to grin at Dad, but he's looking out across the water. I get his chair from the back. He puts very little weight on his prosthesis, and steadies himself by holding on to the truck bed while I open it and place it behind his knees.

Sophia has backed Rega out and I take her lead while she goes back for Free.

"Isn't she beautiful?" I run my hand over her neck. Her lips find my left ear and flick around in my hair.

"She's gorgeous," Dad says. He puts his hand out for Rega to smell.

Dillon comes over with two stiff leather braces, kneels and puts one, then the other on Rega's front cannon bones between her knees and her pasterns just above her hooves. "What are those for?"

"Her tendons will be flexible for years yet. These will keep her from pulling them in the soft sand."

Everyone is standing around looking at me and smiling about something. I have my back to Dad and when I turn to see if he's in on the joke, he stands up, folds his wheelchair, and puts it in the cab behind my seat, then slams the door.

"Let's go for a walk, shall we?"

I nod. I'll cry if I speak.

"Look at that man's leg, Momma," a little boy says. He's riding a bike with training wheels along the sidewalk.

"It's rude to point." His mother thumps his helmet. "Sorry," she says to Dad.

"He lost it fighting in the war." I'm so proud of Daddy right now, I could burst.

Her lips compress and for a moment I think she may say something mean, but she says, "Thank you."

There's an old paved logging road that parallels the street where we are parked. The others lead the horses through the ice plant that grows between them.

"We'd better stick to the pavement," Dad says.

"Are you sure you're okay to walk this far?"

He smiles. "Pretty sure."

"The therapy riding is really working?"

"It certainly is. This thing is still a bit uncomfortable, but I'm getting used to it. I've even ridden wearing it."

About a hundred yards north is a gravel parking area. There's a paved trail that connects the street to the logging road. Dad and I cross and walk along behind the others. Rega looks like a Chihuahua surrounded by Great Danes.

A couple of years ago a winter storm washed out nearly two miles of the road, leaving a jagged asphalt edge and a thirty-foot drop-off to the beach. About twenty yards short of where the pavement ends, people have cut a deep trail down to the beach. Dillon and the others are there with the horses, waiting for Dad and me to catch up.

"I'll wait for you here," Dad says.

"Hannah, will you take Rega?" Sophia holds her lead out. "She's too bouncy for me."

I was hoping she'd let me take her. "Sure."

Sophia starts down the deep gully leading Free.

I haven't entirely forgiven her for not loaning me the money to buy the filly. At least it made me get a job, and I've saved two thousand and ninety dollars so far.

"By the way, Hannah." She looks back at me. "Do you remember what *el regalo* means?"

Dillon, Meg, Sophia, and Dad are smiling at me.

"Yes . . ." My heart starts to pound. "It means the gift."

"Exactly. Happy half birthday." Sophia smiles, turns, and continues on down toward the beach.

Tears swim in Dad's eyes. "Congratulations, honey."

I say, "Really?" even though I know it's true.

The others file past me with their horses. Meg kisses my cheek; Dillon pats my back. "She could never have belonged to anyone else."

Sophia would not have done this without asking him, which means he said yes. "Thank you, Daddy."

"You earned her, sweetheart."

I take my shoes off, then lead my horse down the gully. *My horse.* I turn and grin at Dad, who gives me a thumbs-up.

The big horses are freaked by the waves. They let themselves be led into the water, then, as a wave nears and prepares to break, they whirl and trot to shore. Rega is actually less afraid. I wade in and, without any coaxing, she follows, lowers her head, and tastes the salt water. Standing in the frigid shallows, I listen to the hissing of the sand and feel it being pulled from beneath my feet. When the first wave rolls toward us, Rega leaps sideways and bolts from the water. She stops when she feels the tension in the rope. I reel her back in. "Don't be afraid," I tell her. "I'll never let anything happen to you."

"Make them follow what they are afraid of," Dillon calls

to us. She and the others brought Carrot Sticks and are a little farther down the beach. They begin to play Parelli games. When the horses are sent in a circle, Bobby, Free, and Super Dee trot in perfect arcs until they get close to the water, where they canter to get past the breaking waves. Dillon, Meg, and Sophia move closer each time, until the horses, to make the complete circle, have to run through the water.

I stay where Dad can watch us and lead Rega back into the surf. When the next wave rises up to break around our feet, she tries to run, but I don't let her go as far this time. When the next one after that breaks, she makes a tight circle and ends up standing behind me. I lead her out again, and this time she swings only her butt around when water splashes up our legs. "You're my brave girl."

Rega nuzzles my shoulder. I glance up at Dad and remember imagining myself riding Rega along this very beach with him watching us from the dunes. It's almost like that, except he isn't in his wheelchair and he doesn't disappear.

"That's your grandfather, Rega. He's a fisherman." I put the side of my head against hers.

39

WEDNESDAY, SEPTEMBER 5

I wake, sit straight up in bed and listen. There's no sound except the ticking of my alarm clock. I used to wake like this when Dad was still rolling from room to room, guarding us, but he's back in his own room down the hall and, though he still has the occasional nightmare, that isn't what woke me. Outside the sky is just graying. *Thirty more minutes.* I fall back on my pillow, then sit up again. Something's wrong.

I go to my door and listen. Dad's snoring echoes off the walls. I have a knee on my mattress ready to climb back into bed when I suddenly know. I grab my jeans off the floor, jam my feet into my Uggs, and pull a sweatshirt over my head. Rega needs me.

I hear one horse screaming and the others whinnying, snorting, and kicking inside their stalls before I even see the stables. My heart thunders as I whiz down the driveway. *Please, not Rega.*

I can't tell who's in trouble, but I go to Rega's stall first and yank open the top half of the door. A rectangle of light floods the archway to their outside run. Free is near the back fence, rearing and striking at something she has trampled to death.

The screams *are* Rega's but she's in shadow made blacker because of the bright doorway. Something growls, then the rear end of a dog swings into the light. It's one of the dogs from across the street and his teeth are sunk into Rega's right front leg. I fling open the door, fall on the dog, and wrap my arms around its neck. Rega backs into the corner between the wall and her feed bin, dragging both the dog and me across the stall. His grip is iron on her leg. Pulling on him only hurts her more. I let go, jump to my feet, and run to the tool shed, Rega's terrified screams ringing in my ears.

By the time I get back with a pitchfork, Rega has slipped and fallen in her own blood. The dog still has her by the leg. I raise the pitchfork as high as I can and drive it into the dog's rear end. His muscles are so tense, it bounces off. I raise it again and aim for his middle. This time I feel it puncture his skin. He lets go of Rega and turns on me, snarling; her blood stains his teeth and gums. I attack him again, miss his head, and strike his back. He snaps at me, then dashes into the run with Free, who charges, rears, and strikes out with her hooves. From just over my right shoulder, there is an explosion. The dog lifts into the air, then hits the ground in a bloody cloud of dust.

It's the man who lives just on the other side of the fence from the stables. He lowers his rifle. "I expected a mountain lion."

I reach up and pull on the ceiling light string. Rega is on the ground, her sides heaving. Blood is everywhere. Its metallic smell fills my nose.

The man has a cell phone on his belt. When he sees me look at it, he hands it over.

Joanne's cheeks glisten when she looks up at me. "I'm so sorry, Hannah. I'll give her something to keep her quiet, but she's pretty torn up. Sophia said she's yours, so what we do is your decision."

"What do you mean?"

"The kindest thing would be to put her down."

"No." I drop to my knees beside her. Her breathing is ragged. I put my hand on her neck, which is sticky with blood. "She's mine. I won't let you kill her."

"Hannah, you have to think about what's best for her." Joanne settles back on her haunches and looks at me. "There are a dozen wounds and she's lost a lot of blood, but her right foreleg is mangled."

I can't breathe. I shake my head, afraid that if I can't talk she will take that for my okay and put her down. "You have to try to save her," I gasp. "You have to. I've got money. I can pay."

"Oh sweetie," Joanne says. "It's not the money. She's suffering."

"Please try. Please. I love her. Please."

For a long time I sit in the corner of the stall watching Joanne bandage her legs. When she cleans the right one, she plucks bone splinters out of the wound, then sews and stitches the muscles. "The only good news is there's no damage to her knee or above."

I don't hear a car but look up when I hear Joanne speaking to someone. Dad is standing in the stall door. I get up, step over Rega's hind legs and into his arms.

"I'm so sorry, Hannah," he whispers against my hair.

"Joanne's treating her," I say. "She'll be okay."

I'd lost track of time until the school bus went by. Joanne has sewn up all she can and rigged an IV. I'm in the corner of the stall with my arm on the rim of Rega's water bucket, my other hand on her neck. Free tries to nudge her, but I've strung a rope across the door so she can't get into the stall with us. I took off one of my shoes so the foot that's pressed to Rega's rump is bare. Free's muzzle bumps my shoulder. I lean my head back against the wall, rub her ear, and try to convince myself that Rega will be okay.

Dad left an hour ago. When he comes back, it's with lunch for me.

"How's she doing?"

I shrug. "Joanne gave her something for the pain. She's sleeping. The guy from across the road came for his dogs. Said he didn't know how they got loose. He didn't say he was sorry or anything, just some bull about how gentle they usually were."

Dad unwraps the sandwich he's made and hands it to me. "You have to eat something."

"I told him his dogs got loose all the time and barked and snapped at me." I start to cry again. I think about the day that boy nearly ran over one and wish now that he had. "I'm glad they're dead."

Dad leans against the wall with his hand on the top of my head.

Joanne comes again in the afternoon and gives Rega another shot for the pain and antibiotics to keep the wounds from getting infected. I stay with her the rest of the day until Dad comes back. "You need to come home, Hannah."

"I want to stay here."

"Come home for dinner and you can come back later."

A little while after Dad leaves, I pack extra hay under Rega's head and cover her with a blanket. "I'll be back in a little while," I tell her.

When I get home, Dad has Mom's recipe box out and is making shepherd's pie, which I used to love. He holds his arms out. I walk into them and start to sob.

"Get it all out, baby. No one deserves this cry more than you do," Daddy says. "All I've put you through for the last year and a half and now this." He holds me and lets me cry until there is nothing left.

Instead of the TV trays, he's set two places at our little dinette. He pulls a chair out for me. "You have to prepare yourself, sweetheart."

"For what?" I say, but I shake my head 'cause I know what he's thinking.

"Just in case."

"How do I do that, Daddy?"

"You accept that she might not make it."

"No. If I don't give up, Rega won't."

"You don't want her to suffer. You don't want to keep her here if she's in pain, do you?"

"How can you ask me that, Daddy? Don't you think between you and Momma, that I know the difference?" I push away from the table. "We should have made it easier for Mom, like they did for Jack, but I'm not giving up on

Rega just hours after it happened. I never gave up on you. I knew you could get better. There's a big difference between no hope and some hope."

After dinner, Dad drives me back to the stables. Rega is awake, but otherwise hasn't moved. She lifts her head, then relaxes when she sees it's me. Joanne must have been here while I was gone, because there is a fresh IV bag hanging from the spike in the wall. Rega's peed and I clean the wet hay away from her as well as I can, then pack more around her and cover her again with the blanket.

I've brought Dad's old sleeping bag with me. It smells of fish, and the outside is still sticky from salt-spray. Rega sighs heavily when I snuggle down with my head beside hers. For a long time, I lie awake watching the moon move across the sky between the tops of the redwoods. I can't stop thinking about Barbaro and how long it took him to die. His owners had lots of money. I try not to think about how much it took to keep trying to save him.

40

THE NEXT MORNING

The call of a raven wakes me. I open my eyes and stare up at the rafters, confused for a moment about where I am. Rega puts her warm muzzle against my cheek. She is standing over me and favoring her right foot by not putting any weight on it.

I want to hug her, but some time during the cold night, I zipped myself completely up in the sleeping bag and now the zipper is stuck. I work on it from the inside while Rega tries to push me around with her nose. I finally get an arm free and zip it open from the outside, then shed the bag like a cocoon.

I pull the string to turn on the overhead light. A little blood and pus has seeped through the bandage on Rega's right front leg, but the others look clean. She's covered with bits of straw. "Are you hungry?"

She bobs her head.

"Good girl." I carefully wrap my arms around her neck. "I told them you'd be all right."

The top of the stall door is open. I reach out and throw the bolt on the bottom half. It takes a couple of trips to collect a wheelbarrow, a muck-rake, a pitchfork full of hay, and a bucket of oats. I fill and carry a bucket of water to her stall, slopping it over my feet.

Rega buries her face in the bin of oats while I muck her stall. She looks at me once, her black face covered with hulls and dust. I get a curry comb and start to brush, careful to avoid all the places she's stitched. She looks okay except that she's favoring her right leg, putting her weight on the other three.

I'm just getting ready to ride my bike home when Joanne pulls in.

"She's up," I say.

"Sorry." She puts her second hearing aid in. "What did you say?"

"She's standing and eating."

Joanne pats my back. "Well, that is a good sign, but she's not out of the woods."

Rega snorts when Joanne enters the stall, blowing bits of grain all over her. "Hey, baby girl," Joanne coos. She strokes her neck and runs her hand down Rega's leg. "Let's have a look, shall we." She kneels and lifts Rega's foot, takes scissors from her bag and begins to cut away the bandages. When she peels them off, I can smell the wound.

Rega is so good. She stands very still while Joanne cleans it again and when it hurts her she only lowers her head and pushes a little against Joanne's shoulder. "Sorry, sweetie. Just a little longer."

When she finishes, she bandages her leg again, gives her another shot of antibiotics, disconnects the IV, then sticks a thermometer in Rega's butt.

"I don't know, Hannah," she says, withdrawing the thermometer. "She's got a temperature and that leg doesn't look good."

"She'll be fine," I say, but there's this terrible pain in my chest.

Joanne picks straw from my hair, then pats my cheek and nods.

Dad makes me come home, shower, eat, and get ready for school. I call Donna at the nursery and tell her what happened and ask for the rest of the week off.

Lacy, Melissa, and I always have lunch together. I'm sitting at our picnic table when they bounce up. Lacy takes one look at my face, sits down, and covers my hand with hers. "What's wrong? Your dad?"

I shake my head. "Rega."

After school Lacy gets off the bus at the stables with me. Rega's outside lying in the sun. She lifts her head, looks at me with glassy eyes and doesn't get up. I go in and sit beside her. The smell coming from the bandage on her leg is sickly sweet.

Lacy stays with us and I'm grateful that she doesn't expect me to talk. After a while, she leans, hugs me, and gets up to leave. "I'm so sorry, Hannah."

Tears come again. "She'll be okay," I say, but I'm not sure anymore.

I stay there with Rega, my back against the fence until the sun moves and we're in the shadow of the trees. Free stands nearby like she knows.

Joanne comes by to check on her and tells me she has held her own since this morning, but I see the look she gives Dad when he shows up to drive me home.

Dad and Joanne stand by the car, talking. After a couple of minutes they come toward me like a human wall. "Go away."

"Hannah," Daddy says. "She's suffering."

"No!" I scream. "You don't know that."

Joanne kneels beside me and puts her hand on my shoulder.

I jerk away. She's supposed to save her.

Tears roll down her cheeks. "You have to love her enough to let her go."

"I do love her that much," I sob. "She's not ready."

Rega watches us.

"How do you know that?" Daddy says.

"I don't know exactly, I just do. Didn't you know when Momma was ready?"

Dad nods. "Yes, I knew because she told me."

"Rega hasn't told me yet."

"Her leg is infected and the infection is spreading," Joanne says.

"Are you sure it's Rega you're listening to, sweetheart?" Daddy says.

"I'm sure."

Rega lifts her head, then gets up to her knees and stands. She tests her right leg a couple of times, putting a little weight on it, she limps to her stall. Inside she drinks some water, looks back at me, and begins to eat her oats.

Joanne sighs. "We'll see what tomorrow brings."

41

FRIDAY, SEPTEMBER 7

At home, Dad is quiet, which is good 'cause I don't want to talk. He fixes spaghetti for our dinner, but I'm not hungry and push away the bloody-looking pile of noodles. I keep seeing him for the first time in the wheelchair in Palo Alto and hear him say again, "If I'd been a horse, they'd have shot me." I look at the umbrella stand with two prostheses still sticking out like someone was jammed in there upside down. Daddy wanted to give up and I wouldn't let him.

The TV's on, but the sound is off. There's an ad on for motorized chairs for people who can't walk. I try to visualize something for Rega, like those walkers old people use. I glance again at Dad's leg assortment and my heart starts to pound. *Why not?*

"That's ludicrous, Hannah." Dad shakes his head. "There's no such thing as a prosthetic for a horse."

Because Joanne is deaf, I have to go through a special operator to call her. I've got the phone to my ear waiting for the TTY operator to answer. "Why not?"

Dad shrugs. "There just isn't."

"Yes, please. Dr. Joanne Willis." I give the operator the number, then put my hand over the mouthpiece. "I saw a dog once with wheels for back legs."

"Did it weigh a thousand pounds?"

"Rega doesn't weigh that much."

The TTY relay operator is on hold at the vet's office, waiting for Joanne to come to the phone.

"My point is she will one day."

"She's on," the operator says.

"Ask her if taking Rega's leg off will save her life."

"How do you spell Rega?"

I tell her and hear her typing my question into the TTY for Joanne to read.

"Short term, perhaps," the operators says for Joanne. "But, Hannah, no three-legged horse can survive. She'd have to rely too heavily on the other legs, and will surely develop laminitis. That's a disease ..."

"Tell her I know what it is."

"Look," the operator says. "Let's meet first thing tomorrow morning and talk about this, okay?"

———

I'm there when Joanne pulls in at seven thirty. Dad sits on the picnic table watching me brush Rega, who is holding her infected leg so only the edge of her hoof touches the ground.

Joanne has scissors and cuts off the bandage she put on last night. She looks at the seeping wound and shakes her head. There's swelling above it, which means the infection is moving up her leg. Rega smells Joanne's hair while she puts a fresh bandage on.

"Hannah, Mr. Gale, I've thought about this and I have some questions. First of all, the only good news here is that her knee is not involved. There's a chance if we take her leg off below the knee she will live. You have to think about what that will mean to her, though. She's fourteen months old—not fully grown. Her other legs will have to bear all her weight."

I open my mouth, but Joanne puts her hand up to silence me.

"Then there is the suffering and pain she will experience, and if she survives, you will have to house and care for a horse you can never ride. She'll be of no use to anyone."

"I don't care about riding her. Rega wants to live and she's trying very hard to get better."

"But a three-legged horse—"

"Not three legs. Four." I point to Dad's prosthesis.

Joanne shakes her head like she's got water in her ears. "I've never heard of a prosthetic for a horse." She looks past me at Dad, but I don't turn fast enough to catch his reaction.

I look back at her and see her shrug. "Let me call Davis."

"Who's Davis?"

"The U.C. Davis vet school."

It's a vet school. Of course they say yes.

We take Sophia's trailer and rig a sling so that Rega can touch the floor with her three good legs but not have to balance herself on the twisty ride from Fort Bragg to Davis, which is a four-hour drive away. Tomorrow they will decide whether it's her only chance or any chance at all. I promised Dad that if the doctors don't think taking her leg off below the knee will save her, I will let her go.

The next morning, on the ride over, I keep thinking about the ups and downs Mom and Dad must have gone through when she got sick. I was too young to remember, but I can imagine the hopefulness they felt when the doctors took off her first breast and said they'd gotten it all. Then cancer was discovered in her other breast. There were weeks and months of chemotherapy and radiation followed by a year of good health. I do remember the day she fell on the stairs. I found her when I came home from school. I was in second grade.

I also remember their faces when the oncologist came into her hospital room and told them it was in her bones. I didn't understand how final that was, but my parents did: The battle was all but lost. They found each other's hands, then turned to smile at me with empty eyes.

The doctors replaced the bone in her leg, which had crumbled and caused her to fall, with a metal rod and sewed her up. Radiation and chemo started again, and the wait for a bone marrow transplant match, which never came.

Dad's in front with Sophia. I'm in the back so Rega can see me. I think about leg bones: Mom's, Dad's, now Rega's. I twist so my back is against the door and put my legs out straight across the backseat so I can look at them. Rega watches me through her little window. I smile at her and hope my eyes don't give away how terrified I am for her and for myself if I have to keep my bargain with Dad.

42

MONDAY, SEPTEMBER 10

We get to Davis at 2:30. The vet school has a nice stall waiting. The vets will examine her later this afternoon and talk to us in the morning. I want to stay with her, but they say it's not allowed, so Sophia takes us to a motel near Interstate 80 and goes to see about adopting another Premarin mare in Galt where she got Free. I run a bath and sit in it so long, the water gets cold.

"Are you okay, sweetie?" Dad's at the door.

"Yeah." But I'm not.

When I come out on my prune feet, Daddy is standing at the window looking out at the parking lot. He turns. "How are you doing?"

I shrug and flop into a chair. "What if this isn't the right thing? I just don't know."

"Yes you do, Hannah."

"But I don't."

"You have to go with your gut, sweetheart. Just like you did with me. It was you who dragged me screaming and kicking . . ." He smiles. "As well as I could—out of my hopelessness."

"You'd have gotten better someday."

"Maybe, but I was awfully busy wallowing in my anger."

"Then you think this is the right thing to do?"

He takes my chin and lifts my head so I have to look into his eyes. "Honey, you said it yourself—of all people, you know the difference between no hope and some hope. If she's beyond help, you'll be the first to step in and let her go. I know that, and until then I won't let anyone try to make that decision for you." He hugs me, and I think about all the months it took to bring him back from where the war left him. His arms tighten around me.

"If she keeps having to have new prostheses as she grows, how will we pay for them?"

"I don't want you to worry about that."

I lift my head and look at him. "Not the *Hannah Gale*."

"I've already called the man who wants her."

I push away from him and shake my head. "I can't let you do that, Daddy."

"Yes you can. The first two times I thought about selling her were for the wrong reasons, but this is for the right one—and just in the nick of time."

"What does that mean?"

"The question of whether I'll fish again is nearly moot. There are too few salmon left anyway. I bet by next year the Feds will shut down the fishery."

"Then why does that guy still want to buy our boat?"

"He's going to use it during crab season and for whale watching during the migration."

"Are you sure, Daddy?" I watch his face for any sign of regret.

"I'm positive."

"What about making a living?"

"I've thought a lot about that. Congress is considering upgrading the G.I. Bill. If they do that, it will pay for me to go to college. In the meantime, I've been talking to Erin. She's NARHA certified and I got to thinking I could do that."

"What is it?"

"The North American Riding for the Handicapped Association. I could become a certified therapeutic riding instructor and if the Feds pay my tuition, I'll become a physical therapist too. Between Rega and me—two peg-leg pirates—we'll be models for beating the odds."

"Why didn't you tell me?"

"It's always easier not to change, Hannah. I guess thinking about it was fun, but doing it—well, I needed a push—a better reason. This is it."

318

"There's no question about removing the lower portion of her leg; it's lost its blood supply," Dr. Harris tells Dad.

"The horse belongs to my daughter." Daddy pulls me over to stand in front of him and keeps his strong hands on my shoulders.

Dr. Harris nods. "I have to tell you we've never amputated a leg for a prosthetic before," he says to me, then goes back to explaining things to Dad. "We've done a couple of mares that are to foal soon because their owners wanted to keep the mare alive long enough to deliver. But I've never known of an amputation for any other reason."

"Are you saying that's the only reason you would do it?" I ask.

"No. It's just the only reason that makes any sense. You'll never—"

I hold my hand up. "Please don't tell me how useless she'll be."

He shrugs. "Even if we can get a prosthetic made, you'll have to keep having new ones made until she's grown. It's going to be an ongoing expense."

I look at Dad.

"My daughter loves Rega and I love my daughter."

He nods. "I understand. I have a daughter too. I'm just saying it's going to be costly. If you understand that, we're willing to try."

"I'm . . . I was a fisherman," Dad says. "I'm selling my boat to pay for this."

"Is that wise, Mr. Gale?"

Daddy bends and pulls up his pants leg, exposing the metal rod from his shoe to his knee. "I lost it in Iraq. My daughter saved my life. I owe it to her to try to save the one thing she loves as much as she loves me. I want you to do the very best job you can. Is that clear?"

"Completely, sir, but it's not all up to us. She seems to be a very sweet horse, but she has to be willing to lie down a lot after the surgery."

"She likes to lie down," I say.

"Okay then. We'll give it a shot." He shakes Dad's hand, then mine.

"You're not in training, are you?" I ask.

"No, miss. I'm one of the professors."

I smile. "Okay then."

It's September 11, and Dad and I sit across from each other in a waiting room. I can't keep my eyes off the clock on the wall. It's like the one we have at school where the hand jumps to the next minute with a little click, which makes it seem like hours between clicks.

"What do you remember most about Nevada?" I want to talk so I don't have to think about what's happening to Rega.

"Not fishing."

"No, really. For a summer you got to live your dream of being with horses. What did you love best?"

"It wasn't anything like that, Hannah. I had no special fondness for horses."

I sit up. "You're kidding."

"No. Horses were just transportation. We were rounding them up to thin the herd. Most were shipped to slaughter. The ones I broke were young and salable."

Maybe I was already at an emotional breaking point, but tears come and spill down my cheeks. "I thought we loved horses. I went to the stables to watch them all the time to feel closer to you. Why did you lie to me?"

Dad leans forward and takes my hand. "Honey, I never lied to you. I was a fourteen-year-old kid who ran off to Nevada because I didn't want to come home every night smelling like my father."

I ignore the guilt in his eyes at having to tell me that. "But all this time, I thought you loved horses and loving them would make you better."

"Loving you made me better."

"But . . ."

He takes my hand and won't let me pull away. "I never had the chance to make the kind of connections with horses that you have. Jack was my first, just like he was yours. My experience with them was brutal. Don't you see? You can only love what you care about, and you only care about what you take the time to know. You understood that long before I did, but now I truly do love horses."

They started at ten. At three, Dr. Harris comes into the waiting room. "That's some little horse you have there."

"Is she okay?"

"She's fine. Would you like to see her?"

I wrinkle my nose trying to hold back tears, but it's no use.

Dad and I follow him down the long hall to the nice air-conditioned stall. When we come in, the room is crowded with men and women in green scrubs and paper booties over their shoes.

"These are a few of our students," the doctor says.

They part to let us through. Rega is standing on a cast with a wooden leg attached. She stretches her neck until my wet face is against her soft, warm lips. I put my arms around her and she folds me against her neck with her head. "You're supposed to be lying down," I whisper.

"She was until she heard you in the hall."

"We used her own tendons to make a pad at the end of the bone. She seems comfortable. She actually walked in here after she woke up, then lay down to wait for her friend." Dr. Harris pats my shoulder. "She'll be okay."

43

LATER THAT DAY

Sophia calls the motel to ask about Rega.

"She did great," I tell her. "They made her a temporary leg so she looks like Captain Ahab. She walked from surgery to her stall on it."

"When can she go home?"

"In a couple of weeks. Did you find another horse?"

"I'm afraid I did. I'm calling to see if Rega needs a ride or whether I can bring the new one home with me when I come to get you."

"Is it a Premarin mare?"

"Not this time. Most of the Premarin stables in Canada have closed, thank God, so the few horses this rescue place had were moved to their facility in Bakersfield."

"Then what did you get?"

"A racehorse."

"Cool."

"Wait 'til you see him."

There's no way to explain to Rega that I'll be back for her. I have to hope she knows. I lie beside her and tell her for the millionth time that I love her. She puts her lips against my left eye. When I was little and hurt myself, Momma used to kiss away my tears. Rega's horse kisses feel like that—except her lips cover the whole side of my face.

Sophia arrives a little after one on the twelfth with a horse as tall as Super Dee, but cow-hipped like the starving ones from Haven Creek. His eyes are dull, his coat is full of dirt, and his face is scarred from a halter burn. No one would guess he's a Thoroughbred.

"He looks too old to be a racehorse," I say.

"He's four," Sophia snaps. She's not mad at me. She's mad at whoever let this happen to him.

"Where'd you find him?"

"I outbid a lip-flipping kill buyer for him." Her eyes narrow. "There were twenty-eight more I couldn't save. I've never felt so helpless in my life." Her voice trembles. "These were headed to Mexico. Watching those terrified horses being loaded onto a cattle truck where they will ride for thousands of miles in hundred-degree heat with no rest and no water only to be . . ." She glances at Dad and stops.

"Only to be what?"

"Let's just say the lucky ones will die on the way."

I look at Dad. "Are you two protecting me?"

"No," he says.

"Well then tell me," I say to Sophia.

Dad nods his okay.

"Before they closed the slaughterhouses in the U.S., horses headed to slaughter were knocked out with a bolt gun, which shot a metal rod into the brain. It didn't always work and often they were still conscious when they were hoisted by a back leg and their throats cut . . ." Sophia closes her eyes for a moment. "It's still the way they do it in Canada, but in Mexico . . . Are you sure about this?" she says to Dad.

"I'm sure." I jam my hands into my pockets to keep them from shaking.

"In Mexico each horse is stabbed, often multiple times, in the neck with a puntilla—a knife used to sever its spinal cord. It's not meant to stun the horse or to render it unconscious, it's to paralyze it. It's then left twitching on the ground, unable to move or breathe, until it suffocates, bleeds to death, or is hoisted and dismembered alive."

A picture of Rega, terrified and calling for me, fills my

mind. I must have made some sound, because Dad puts his hands on my shoulders.

"Of all of them, why did you choose this one?" he says.

I tilt my head back and look up at him. For some reason stronger than pity, he's connected with this horse. I can see it in his face and I have an overpowering feeling that our lives have just changed.

"I don't know," Sophia says. "They were all terrified and racing around the inside of the corrals, but this one stood apart. In spite of his condition, he looked regal. Maybe it's his breeding, or memories of the winners circle. I don't know. He seemed determined to accept his death with dignity. I wanted to know him better."

"Do you know his name or anything about his racing career?" I say.

"No, but all racehorses have tattoos on the inside of their upper lips. We can trace him through that. And I plan to," she says. "They used him up and discarded him. I want to know who did that."

"What will you do if you find out?"

She shrugs. "I don't know. Write an editorial. Try to embarrass them. I took lots of pictures. Maybe start a blog in his name. Let people watch him recover."

"We should put Rega on the blog too. Maybe other people will try to save their injured horses."

"Maybe." Sophia looks at Dad. "When I called last night, Hannah told me you might start a therapy practice. If and when you do, would you consider taking Free?"

"Of course we would," I answer before Dad has time to think about the expense.

"I'll take care of her until then," Sophia says, "but I thought you could start working with her when you're ready. I'm going to have my hands full bringing my new boy back from the brink."

Rega stayed in Davis for two weeks just to make sure there was no leftover infection. The vet school found a place in New Orleans to make her prosthesis, which they donated. It turned out to be their second request. The first was for a pony named Molly who was rescued after Hurricane Katrina.

On September 29—the nine-month anniversary of Barbaro's death—Sophia lent us her truck and trailer to bring Rega home. When we pull into the driveway at the stables, Rega whinnies and the other horses answer. Free is alone in the paddock. When she hears Rega, she races to the fence, whinnying and rocking her head from side to side. Dillon, Sophia, Meg, and Joanne are all there waiting.

"Watch this." I lead Rega to Free's paddock. When I unclip her lead, she trots all the way to the far end, shaking her head and snorting, then canters back.

"That is astonishing," Dillon says. The others applaud.

"Dr. Harris told me the only thing wrong with Rega—thanks to the vet students—is she's addicted to peppermint candies."

EPILOGUE

MID-FEBRUARY 2008

I'm at the stables every afternoon, and now Dad comes with me. He works with Free and I play with Rega. Rega seemed to know how to take care of herself from the beginning. She doesn't like to sleep with her prosthetic on. When I'm getting ready to close her stall for the night, she holds her leg up for me to take it off. In the morning, she holds steady for Dillon to put it on for her. She wears a brace on her left leg for added support.

Today, Dad and I stand back to back in the center of the arena and watch Free and Rega run at liberty. When we look at their butts, they stop, come and face us. Dad gives Free an oat cookie and I give Rega a peppermint candy, then I put my hand on her withers, and side by side we trot to the wall and back, like we're dancing.

Lacy has moved her horse, Blue, here to Redwood

Springs and she's learning Parelli. Zoey, a girl in my class who is blind, asked to be Dad's first client. He isn't charging her anything because he doesn't have his NARHA certification yet, but she's a willing guinea pig. She comes every Saturday.

Rega is her favorite. She brushes and talks to her like they've known each other forever. Zoey uses her hands as her eyes and she gets me to close my eyes and just smell and touch Rega and Free and Sophia's new horse—Caspar. Sophia never did check to see who used to own him. She decided that knowing would fill her with hatred, so she named him after the town between here and Mendocino where she lives.

Zoey can tell the horses apart just by their smell and how their skin feels against her hands. I can't, of course, not like she can, but I can smell their cookie-breaths, the blankets and leather saddles, the dirt floor, even the arena walls.

When Dad was sick, I didn't want any friends. Last weekend, I had a sleepover. Lacy, Melissa, and Zoey spent the night. Dad had a nightmare, and woke us shouting, but once they got over the jolt of being awakened like that, it was Melissa who hugged me and said she was sorry, then grinned and said, "I can lick my elbow."

"So can I." I licked my finger and touched my elbow.

"Not like that." She stood up, put her hand flat on my

nightstand, leaned over, popped her elbow out of joint, and put her tongue on it.

Zoey ran her hand down Melissa's arm until she touched Melissa's tongue. "Yuck."

I laughed until I couldn't catch my breath.

Rega's leg still hurts her a little. When she's ready to quit playing, she comes over and wants her prosthesis off for a while. She likes getting a bath, so if it's not too cold I always lead her to the wash station, take her artificial leg off, and rest it against the wall.

It rained last night and the ground is damp. After Rega's bath, I put her leg back on to lead her to her stall. Behind us we leave our tracks on the damp ground—my boots, three hoof prints and one circle with a heart in the center. The people in New Orleans etched a raised heart into the bottom of her prosthetic hoof. It reminds me that Rega's heart may not weigh twenty-one pounds like Secretariat's, but it was always big enough to handle this.

Dad and I have two tickets for tonight's Knights of Columbus Crab Feed, so we're at Harvest Market getting horseradish, Dijon mustard, hot sauce, and light mayo for Dad's special mustard sauce. We divided the shopping list and I've found all the stuff on my half and am now going aisle to aisle looking for him. When I find him, he's in the produce section holding a bag of organic grapes. He's staring at the back of a woman over by the lettuces. It's Sondra.

I look from my dad to her and back. His expression is soft and sad like someone looking at pictures of dead people in a family album.

Sondra shakes the moisture off a bunch of spinach, drops it into a plastic bag, then into her cart.

"Banna!" Jeffy runs at me from between the stand of potatoes and the one of onions and wraps his chubby arms around my knees.

Dad looks at me—startled to find me beside him.

Sondra's head snaps around. There is shock on her face, but she recovers quickly. "Hello, Jeff. Hannah."

I squat down and lift Jeffy, hugging him and giving him slurpy-sounding kisses on his neck. "How's my big boy?"

"I'm three." He holds up four fingers.

I take his hand and kiss it. "Can you give Daddy a hug?"

He leans toward Dad, but covers his face with both hands.

Dad takes him in his arms, puts his nose against his head, and breathes him in.

Sondra wheels her cart over next to ours. "You look good, Jeff." She hugs me and brushes my cheek with her lips, then takes Jeffy from Dad and stuffs his kicking legs through the gaps in the wire kiddy seat. It's when she snaps the little seat belt across his stomach that I notice she's still wearing her wedding ring.

"You look wonderful," Dad says.

She ignores his compliment. "How long have you been . . . out of the chair?"

If she hadn't made herself scarce every other Saturday, or if her mother had bothered to mention it, she'd have known.

"Six months."

Her eyebrows go up. "Wow. That long." She touches his arm. "I'm glad for you, Jeff."

"Thanks." He looks down at her hand.

"Are you back fishing?"

"We sold the *Hannah Gale*," I say.

Sondra blinks. "Oh, Jeff. I'm sorry."

"Don't be. It went for a good cause." He smiles at me.

"Really?" She looks back and forth between us.

"For Rega's leg," I say. "She's doing great."

"And I'm just finishing the course work for my NARHA certification," Dad says. "Another month or two and I'll be a full-fledged therapeutic riding instructor, and Hannah has Rega, who's an inspiration to all sorts of people with disabilities—especially me."

Sondra smiles at me. "I read all about your little horse in the paper."

"We own Free now too." I grin. "You should bring Jeffy over and let me teach him to ride."

"Maybe when he's older." She bites her lip. "Well, it's great to see you both."

"You too," we both say.

"Grapes look good," Sondra says.

Dad's still holding the package of them. He nods. He's looking at her and she's looking at him, but she looks away first. "Well . . ."

"Sondra," I say.

"Yes." She turns back.

"Would you consider letting me babysit sometime? I'm fifteen now."

"I know. I have a couple of cards I'm late sending. Of course you can babysit."

"How about tonight?"

"I don't have any plans for tonight, maybe . . ."

"The crab feed is tonight, and Dad has an extra ticket."

She glances at the things in our cart. "I should have known. All the ingredients for your mustard sauce."

Dad's slow to get what's happening. "You remember?"

"Of course I remember. It nearly blistered the inside of my mouth."

I elbow him and grin. "The extra ticket?"

"I guess I do have one. Would you consider . . . ?"

We just stand there for a moment—awkwardly. Even Jeffy is momentarily still.

Geez, I think and almost open my mouth to say, *Well, will you*, when I see her shoulders relax. She smiles. If she were a horse, Daddy could turn now and she would hook on and follow.

AUTHOR'S NOTES

I was a National Airlines flight attendant—not a writer—in 1977 when I was preparing for my first flight from Miami to Paris and saw animal carcasses being loaded into the cargo hole of our DC-10. They were frozen and wrapped in plastic but looked too long-legged to be beef cattle. I asked John Behrens, a friend and head of the cargo department, what they were. "Horses," he said. And the consignee? A popular fast-food restaurant.

When I was growing up, I remember seeing an old horse and my dad saying the poor thing was ready for the glue factory. I loved the whole idea of horses, though I never had one. I rode a mop with rope reins, or a flat and folded old inner tube strung between two trees in our side yard. Still, I hated to think that being rendered down for glue was the fate of old horses.

In truth, most glues are now synthetic, but certainly when I was growing up, many different animal parts were used to make glue. The skin, bones, tendon, and other tissues were subjected to prolonged boiling to extract the gelatinlike collagen. Kolla, from which the word *collagen* is derived, is Greek for *glue*.

By 2007, I'd known for nearly thirty years that people in other countries ate horses. I even knew that during World

War II, we ate them here in this country, but it wasn't until 2007 that I learned that the slaughter of horses for human consumption and for pet food is a huge business. I was watching Katie Couric and the CBS news on June 8, 2007, when she did a segment on the slaughter of racehorses. The statistics were appalling. In 2006, 100,800 horses were slaughtered to satisfy the appetite for horsemeat, primarily in the countries of France, Japan, and Belgium. At the time that program aired, the last U.S. slaughterhouse had just been ordered closed in DeKalb, Illinois, by the now famous Governor Rod Blagojevich.

That same year, an additional 30,000 horses were sent to slaughter in Canada, Mexico, and Japan. By the time that June eighth story aired in 2007, an additional 50,000 horses had been slaughtered here and abroad.

According to the Humane Society of the United States, ". . . horses slaughtered for their meat come from many sources—wild horses, pet horses, racehorses, miniature horses—all have been used for this purpose. The number of wild horses rounded up and killed has depended on the legal protection afforded them at any given time. Most of the horses going to slaughter are losing racehorses, horses from riding schools and camps, stolen horses, and surplus mares raised on farms for use by pharmaceutical companies that produce hormone replacement drugs for humans, notably Premarin (which uses the urine of pregnant mares)."

The closing of the last U.S. slaughterhouse was met with praise, as it should have been. Unfortunately, it didn't mean there was a decrease in the number of horses being sent to slaughter, it only meant they were no longer being killed here, where they had some degree of humane protection. Instead, they are loaded into livestock trucks and driven either north into Canada, or worse, south into Mexico. The trips can last for hours, or even days, with horses crowded together without food or water and often through unbearably hot temperatures.

In the summer of 2007, I was still casting around for subject matter for a new novel. I'd written two books since the publication of *Hurt Go Happy*, but no one seemed interested in either of them, and I had two other false starts on a shelf in my closet. So on July 4, I was again plunked down in front of the TV watching the CBS news. This time the story that caught my eye was about the horses that pull the caissons at Arlington National Cemetery. When they are not transporting the caskets of our Iraq and Afghanistan war dead, they are used for physical therapy for soldiers who have lost limbs in the war.

With that newscast, all the pieces for a new novel fell into place. Just a year earlier, Barbaro, the 2006 winner of the Kentucky Derby, was expected to sweep the Triple Crown, taking both the Preakness and the Belmont Stakes. Instead, he broke his right hind leg coming out of the starting gate at the Preakness. The nation was gripped by the ups and downs of his battle to recover, until he was euthanized in January of 2007. As equally disturbing was the 2008 running of the Kentucky Derby, when Eight Belles, who came in second behind the winner, Big Brown, collapsed with compound fractures of both front ankles and was euthanized on the spot. Veteran *Washington Post* sportswriter Sally Jenkins wrote of Eight Belles: "She ran with the heart of a locomotive, on champagne-glass ankles." Blaming the breeders and investors, Jenkins claimed, "Thoroughbred racing is in a moral crisis, and everyone now knows it"

The moral crisis is that racehorses start racing before their skeletons can withstand the punishing pace and training. All racehorses are given a foaling date of January 1 in the year of their birth, which means they are sometimes less than two when their training begins. Barbaro was born on April 29, 2003. He won the Kentucky Derby less than a month after his third birthday. He never reached his fourth.

One of the other moral issues surrounding horseracing is that about 33,000 foals are born annually. If the foal is deemed unsuitable as a potential racehorse at birth, it is killed before it stands up. The stud fee must be paid if the foal stands and begins to nurse. Of the foals who survive this elimination process and are groomed for racing, the average life expectancy is about five years. They either fail to become income producing, break down from the stress and strain on their young skeletons, run out of steam, or, like Super Dee in this book, stop producing sufficent income for their owners. Until recently most were sold to be slaughtered. Just this last year, criticism of this practice has reached a peak, and more and more stables are making the selling of racehorses to meat men a firing offense.

The sport remains a dangerous one for a horse. Nearly two horses die for every 1,000 starts. The estimate by the U.S. Jockey Club in New York is that 600 died on U.S. racetracks in 2006. The sport is worldwide. The cost in lost equine lives is staggering.

The Outside of a Horse is a fictionalized compilation of true stories.

There are dozens of horse rescue facilities across the nation. This is a website with the locations of horse rescue centers by State. http://www.horseshowcentral.com/hro_search.php

Those interested in the NARHA certification program or locating NARHA certified therapy programs near you can use the website http://narha.org

Readers can also use *Google Alerts / The Slaughter of Horses* to receive e-mail alerts with the latest information on Bills before Congress, BLM roundups, and the names of groups working to stop the killing.

If you have a horse you can no longer care for, please make every effort to find it a suitable and safe home. If you are considering getting a horse, please keep in mind the commitment you are taking on.

To learn more about the Parelli method of training horses or to find a qualified instructor near you, please follow this link. http://www.parelli.com/home.faces

Remember, there are millions of abused and homeless animals in shelters everywhere. If you can't adopt, you can become a volunteer dog walker, or spend a little time petting a cat.

ATTENTION TEACHERS

If your class or book club has read *The Outside of a Horse* and would like the opportunity to speak with the author by phone about the research and writing of this book or her other books, please check my website www.ginnyrorby.com for contact information and to set up an appointment.

Appointments can be made for any time between 8 a.m. and 2 p.m. (Pacific Time) Monday through Friday.

ACKNOWLEDGMENTS

I'm blessed to be surrounded by so many great writers and gentle critics. Their praise, criticism, and encouragement keep my sails full and the wind at my back.

The Outside of a Horse would have never been written if Kelly Doaust, Erin Clarke, Vanessa Grosjean, and Prue Emerson hadn't let me hang out with them and their horses for a full year. Nearly all I know about these remarkable animals, I owe to them. In the same vein, my undying gratitude to Erin Livingston and Ellen Bartholomew of Ridgewood Ranch, and to June May Ruse, who treated this project as real and valuable before it was either.

A huge thank you to the absolute best writing group in the world, the Mixed Pickles: Norma Watkins, Katherine

Brown, and Charlotte Gullick. When I was floundering in the early stages Kate Erickson, Zida Borich, Maureen Brogan, Jill Myers, and especially Cynthia Wall kept me from giving up. Thanks also to Jeannie Stickle and Katy Pye, who waded through this more than once. Thanks always to Teresa Sholars for her scholarly insights, Linda Foote for much needed moral support, and Andarin Arvola, whose edits kept how little I know about horses from becoming an embarrassment.

I also have to thank other members of the community who so willingly lent their expertise and assistance so that other details in the book were correct representations: Henri Bensussen, Susan McKinney, Angie Herman, Linda Perry, Nancy Barth, Elizabeth Andriot, and Heather Shandel. My dear friend Joanne Mansell got me through the technical veterinary stuff; kudos to Kaye Harris, who saved Molly, and Dwayne Mara of the Bayou Orthotic and Prosthetic Center, who made Molly's new leg. Thank you also to my young critics Shelby Co and Jessica Kotnour, and to Savi Green, who'll always be Hannah to me. Of course, the sun rises and sets on Laura Dail, my agent, and on Kathy Dawson, the best editor in the business.